KISS IN THE DARK

MARCIA LYNN McCLURE

Published by Distractions Ink
P.O. Box 15971
Rio Rancho, NM 87174

©Copyright 2009, 2011, 2013 by M. L. Meyers
A.K.A. Marcia Lynn McClure
Cover Photography by ©Yuri Arcurs/Dreamstime.com
Cover Design and Interior Graphics by Sandy Ann Allred/Timeless Allure

First Printed Edition: 2011
Second Printed Edition: 2013

McClure, Marcia Lynn, 1965—
Kiss in the Dark: a novel/by Marcia Lynn McClure.

ISBN 978-0-9835250-9-7

Library of Congress Control Number: 2011931074

Printed in the United States of America

To true and enduring friendship...
A rare and beautiful gift that I have been so blessed to know!

CHAPTER ONE

"Boston!"

Boston skidded to a stop, wishing she were wearing cross-trainers instead of heels. Leaning back, she glanced into Mr. Mercer's office. Dominic Mercer hurriedly rose from his chair, snatching a piece of paper from his desk.

"Yeah?" Boston asked as he strode toward her.

"Are you heading to the set?" he asked.

"No…but I can stop there on my way," she replied. Awkwardly, she rearranged the box, envelopes, and papers piled in her arms.

"Good," Mr. Mercer said, stuffing the paper on top of Boston's already precarious pile. "Then make sure Atkins gets this ASAP! It's an update on that downtown murder."

Boston pressed her chin to the top of the pile to secure the added task. "Got it," she said.

"That's my girl!" Mr. Mercer chuckled, slapping Boston on the behind.

Boston gritted her teeth, nodded, and simply set out anew toward the news desk set. Mr. Mercer was a pervert, and she couldn't stand him! Yet Lara Hoffstetter was leaving the network, meaning the assistant news scriptwriter's job was about to open up. Boston wanted the Channel 7 News assistant scriptwriter's job more than anything. And she was fairly certain she'd get it—as long as she could put up with Mr. Mercer's harassment for a little while longer.

Therefore, she didn't reprimand her lecherous boss, nor would she report him to human resources. She wanted that scriptwriter's job, and she knew she wouldn't get it if she rocked the boat now. Instead, she raced to the news desk, set her pile down just long enough to hand the update on the downtown murder to the media news editor, and hurried on.

Her feet were aching something awful! She'd known she shouldn't have worn new shoes—especially heels—especially on a Friday! Glancing to a wall clock as she rushed down the hall, she breathed a little sigh of renewed determination, knowing she could take her shoes off in just fifteen more minutes. She decided she'd drive home barefoot; she wouldn't wait until she got home to give her feet a break.

"Did you drop that promotional stuff off in advertising for me, Boston?" Ms. Shafer asked as Boston passed an open office door.

"Yes, ma'am, I did," Boston called, not pausing to glance at the woman or give the arrogant promo VP any other opportunity to criticize.

"Fifteen more minutes," Boston mumbled as she tossed a manila envelope onto the desk of one of the weekend anchors.

Fifteen more minutes and she'd be free! Fifteen more minutes and she'd be on her way home to change so she and Steph could go over to Danielle's apartment for dinner.

Boston's mouth watered as she thought of the delicious chili dogs waiting at Danielle's. She could almost smell the onions and cheese, and she smiled. It was always best to have something to look forward to. Boston adored her little secret delights, like knowing a fun evening with friends and chili dogs awaited after a long work week.

"Don't forget the chocolate milk mix," she mumbled. She and Steph were supposed to bring the chocolate milk mix for dinner. Danielle was out.

"Come on, Boston! I need those printouts now!" Mr. Stafford growled as she approached his office.

"I'm sorry, Mr. Stafford," she apologized, handing him the printouts he'd sent her to retrieve. "The printers were out of ink, and I had to change them myself."

"That's no excuse," he growled, snatching the papers from her hand. "I needed these five minutes ago!"

"I'm sorry," Boston said, apologizing once more—though she really felt like slapping him soundly across the face, telling him he should've gone to get his own printouts. She glanced at his potbelly, thinking the walk would've done him good. She kept a civil tongue, however, and turned to drop off the last item she still carried, a box of paper for Samantha Sang's office.

"Thanks, Boston," Samantha said as Boston set the box on her desk and heaved a sigh of relief. "I hope it wasn't too much trouble."

"Not at all," Boston told the head news scriptwriter for Channel 7. "It was on my way," she lied.

Samantha smiled. "I'm sure that's not true...but thank you anyway."

Boston smiled and said, "You're welcome."

Samantha opened the box, lifted out a ream of paper, and proceeded to load her printer. Boston liked Samantha Sang. The woman had retained a good measure of humility, even for her high position on the news staff. She was in her mid-thirties and always dressed well, in business skirt suits. Her overall appearance was very professional and, at the same time, very feminine.

Samantha tucked a strand of short brown hair behind one ear.

"Have you got plans for this evening, Boston?" Samantha inquired.

"Nothing too exciting. Just hanging out with some friends," Boston answered.

"Girl friends...or guy friends?" Samantha asked, winking.

"Girl friends," Boston said, her smile broadening. "We're doing chili dogs and a movie. You know, sloppy clothes, overeating...watching a chick flick."

Samantha giggled. "Sounds like fun!"

"Yeah," Boston said. However, she did not want to overstay her welcome in the office of the woman she hoped to be working for in a few weeks. So she said, "Well, you have a good weekend, Ms. Sang."

"You too, Boston. Eat a chili dog for me, will you?" Samantha said as Boston left her office.

"Of course!" Boston exclaimed.

As she walked down the hallway away from the news scriptwriter's office and back toward the chaos of the news desk set, she crossed her fingers. In truth, she hadn't put in much time at Channel 7 News—only a year—but she'd worked hard, even made some last-minute script changes at Samantha's bidding on occasion. Now she hoped her hard labor, good work ethic, and cheery amity with everyone on the staff would soon pay off.

She felt the buzz in her pocket and retrieved her cell, smiling when she saw the text from Danielle.

Don't forget the chocolate milk mix, it said.

Quickly, Boston responded, *Oh, don't worry...I won't!* speaking the words aloud as her thumbs raced over the keys.

She smiled when Danielle's next text said simply, *Fabulous!*

Boston dropped her phone back into the front pocket of her pants and glanced up at the clock on the wall. Five more minutes—just five more minutes! Yet as her feet ached for relief, she wondered if there would be any feeling left in them at all when she finally got those stupid shoes off.

She raced back to her cubical, quickly straightened her work station, grabbed her purse, and headed for the exit door. As she left, she heard the office go quiet and the Channel 7 theme music begin piping through the building—she knew the 5:30 newscast had begun. Her work week was officially ended!

Boston paused a moment as she stepped from the building and into the warm evening sun. She reached into her purse and dug around until she found one last chocolate Tootsie Pop. She removed the wrapper from the sucker and popped it into her mouth, exhaling a long, relieved sigh of delight. As her mouth began to water from the sweet taste of the candy, she took hold of the white cardboard stick protruding from her mouth and pulled the lollipop out for a moment. She closed her eyes—inhaled a deep breath of city air. All the scents she loved about the city were there: the mingling aromas of the good downtown restaurants, the warm smell of hot pavement, stale pipe smoke wafting from somewhere, a hint of chlorine from the enormous fountain in the plaza one building over.

Boston opened her eyes, popped the chocolate Tootsie Pop back into her mouth, and smiled. She liked working downtown; she wouldn't want to live there but liked working there. As she walked to the parking garage, she passed the Little Christmas Shop. She wished she had time to pop in. She loved wandering through the high-end Christmas decorations, the little lighted porcelain villages. But it would have to wait. Steph would no doubt beat her home and be as impatient as ever to get over to Danielle's.

As she walked, rolling the sucker in her mouth back and forth with her tongue, Boston wondered how Halle's job interview had gone. She wondered if Kara's boyfriend, Max, had managed to get up enough nerve to propose. Surely Kara would've texted if Max had asked her to marry him. Likewise, Halle would've texted if she'd gotten the job. Still, maybe they were just waiting until they were all together at Danielle's for dinner.

Boston slid into the seat of her car, turned the key in the ignition, and backed out of her parking spot. As she drove home, she continued to think about her friends, smiling to herself as she thought of the way they'd all met. The summer after Boston's first year at college, her uncle had secured a job for her at the little Santa's Workshop and North Pole theme park in Cascade, Colorado.

Nestled in the foothills of Pikes Peak, the North Pole had always been Boston's favorite summer vacation destination as a small child. Amid the tall pines and roaming deer, the North Pole had Christmas-themed rides, like a roller coaster that looked like a candy cane, a giant peppermint slide, and a little train that slowly circled the theme park. Santa's house was there, cozy and warm, a fire glowing in the hearth even in summer. There were other little buildings and shops as well—colorful buildings constructed and embellished to mimic a tiny, vibrant alpine village of sorts. Small cafés served hot chocolate, warm cider, cookies, and sandwiches. Deer roamed the park freely, and there was even an area where guests could feed Santa's very own reindeer. All in all, it was the wonder of a small child's dreams come true. Thus, she had been thrilled when her uncle had called with the news he'd procured a summer job for her at the North Pole—for it was just about her favorite place on earth!

Boston stayed with her aunt and uncle in Manitou Springs while she worked that summer. It had been the most delightful job she'd had! Boston smiled as she turned onto Main Street, thinking it still the most delightful job—ever. That glorious summer, she'd started working as the operator for the Candy Cane Coaster but had soon managed to work most days in Carousel Café. It was while serving ice cream and milkshakes at the café that she had first met Halle. Halle worked in the café too—worked in the café or sometimes operated the Christmas Tree ride. Halle and Boston had become fast friends, and they'd soon gotten to know Danielle, who manned the camera at Santa's house. They'd met Dempsey there too, the coolest male elf Santa had ever employed.

Boston giggled out loud as a remembered vision of Dempsey, dressed like one of Santa's elves and operating the world's highest Ferris wheel, flashed through her mind. Dempsey was what Halle liked to call "a character," always into mischief, always finding amusement in the smallest things in life. It was hard to imagine him as the big hotshot he was now—not so hard to imagine that he made his money writing humorous advertising gimmicks and jingles.

Boston, Halle, Danielle, Dempsey, and Dempsey's sister Kara had worked nearly the whole summer together that year before figuring out that Boston's uncle knew all their parents and had procured jobs for each one of them. Thus, the five University of Oklahoma, Oklahoma-born natives found themselves working as Santa's helpers at the North Pole in Colorado for one glorious summer—a summer that forged vastly enduring friendships.

Steph was the only one of the group whom they'd met back at school. She'd worked at small café with Dempsey during their second year. Steph had harbored an insane infatuation with Dempsey and somehow managed to insinuate herself into the group. After graduation, as everyone managed to secure jobs in Oklahoma City, somehow Boston ended up sharing an apartment with Steph. It was a character flaw of Boston's—the inability to say the word *no* when someone acted pitifully enough. Steph had begged Boston to share the apartment, and though her gut churned in telling her she shouldn't cave, she did. Thus, she'd been roommates with Steph for over a year—and in truth, it was wearing.

Boston sighed. Steph was a good girl—and as good a friend as she knew how to be. Yet Boston didn't quite understand why thoughts of Steph caused such anxiety to rise in her. Still, they did, and it seemed the feelings were accelerating. In fact, Boston had been considering getting her own apartment, but she knew that would make Steph angry and hurt.

Scraping the remaining hard candy and Tootsie Roll center off the stick with her front teeth, she deposited the empty stick in the cupholder in the center console of the car—where it would linger for who knew how long with the twenty or thirty other discarded lollipop sticks. Boston shook her head and bit into the now-softened Tootsie Pop. She decided she wouldn't nest on dismal thoughts—not when a fun night at Danielle's was just around the corner. Still, she frowned a moment. It was fun to go to Danielle's nearly every Friday, but secretly Boston wished for something a little more—something a lot more, actually. She dearly loved her friends, but she was beginning to feel stagnant, as if life had begun to pass her by. She hoped then that Max had found the courage to ask Kara to marry him. At least then someone would be stepping into a new adventure—the adventure she secretly yearned to live for herself, the adventure of owning a loving husband and children.

Again she shook her head. She wouldn't think about it. She had a great job—hopefully soon a great career! She would be happy with that, with that and her good friends—Santa's elves or not.

❧

"Do you think I need to have Sylvia put a few more highlights in my hair this time?" Steph asked as Boston pulled into a parking space just in front of Danielle's apartment.

Boston forced a smile and looked to Steph. Green-eyed and brown-haired, Stephanie Crittendon was a pretty girl—at least outwardly. She was tall with a perfectly slender figure and more self-confidence than Boston could ever imagine owning. Yet she was often pretty shallow—very often. Steph had done nothing but talk about her hair all the way to Danielle's. Boston wasn't really just tired of offering reassurance that Steph's hair was perfect; rather, she was more irritated because Steph had answered Boston's cell while she'd been in the bathroom before they'd left the apartment. Logan West had called while Boston had been brushing her teeth, and when Steph had seen the name on Boston's caller ID, she'd taken the liberty of answering instead of just letting the call go to voicemail.

Boston had stepped out of the bathroom just in time to hear Steph flirting with Logan as she promised to give Boston the message he'd called.

"He says he's still at work so he'll call you later…if he gets another chance," Steph had explained. "I didn't want you to miss the call entirely, Boston."

Boston had been inwardly furious! She couldn't count how many times she'd kindly asked Steph not to answer her phone. Further, she knew Steph had answered exactly because it was Logan West. She wouldn't have answered if it had been anybody else.

Logan West was simply the most attractive man Boston had ever known. He'd worked at Channel 7 News until he'd landed a head scriptwriter's job with a competitor. She'd secreted a crush on him simply forever and had been ecstatic when he'd called and asked her out the week before. He'd taken her to the zoo, and they'd had a wonderful time—at least Boston had a wonderful time. Yet she figured Logan had too since he said he'd call again. He had called, and it irked Boston to the tips of her toes that Steph intercepted it. If there was one thing about Steph that she couldn't tolerate (yet still did for the sake of keeping the peace in their apartment), it was Steph's attempts to infiltrate every relationship Boston had. She knew Steph would love nothing more than to steal Logan West's attention—and it was boiling Boston's blood.

Yet as Steph repeated her question, Boston simply bit her tongue, hoping Logan would call back—soon.

"Well? Do I or don't I?" Steph asked.

"I think you have plenty of highlights, Steph," Boston said, forcing a smile. "Maybe you need a few lowlights. Maybe that's what you're thinking is missing."

"Hmm. That could be it," Steph said, pulling down the sun visor, lifting the lighted courtesy mirror flap, and studying herself again. "I'll ask Danielle."

Boston exhaled a heavy sigh. She didn't even know why Steph asked her opinion on anything. She never took it to heart—always had to ask someone else instead.

Boston pulled down the sun visor on the driver's side. She wiped a fleck of dry mascara from underneath one eye—thinking how grateful she was that her own auburn hair held natural gold highlights—closed the mirror, and opened the car door.

"Will you grab the chocolate milk mix, Steph?" she asked.

"Sure," Steph agreed, retrieving the mix from the backseat before getting out of the car herself.

As they started up the sidewalk toward Danielle's house, however, Boston felt her phone buzzing. Quickly she plunged one hand into the depths of her purse, rummaged around a moment, and retrieved the device. She smiled as she looked at the caller ID— Logan West!

"Go on in, Steph," Boston said. "I've gotta get this."

"Okay," Steph said, continuing up the sidewalk while Boston remained still and turned her back to the direction of Danielle's door.

She pushed send, put the phone to her ear, and said, "Hello?"

"Hey, Boston," Logan responded. Boston smiled, delighted by the way his deep voice spoke her name. "This *is* Boston, right?" Logan asked.

"Yep! This time it's really me," she said. Her smile was so broad it hurt. "How are you, Logan?"

"I'm well," he said. "Just wondering if you have time to go out with me tomorrow."

"Of course!" she exclaimed. She worried her excitement was perhaps a little too obvious. "What were you thinking?" she asked, trying to tone down the excitement in her voice.

"Oh, I don't know. Do you golf?" he asked.

"If you can call it that...the way I play," she said. Boston liked golf well enough; she just wasn't very good at it.

"Then we should make a perfect couple out on the course," Logan chuckled. "I stink at it."

She laughed. "Good!"

"I'll get us an early tee-time...like maybe eight a.m. Sound good?"

"Sounds great!" Boston giggled.

"Awesome! I'll pick you up at your place at, say, 7:30?"

"Perfect," Boston said. She smiled at the goose bumps suddenly prickling her arms. Logan West? It was too dreamy!

"Don't worry about clubs. I've got two sets," he said.

"I thought you said you were no good at golf," Boston reminded, mortified that she might have to play with a good golfer.

"I'm not good at all. Just thought it was the clubs' fault the first six months...so I bought another set."

"Did it make a difference in your game?" she asked.

"Not one bit," he chuckled. "See you in the morning then?"

"Of course!"

"Okay. Have a good night."

"You too. I can't wait!" she exclaimed.

"Me neither! Bye, Boston."

"Bye."

Boston sighed with delight, dropped her phone in her purse, and hurried toward Danielle's apartment.

"I cannot believe this!" she exclaimed, giggling to herself. "Logan West! I can't believe it!"

Bursting into Danielle's apartment, Boston began, "You guys will not believe this, but—"

She gasped slightly, startled as Steph stepped directly in front of her and said, "First come, first served. I saw him first. Just remember that, Boston."

"What?" Boston breathed. The determination and warning flame in Steph's eyes confused Boston as much as the threatening tone of her words.

"What the heck, Boston?" Halle asked, rather pushing Steph out of the way and embracing her in a friendly greeting. "What has you all wound up?"

"Just Logan West," she giggled.

"Did he ask you out again?" Kara asked, embracing Boston next.

"He did. We're golfing tomorrow!" Boston said.

"Oooo! That's an all-day event," Danielle said, coming to hug Boston.

"I know! I'm so totally excited!" Boston sighed.

Her friends—they were so important to her. She realized in that moment, consciously realized, how stifling Steph was to her mood—to her very soul. When Boston was in the company of her good friends, she was able to be herself—say and do the things her character and personality naturally did. But when she was sequestered at home with just Steph for company, she was self-conscious, often frustrated, and unhappy. As she gazed into the smiling faces of her true friends, she sighed. Yep, it was time to get an apartment—an apartment of her own.

"Logan West! Mmm! Maybe tomorrow will bring on the first kiss," Halle teased.

"Don't even say that! You know it wigs me out. I get all nervous. The anticipatory anxiety freaks me out!" Boston scolded, smiling.

"But golf is a long game. You have to do *something* while you're walking to the next hole," Danielle said.

"I know!" Boston giggled. She sighed as she thought of Logan's dazzling smile, tawny hair, and broad shoulders. How had she rated a date with him? How had she rated a second date?

"Excuse me."

Boston's smile faded—but only slightly—as a tall, muscular guy pushed his way through her friends and to the door. She recognized him at once from the family photos Danielle had around her apartment—Vance Nathaniel, Danielle's older brother. He was dressed in a pair of swim trunks, a rather ragged white T-shirt, and sandals, and he boasted dark hair, smoldering green eyes, and a rugged five o'clock–shadowed jaw. Vance Nathaniel was even more handsome in real life than he was in photographs. Boston couldn't help but find her smile suddenly broadening again. Danielle's brother resembled his sister so perfectly—as perfect an example of gorgeous, iconic masculinity as Danielle was the ideal representation of flawless femininity.

"Oh, Vance," Danielle began, "this is Boston."

"Hey," he greeted almost warily it seemed.

"Boston, this is my big, bratty brother, Vance," Danielle said. "And don't let him fool you. Tall, dark, and handsome he may be…but he's a total brat."

"Nice to meet you," Boston greeted.

"You can stay and have dinner with us, Vance," Danielle suggested.

"Yeah! You should totally stay!" Steph exclaimed.

Boston nearly laughed out loud. So Danielle's brother was what Steph had been talking about when she'd nearly growled to Boston, *I saw him first.*

"It's okay," Vance said, shaking his head. "I'm going down to the pool. And besides, nothing messes up a chick party like a ratty, old rooster." He smiled a little, and as Steph sighed with obvious admiration, Boston fought to keep from rolling her eyes with disgust.

"Looks like Steph has chosen her next victim," Halle whispered.

Boston giggled, feeling only sympathy for Danielle's brother. No doubt Steph would pursue him like a rabid pit bull. The guy didn't have a chance.

"You ladies have fun with your chili dogs and girl movies," Vance said. "It was nice to meet you all."

He left the apartment. As soon as Vance had closed the door behind himself, Kara said, "I thought he wasn't coming until next week, Danielle."

Danielle nodded. "He wasn't going to…but his landlord was pressuring him to get out of the apartment so the new renters could move in."

"When will his house be ready?" Halle asked.

"A month, I think. He's just gonna stay with me until it's ready."

"So he's a zookeeper?" Steph asked.

"He'll be the curator of exhibits at the city zoo," Danielle explained. "But he doesn't start for three more months."

"What'll he do until then?" Steph asked.

Boston sighed. It was so obvious that Steph was already planning her wedding to Danielle's brother, wondering how she could time the nuptials just right so she and Vance could move into his house and have a month or two of marital bliss before he started his new curator job.

"He's gonna work road construction," Danielle answered.

"Ooo! That's a brutal job this time of year," Halle exclaimed.

"Yeah…but Vance likes physical work. He likes to keep busy," Danielle said.

"Well, he's gorgeous, I'll give him that!" Steph said.

"I guess so…if you like that kind of thing," Danielle said.

"You mean like rippling muscles, washboard abs, square jaw, handsome face, shoulders like a Viking…" Halle teased.

"Whatever, you guys. He's my brother…so to me he's just the brat who used to drop toads in the tub when I was taking a bath and is way too overprotective of me now," Danielle laughed. "A Viking?" she giggled, looking at Halle. "Maybe a Vulcan?"

Halle frowned. "Like in Star Trek? He doesn't look anything like—"

Steph laughed out loud, shaking her head at Halle's innocent assumption. "Halle," Steph began, "I swear…you're so stupid sometimes. A Vulcan…like in Roman mythology, not Star Trek. Vulcan was the Roman god of fire and metalwork, and he was ugly.

Vance is far from ugly. Sheesh, Halle! Can you at least pretend to have a brain?"

Boston felt sick. She hated when Steph belittled people! She could be so cruel. How had they all put up with her for so long? But the answer was simple: they didn't know what else to do. What could they do, show her the same cruelty she often showed others? Of course not! That kind of cruelty wasn't in any of them—especially Boston. Still, what she'd said to Halle was so unkind.

"Then we'll stick with a Viking," Halle said cheerfully. Boston was ever astonished at the way Halle seemed to let Steph's cruelty just slide away, like water off a duck. "Vance the Viking," Halle giggled. "Can Vikings have dark hair though?"

Everyone laughed. Halle's questions were often so simply—yet so entirely—amusing.

Even Steph laughed, though Boston was certain her roommate was still silently planning her wedding to Danielle's brother, the black-haired Viking.

"So Boston, tell us about Logan," Kara said then, entirely changing the subject, thankfully. "Are you totally stoked or what?"

"I am," she admitted. "I can't seem to settle down. I mean…I never in a million years thought he'd give me a second thought!"

"Everyone gives you at least a second thought, Boston," Halle giggled. "Those green eyes, that gold-streaked auburn hair, that perfect complexion."

"Whatever," Boston said, rolling her eyes. Halle was always trying to build Boston's self-esteem where her appearance was concerned. "But the question is, did you get the job, Halle?"

"I did!" Halle exclaimed. "I start Monday!"

Everyone squealed congratulations and took turns hugging Halle. Boston glanced to Kara's left hand—no ring on her finger. Max was so in love with Kara—so intimidated by her beauty and self-confidence—and Kara loved Max desperately. She determined she was going to have to give Max a little talking-to—a little more ego boosting. After all, Max already had the ring; he'd shown it to

Danielle and Boston only two days before. What the heck was he waiting for?

"Everything's ready for dinner, you guys," Danielle said. "Let's eat…'cause I skipped lunch today!"

At that moment, the apartment door opened, and Vance stepped back in. "I forgot a towel," he mumbled. Boston noted the way he seemed to avoid looking at any one of them directly in the eye. As he strode through the room, her eyes fell to his right leg—to the large, deep scars marring his calf. They literally looked as if something had torn chunks of meat out of him. It was obvious the wounds had been skin grafted. Even though the scars appeared to be very old, the thought of the pain that must've accompanied the injuries that caused them made Boston's stomach flip-flop with sympathy. She wondered what had happened to Danielle's brother to leave such scarring.

Vance disappeared into Danielle's bathroom and returned a moment later with a red towel clutched in one hand.

"Red towels, Danny?" he asked, grinning at her.

"Yeah?" Danielle giggled. "What's wrong with red?"

Vance winked at her and said, "Nothing." Holding the towel with both hands lengthwise out at his side, he stomped one foot and quickly spun the towel around itself, whipping one end out and hitting Danielle on the behind. "Olé!" he chuckled as he left the apartment once more.

"Oh my heck! He's so hot!" Kara giggled. "The girls must be rabid after him, Danny."

Danielle nodded. "Yeah…pretty much," she said, rubbing the cheek of her bum where her brother had whipped her with the towel.

Halle frowned for a moment and seemed lost in thought. "Maybe he'd be a better matador than a Viking," she said.

Everyone giggled and headed for the kitchen area.

"Well, I'm starving," Boston said, picking up a paper plate from the counter. "I skipped lunch today too. I didn't want to be late."

"Me too!" Kara said. "I want extra cheese, by the way."

Boston giggled as she and her friends nearly dove into the buns, boiled hot dogs, slow cooker of chili, and condiments. She loved Friday nights. And she was going to love golfing on Saturday even more!

"Mr. Mercer grabbed my butt again today," Boston said as she sat at the table eating her chili dog.

Danielle put an extra scoop of chocolate milk mix in her glass. "That guy's a jerk," she grumbled. "I don't know how you put up with his behavior, Boston. You should go straight to HR."

"I don't know *why* you put up with it," Steph said.

"Next time he does that, just turn around and drive a knee right in his—" Halle began.

"Oh, don't worry," Boston interrupted. "As soon as I land that assistant scriptwriter's job, I plan to do just that!"

There was a pause as everyone ate in silence for a moment.

"Max and I are helping Dempsey finish his pond thing tomorrow...if any of you want to help," Kara said.

"Well, Boston's going to be making out on the golf course," Halle giggled, "but I can come if you need me. That reminds me—what brand of bra do you wear, Kara? I need to go bra shopping. That's always such a nightmare!"

"Oh, I hate shopping for bras," Danielle whined. "It's torture!"

"It totally is!" Steph added. "I'd rather clean bathrooms than shop for bras."

Boston giggled, enjoying the lighthearted conversation of her friends. She opened the fridge and took out the gallon of milk, closing the door with her knee. Her eye was drawn to a photograph on Danielle's fridge. A magnet that read, *Eat Beef—The West wasn't won on salad*, secured a picture of Danielle and her brother Vance to the freezing compartment door.

Both Vance and Danielle were smiling, standing in front of a hotel signboard announcing, *Sam Elliott slept here!* Boston gazed at the photo for a moment. Vance's smile was broad—dazzling. Both he and Danielle were much younger in the photo—teenagers—and

Boston noted the sparkle in Vance's eyes, a sparkle that had been absent when she'd met him a short time before.

She shook her head, glanced down at her second chili dog, and wondered. Did her mouth water in anticipation of the chili dog on her plate or because a vision of Logan West had just leapt into her mind?

CHAPTER TWO

"You know, it's interesting to think about how couples have met…or how they might meet," Steph said as she sat in the passenger's seat of Boston's car. "I mean, some people tell the most random stories of how they got together with their mate. Wouldn't it be interesting if this became my story—that I just dropped by my best friend's house one night and met her brother…and the rest was history? I mean, you do hear the most random 'how we met' stories. I think this might be the beginning of mine!"

Boston gritted her teeth and tried to keep her level of inward irritation from increasing. Steph had talked about nothing but Danielle's brother since the moment they'd left Danielle's apartment. Sure, he was incredibly hot, but he was a complete stranger! Still, it never ceased to astonish Boston the way Steph would obsess over men, whether or not she knew them. The first time Steph had set eyes on Dempsey, she'd nearly fainted. She'd been certain she was going to marry him, she'd once confessed to Boston. But, in the end, Dempsey just had too many faults that couldn't be tolerated. Boston knew the truth, however—that Dempsey Mattice just hadn't been interested in Steph, not one breath of interest. Therefore, Steph decided he just wasn't worthy of her heart. Boston couldn't begin to count the times Steph had dogged men who didn't immediately fall at her feet and confess their undying love. It was routine—Boston knew it was—but for some reason, she just didn't want to go through the same routine for the billionth time.

"Maybe he already has a girlfriend, Steph," Boston said as she drove toward home. "Have you thought of that?"

Steph shook her head with indifference. "Oh, I can remedy that easy enough," she said.

Boston felt her mouth gape open; the chocolate Tootsie Pop propped in it almost fell out into her lap. "Stephanie! You cannot just plan on breaking up a relationship! You can't just plan on dating someone without his consent," Boston exclaimed. She was feigning a jovial demeanor, but she felt anything but jovial. Steph had set her sights on Danielle's brother. Boston knew she'd settled on him the moment Steph had stepped into Danielle's apartment and seen him. Yet how could she settle on someone that way—after just one look—without any consideration for the guy or the other woman that might be in his life?

"Sure I can!" Steph argued. "He's not married, that's obvious. So he's free prey...and I'll get him. You just watch me, Boston." Steph looked to Boston, her eyes narrow and threatening. "And in case you've got any bright ideas of your own...stay out of my way."

That was it! Absolutely it! Not because Boston had any designs on Danielle's brother herself but simply because she could no longer align herself with the likes of Stephanie Crittendon—she didn't care how pitiful a friendless creature she was. She bit hard into her Tootsie Pop with her molars, crunched up the remains as quickly as possible, plopped the naked lollipop stick into the cupholder of the console, and tried to breathe calmly for a moment—tried to gather her thoughts. She and Steph were almost home, and she was grateful. Yet in the next moment, she realized she's be trapped with Steph, isolated in their apartment with no reprieve. Boston felt her shoulders begin to droop at the thought. It was too much—she couldn't endure it any longer—she wouldn't!

"I don't have any bright ideas where Vance Nathaniel is concerned...but I do have something else I've been wanting to talk to you about," Boston said.

"What's that?" Stephanie asked.

Boston glanced to Steph. It was obvious her soon-to-be ex-roommate was unaffected. Steph was probably so relieved to hear Boston couldn't care less about Danielle's brother that she failed to think anything else could be of consequence.

"I'm moving out," Boston said. There—she'd said it! There was a time when Boston would've hum-hawed around about saying something she thought might not be well received. But rooming with Steph had hardened her up just enough that she was able to say what she meant to Steph, rather than beating around the bush the way she would normally do with anybody else.

"Moving out?" Steph screeched.

Boston frowned—began to tremble with anxiety—immediately knew regret for having spoken so bluntly. She shouldn't have been so harsh; she should've eased Steph into the revelation. After all, what had Stephanie ever done to deserve such vile treatment at Boston's hand?

"You can't move out!" Steph continued to screech. "What will I do? I need you to pay half of the rent! I need you in the apartment! Who's going to do the dishes and stuff?"

Some of Boston's guilt subsided. Was that all Steph cared about—the dishes? Boston knew Steph would quickly figure out that if Boston moved out, then Steph might not always be invited to do things with the group of retired elves from Santa's Workshop and North Pole. Deep inside, Boston had always known there were three reasons Steph clung so desperately to her: to feed off Boston's once-elf friends, to feed off Boston financially, and to feed off her cheery disposition—not so unlike some slimy, bottom-dwelling parasite. These were harsh thoughts—Boston knew they were—and she didn't like them. In fact, she scolded herself for even having them. Yet this was another reason she felt she needed to find some space—so she could purge her soul and mind of the unkind, frustrated sort of feelings and thoughts Steph always seemed to provoke within her.

"I just…I just want to try things on my own for a while," Boston said. "It has nothing to do with you, Steph," she lied. "I just want to see if I can be entirely self-reliant when it comes to finances and stuff."

"I had no idea you were so incredibly selfish, Boston!" Steph growled. She glared at Boston and added, "Actually, I did. You don't think about anybody but you! You don't care that I'll have to find a way to make the rent...or find another roommate. What about the car? How do you expect me to get anywhere if you move and take the car?"

"It's my car, Steph," Boston reminded, as gently as her vexation would allow. "And this isn't unusual. I'm just moving into my own place. People do it all the time."

Steph's chest rose and fell with the labored breathing of fury. Thus, Boston quickly countered, "You've always wanted your own place anyway, Steph. You're constantly telling me."

"I only say that when I'm frustrated with your stuff being everywhere," Steph said.

"My stuff. You mean like my pictures on the wall, the lounge chair that my dad gave me last Christmas that I never get to sit in?" Boston said. She'd lost her cool—and she knew she'd pay for it.

"The lease is up in a month," Steph growled. "I want you out in two weeks!"

"Steph...look..." Boston began—not because she wanted to stay in the apartment longer than two weeks but because she loathed contention and hard feelings.

"Shut up, Boston!" Steph shouted as Boston pulled into their apartment parking lot. "Shut up and leave me alone for a while! Go find something to do for an hour or two so I can have time to think!"

Furious, Steph got out of the car, slammed the door behind her, and marched off toward the apartment.

Boston sighed—felt nauseated and worn out. She'd been through this drill before. Stephanie would get mad or in a fit of self-pity over something, and Boston would end up at Danielle's or Halle's for an hour or two until her psycho roommate calmed down. It was a ridiculous, high-school nightmare she kept reliving every three months or so. At first, Boston felt anxious, worried, and tired. But then she began to feel lighter, as if a huge stone had been hung around her neck and was gradually being lifted. She could endure one more of Stephanie's fits; she could hang out with Danielle for one more hour. It would certainly be more pleasant than having to deal with Steph.

Shaking her head, unable to fully believe she had such a wound-up nut bag for a roommate, Boston turned the car around and headed back toward Danielle's. She should've had the guts to stand up to Stephanie the month before when Danielle had moved into her bigger apartment. Danielle had tried to get Boston to move in with her, but Boston had still felt too sorry for Stephanie to do it.

As she drove back to Danielle's, Boston wondered what had finally pushed her over the edge. Why had she finally found the nerve to tell Steph she was moving out? Yet, after several moments of reflection, she decided she'd just reached her limit—finally. She didn't even know which straw had broken the camel's back—but whatever the straw had been, she was thankful for it!

Reaching out, she pushed the CD player button. As Taylor Swift sang "Love Story," Boston smiled. Steph never wanted the music on in the car—especially anything even resembling country music—and Boston suddenly felt quite entirely liberated.

"It's my freaking car!" Boston exclaimed out loud. "I can listen to whatever the heck I want to listen to!"

To further assert her own power, Boston reached out and set the CD player to repeat. All the way back to Danielle's, she sang "Love Story" with Taylor Swift—sang at the top of her lungs and with such a feeling of triumphant freedom that she arrived at Danielle's door smiling, rosy-cheeked, and more hopeful than she'd felt in a long, long time.

"Did you forget something?" Danielle asked as she opened the door.

"Nope!" Boston said, smiling. "I told Stephanie I'm getting my own place, and she told me to leave." Gesturing quotation marks in the air with her fingers, she added, "'Go find something to do for an hour or two so I can have time to think,' is what she said exactly."

Danielle rolled her eyes and laughed with utter disbelief. "Oh my heck," she groaned. "That girl is whacked! How did we ever get ourselves mixed up with her?"

"I don't know," Boston mumbled. She was beginning to feel bad about being so happy at the prospect of ridding herself of Steph's constant presence. "I think our initial intentions were to help her...you know...teach her how to make friends or something."

"Those were *your* intentions," Danielle said. "The rest of us just endure her for your sake."

"Really?" Boston breathed as she stepped into Danielle's apartment.

"Of course not," Danielle giggled. "We all felt sorry for her." Yet Boston wondered if the first reason Danielle offered was more the core truth.

"Well, I'm glad you finally said something to her," Danielle said as they sat down at the table. "Do you want some ice cream?" Danielle asked.

Boston smiled. "Sure. Ice cream always makes me feel better."

Vance was already sitting at the table eating a bowl of ice cream. Boston studied him quickly, feeling sorry for the man. He had no idea what was about to come his way where Stephanie Crittendon was concerned.

"Did you have a nice swim?" Boston asked, still studying him. Mercy—he *was* handsome! She really couldn't blame Stephanie for wigging out at the sight of him. "You must be a complete prune. You were gone forever."

Vance glanced up at her then, and Boston was startled; the way his eyes fixed on her caused her to experience an intense, although pleasant, sort of discomfort.

He shrugged broad shoulders and said, "I didn't want to mess up you girls' evening, so I went for a run after the pool."

"Well, I'm sure that was very refreshing," Boston said. She felt like an idiot! *Very refreshing?* What decade did she think she was in? What century?

"So," he began, "you're having roommate troubles, huh?"

"Oh, yeah," Boston sighed, rolling her eyes. "I've been having roommate troubles for a while. But…you know…it's so sticky…getting out of a situation like that. I mean, she doesn't have her own car. She'll have to do the dishes." Boston paused, frowning as she considered something. "I don't even know if she knows how to do dishes," she said. "Plus, she doesn't have any friends. The only people she hangs out with are us. I feel so awful about it really. I feel worse the more I think about it. Maybe I shouldn't have—"

"So she hangs out with your friends, rides around in your car, and you do the dishes?" Vance asked.

"Pretty much," Boston admitted.

"Let me ask you this," he began. "Does she borrow money from you? Does she whip up a good show of tears whenever you disagree with her on something? You said she told you to leave the apartment so she could have time to think?"

"Yeah," Boston said tentatively. This total stranger sitting next to her at the table was leading up to something, but she didn't know what.

"She's a poisonous friend," Vance said. He picked up the bottle of chocolate syrup to his right and slathered the remaining ice cream in his bowl with a generous helping.

"A poisonous friend?" Boston asked.

"She puts her own wants, needs, feelings before yours…before your friendship. She uses you at every turn and sounds like a manipulative little—" he paused and glanced up at Danielle. Boston saw Danielle arch one eyebrow in warning to her brother, and he finished, "—a manipulative little wench. She's what I would tag a poisonous friend. And I'm guessing you're a very empathetic, caring individual who finds it really hard to say no to anybody about anything. Am I right?"

"Maybe," Boston said, blushing with humiliation. He'd pegged her! Totally nailed her to the wall. How could he possibly have done it? He'd only met her once before.

"I'm pretty familiar with poisonous friends," he began, "So my guard is always up. That's why I can spot them right away. What did she growl at you about when you first got here earlier this evening?"

Boston shrugged, trying to feign indifference. "Just something about something."

"I'd bet you a hundred bucks she was demanding something of you. Am I right?"

Boston nodded, shook her head, and giggled. "Wow! I must be really transparent," she said.

Danielle set a bowl of vanilla ice cream on the table in front of Boston and smiled. "No, you're not transparent," Danielle said. "Vance is just the creepiest people-reader I've ever known. Don't take it too personally. I've seen him peg someone's character by just glancing at them."

"So you're judgmental," Boston teased, reaching for the chocolate syrup and squeezing a generous portion over her ice cream.

Vance chuckled. When he looked at her again, he was smiling, and Boston was astounded that he was even more good-looking when he smiled.

"No. Just...just observant," he said. He laughed and added, "Besides, just before you came back, Danielle was sitting here telling me everything about all her friends. She'd just finished up about you and your roommate."

"Danielle!" Boston exclaimed, laughing. "You were letting me think he was, like, psychic or something!"

Danielle laughed too. "Oh, don't let him fool you. He sort of is!" Danielle said. "Sure, I told him some stuff. But that whole poisonous friend routine...that's purely Vance Nathaniel and his theories."

"But I'm right...aren't I?" he asked Boston.

Boston couldn't help but smile at him—couldn't help being momentarily smitten by how handsome and charming he was. "Maybe," she said.

He chuckled and returned his attention the bowl of ice cream on the table in front of him.

"I'm right," he mumbled.

"So…you've told Steph you're moving out. Now what?" Danielle asked. She glanced to her brother a moment. "I don't suppose it would be appropriate to have you move in here with Vance and me."

"You can share my room," Vance teased. "There's only one bed…but I'm all good with it if you—" Danielle slapping him soundly on the top of the head silenced him.

Boston giggled as Vance mouthed, "Ow!" at his sister.

"But when Vance's house is finished, you can totally move in with me! It's what I wanted you to do before…remember?" Danielle reminded.

"Yeah, yeah, yeah," Boston sighed. "I remember. But I have to be out in two weeks."

"Two weeks? I thought the lease wasn't up for a month."

"She told me I have to be out in two weeks," Boston said.

"You won't last two weeks," Vance interjected.

"What do you mean?" Boston asked.

Vance looked to Boston, then to Danielle, then to Boston once more. "You're kidding me, right?" he asked. "There's no way you'll last two weeks with this chick! You've offended her pride; she's ticked off. You're a girl. Do you really think she can be amicable for two weeks?" He shook his head. "Nope. She's gonna make your life a living hell."

"Thanks for the encouragement," Boston said, stirring her ice cream and chocolate syrup in the bowl. Once it was smooth, she put a heaping spoonful into her mouth and sighed, "Mmm!"

She felt somewhat self-conscious when she noticed both Danielle and Vance watching her—Danielle with apparent amusement, Vance with something akin to befuddled intrigue.

"So I see you're a stirrer," he said.

"I am," Boston admitted.

He didn't say anything else, just looked to his own bowl of ice cream and continued to eat.

"So…the cute guy at work asked me out today," Danielle said.

"What?" Boston exclaimed. "I can't believe you didn't tell us earlier!"

Danielle shrugged. "I don't know. I just didn't want to mention it in front of Steph. You know how she is."

"Oh, I do!" Boston said, stirring her ice cream some more. "No doubt she would've found a way to drop by your office so she could check him out…and then try to steal him. She answered my phone when Logan called the first time today."

"Oh my heck! I don't know how you tolerate her!"

But Boston shook her head. "Let's not talk about it. Worrying about Steph occupies too much of my time anyway. Tell me about the guy at work."

Danielle's face brightened. Her smile was so broad Boston wondered if her face might crack clean in half.

"His name is Theo, and he's *so* cute! He wears these little bow ties that are so adorable and—" Danielle began.

"Danny!" Vance interrupted. "Are you kidding me? Bow ties?"

"Yeah! He sort of looks like Harrison Ford in the Indiana Jones movies. He even wears glasses. He's just the cutest handsome I've ever seen!"

Boston giggled as Vance put a hand to his forehead, rubbing his temples with a thumb and index finger.

"What's the matter? You don't go in for bow ties?" she teased.

"Not necessarily," he said. He chuckled a little and added, "I'm just worried."

"About what?"

"I've only been here one day…and with all you girls around— with no guys in my corner—what will I be like after a month of this? My estrogen level must've already gone out of sync."

"Estrogen levels? Why do you say that?" Boston asked, giggling.

"Because right now, as I'm sitting here, the thought is running through my mind that Harrison Ford *is* kind of cute wearing glasses and a bow tie."

Boston and Danielle erupted into pealing laughter. They laughed and laughed—then laughed harder! Boston couldn't catch her breath. Her lower back began to hurt with the force of the laughter. Danielle was out of control, rocking back and forth, gasping for air.

"It's not funny," Vance grumbled.

But as Danielle and Boston continued to laugh, Vance growled with disgust. He stood, taking his bowl of ice cream with him as he sauntered over to the couch.

"You've got satellite, Danny, right?" he asked, depositing himself on the couch and picking up the remote. "Let's hope the Military Channel or something with a little testosterone is on."

Boston's and Danielle's laughter was renewed, and Boston stamped her feet on the floor trying to gain control of the painful laughter.

"Well, I'll say this for you and your friends, Danny. You sure are easily entertained," Vance said, shaking his head.

"Oh my heck! Oh my heck!" Danielle gasped, finally able to draw a deep breath.

Boston sighed and wiped the tears from the corners of her eyes. "Oh, I feel so much better!" she said. "I swear…there's nothing like a good laugh."

"Oh my heck!" Danielle breathed. "I swear he cracks me up so bad sometimes!"

Boston glanced to where Vance sat stretched out on the sofa, eating his ice cream—his head bobbing back and forth to the rhythm of the *COPS* theme song as images of police officers handcuffing bad guys flashed on the TV screen.

"You go on and talk about your boy toys, girls," Vance said. "Me and Officer Rodriguez are going on a drug bust in New York City."

Boston giggled again and asked, "Is he always that funny?"

Danielle shook her head. Lowering her voice, she said, "Not always...and there's the deal. It's usually accidental like just now! I mean, if he tried to be funny...it wouldn't be nearly as funny!"

"I feel so much better," Boston sighed. She ate a spoonful of ice cream, and a residual giggle of amusement caused her to choke. She coughed and ate more ice cream. "I can't tell you how rotten the atmosphere in our apartment is. I can't wait to get out of there."

"I can't wait for you to get out of there either!" Danielle said. "Steph...she's a piece of work."

"You have no idea," Boston said, rolling her eyes. She looked to Danielle and lowered her voice even further. "You know she's already planning her wedding to your brother, don't you?"

"What?" Danielle exclaimed in disgust. "Oh, please tell me you're kidding, Bost."

Boston shook her head. "Nope. He's all she talked about on the way home," she whispered. "She went on and on and on about how hot he is...how she felt like she'd known him her entire life! Actually, it was after blabbering on about Vance that she launched into this whole thing about how people meet...how interesting it is to hear stories of how couples find their mates."

Danielle stuck out her tongue and put a finger toward her mouth to indicate she wanted to vomit. "How they find their mates?" she repeated. She giggled then and whispered, "Actually, that's kind of funny...considering Vance will be the exhibits curator at the zoo soon!"

Boston laughed, nearly sucking ice cream into her sinuses. Shaking her head, she whispered, "It still nauseates me though. Plus, what if she did manage to catch him? Then we'd be stuck with her forever! At least you would."

"Won't happen," Danielle said. "Not in a billion years. Vance pegged Steph the minute he met her...I know he did. He won't give her a second look. I don't care if she was a dead corpse still hanging out of an anaconda's mouth—he wouldn't look twice."

Boston giggled and wrinkled her nose as an image of Steph being downed by an anaconda entered her mind. She hoped Danielle were right; she hoped Vance Nathaniel wasn't stupid enough to fall for Stephanie Crittendon's ridiculous methods of catching a man—a mate. She'd hate to see Danielle have to endure Steph any longer than she already had. Furthermore, something about the idea infuriated her even further; to think of Steph winning a guy like Danielle's brother bugged her to no end.

"An anaconda?" Boston asked. She giggled as she ate more ice cream. "You crack me up, Danielle."

Vance couldn't help but smile as he continued to eavesdrop. Witnessing an anaconda working its prey into its body would really be something to behold! He liked that his sister knew him well enough to use such an analogy. Furthermore, Danielle was absolutely right: he'd pegged Boston's roommate the minute she'd set foot in the apartment—shallow, self-centered, cruel. He also sensed the girl was far more willing to do whatever was necessary to catch any guy she set her mind on than Boston and Danielle suspected—far more willing—and whatever was necessary.

Danielle's friend was lucky to be moving out. Vance knew women like this Steph person—anybody was better off without their company. He continued to make the pretense of watching *COPS* as he listened to the girls' conversation. He gathered Boston really liked the guy she had a date with the following day; it seemed the guy was taking her golfing. Vance nodded. It was a pretty good date idea—an entire day together. Eighteen holes did take awhile to play through. He hoped this guy—Logan seemed to be his name—was a good guy. He knew Danielle really liked Boston and valued her friendship very much. And, to his senses, Boston seemed to be worthy of his sister's admiration and devotion. There was something very vibrant and sort of sunshiny about her—a rare effervescence. In a different time and place, Boston was just the sort of girl Vance himself would've been drawn to. But it wasn't a different time or place, so he pushed the thought from his tortured mind—or at least tried to push it from his mind. She was awfully cute. That auburn hair looked so smooth and soft he wondered if it actually tasted like cinnamon. She was curvy—

owned a great shape. He liked the way the green of her eyes seemed to deepen when she laughed, the way her smile lit up the room. Yep, in another time and place, he might have looked twice at Boston—whether or not an anaconda was downing her.

"Well, ladies," Vance said, pressing the power button on the remote and standing. He stretched for a moment, and Boston felt her eyebrows arch with admiration at the muscles in his arms and legs as they tightened. "I'm gonna hit the hay. I have to be out on site at five a.m."

"On a Saturday?" Boston asked. She felt an odd pang of sympathy in her chest. She was so relieved to have the weekend off, and she always felt bad for anyone who didn't.

"Yep," Vance said. He walked to Danielle, bent, and kissed the top of her head affectionately. "Good night, baby sister," he said.

She smiled, and he looked to Boston, offering her a hand. Boston accepted his hand, and he gripped it firmly, saying, "It was good to meet you, Boston."

"You too," she said. She was surprised by the giddy feeling that popped around in her stomach for a moment.

He didn't release her hand right away. In fact, he tugged at her a little and nodded toward the back of Danielle's apartment. "The offer still stands, by the way," he said.

"The offer?" Boston asked.

"To bunk in with me if the situation with that chick you room with becomes too intolerable," he teased.

"Oh!" Boston giggled. She was mortified when she felt a delighted blush rise to her cheeks. "Well, thank you...but I'm sure I'll be fine."

"You sure?" he asked, winking at her. He released his firm grip on her hand, yet held to her fingertips—lingered. "I could show you our room right now if you want. Danny's got it all fixed up nice with extra pillows and quilts. It's awful cozy in there."

Boston giggled again—blushed again. "Thank you, Vance...but I'm sure I can make it through a couple more weeks of Steph."

"Okay," he said, releasing her at last. "But don't say I didn't try. When that psycho chick you live with comes after you, you just remember who offered to help you out first."

"Oh, I will. Thank you," Boston said.

With one final nod, Vance sauntered to the back of the apartment.

"So…I see your brother's a bad boy," Boston said when he was gone.

"He likes to pretend he is," Danielle said. "In truth, he's just a terrible tease." Danielle giggled. "You should've pretended to take him up on his offer. He wouldn't have known what to do! He probably would've bolted out the window."

Boston laughed a moment—but only a moment, for a dismal thought she'd been trying to ignore pushed itself to the forefront of her mind then. She was going on her second date with Logan, and a second date wasn't usually something to worry about. But if there was a third—in Boston's experience, it was during the third date that guys often began to push for things.

"I bet Vance has had his share of women, huh?" she asked.

"Oh, yeah!" Danielle said. "Especially when he was younger. The girls would flock to him like you can't imagine…kind of like when you go down to the pond at the park and start tossing a few bread crumbs to the ducks. You know how they get all frenzied and, like, want to eat your ankles? That's how girls were about Vance. Of course, he beats the women off with a stick now—actually, just reads them so fast and chooses who he will deal with and who he won't— that it's not quite as bad as it used to be. Especially since—"

"Since what?" Boston asked.

Danielle shook her head. "Just…just since he's gotten older…and wiser, I guess. He's a lot more selective now."

"I see," Boston mumbled.

"Oh, wait, Boston," Danielle said. "He's not…Vance isn't…he isn't promiscuous, if that's what you mean. And I'm sure Logan West isn't either."

"What?" Boston asked, feigning ignorance.

"I know how your mind works," Danielle said. "You're already getting all worked up over whether or not Logan West is gonna pressure you to—"

"I'm sure he won't," Boston interrupted. "He's such a nice guy. I'm just paranoid."

"You're paranoid because the last four guys you've dated have turned out to have no moral character at all!" Danielle said. "Believe me, I get it. I'm gun-shy too." Danielle giggled, however, and added, "But I still have high hopes where Theo is concerned. Don't you think a man who wears bow ties might have chance of being a good guy?"

Boston giggled. "I think you never got over that crush you had on Professor Farnsworth. That's what I think."

Danielle smiled. "Maybe," she said.

Boston glanced up at the rooster clock hanging over the sink. It was midnight, and she had an early date with Logan.

"I better go," she said, pushing her chair away from the table. "I'll look awful tomorrow if I don't get some sleep."

"Well, we don't want that," Danielle said. Boston stood and Danielle did too. "I just hope Steph has calmed down a little."

"If not, my offer still stands," Vance said in a garbled voice.

Boston looked over to see Vance standing in the hallway wearing nothing but a pair of striped pajama bottoms and brushing his teeth. *Good grief! He's totally ripped*, Boston thought, trying not to stare at Vance's muscular torso.

"Thanks, Vance," Boston said. "I'll keep that in mind."

"You do that," he said, still brushing his teeth.

"Vance! Put some clothes on!" Danielle scolded.

Vance shrugged massive shoulders, an expression of innocent naïveté on his face.

Boston giggled and hugged Danielle. "Thanks for letting me hang out awhile," she told her friend.

"I just wish you'd moved in last month!" Danielle said. "But it won't be long. I'm sure Halle will beg you to stay with her. We'll all be fighting over you."

"Have a good day tomorrow," Boston said. She glanced past Danielle to Vance, still standing there displaying ridiculous muscles and brushing his teeth.

"Good night, Vance," she said.

He nodded and turned toward the bathroom.

"Call me after you get home tomorrow," Danielle said. "You're going to have a great time!"

"I hope so," Boston said. "Bye."

As Boston walked to her car, she glanced up into the starry night sky. The breeze was warm, and everything was still. The crickets were chirping, and it soothed her further. Steph would be in bed when she got back to the apartment. It was her routine—get mad at Boston and tell her to leave, then act like nothing had ever happened and go to bed. Boston was glad of it, however, for she had no desire to talk to Steph one more second that day.

Inhaling a deep breath, she breathed out slowly, calming herself. She would think about Logan—dream about their planned date to go golfing. She couldn't wait! She'd have the whole day with him, a whole day without Steph. Sure, she had to start making plans about what to do with her stuff until she figured out exactly what to do, but she wouldn't worry about it anymore until she'd had her day with Logan West.

Boston got into her car, reached over, opened the glove compartment, and retrieved a chocolate Tootsie Pop. She popped the sucker in her mouth, turned the key in the ignition, and headed for home. The flavor of the candy in her mouth was delightful! She thought about Vance teasing her about sharing Danielle's extra bedroom with him. He was a funny guy. Funny and ripped! She shook her head, for she knew that no matter what Danielle said about her brother's character, Stephanie Crittendon had chosen Vance Nathaniel to be her mate, and Vance Nathaniel was about to be forced into a high-speed chase like nothing he'd ever seen on *COPS*. She thought again of how handsome and built Vance was—about the fact he was a zoo exhibits curator.

It suddenly seemed too ironic that Steph would look to Danielle's brother as her selection of "mate"—Vance, who would soon be working as part of the city zoo staff. A vision of a gorilla, a female gorilla named "Stephanie," popped into Boston's mind. She giggled at her mind's illustration, thinking Steph's temperament would probably be a lot easier to deal with if her soon-to-be ex-roommate were a primate in one of Vance's zoo exhibits.

CHAPTER THREE

Golfing with Logan had been fabulous! Not that Boston did well—her score was actually pretty pitiful, but so was Logan's. Though the golf scores weren't anything to brag about, the company, the beauty of the day, and the experience were wonderful. After they'd finished golfing, everything just got better. Logan took Boston to lunch, to a movie, and then to dinner. They'd spent nearly sixteen hours together! Boston couldn't think of a time she'd spent sixteen hours on a date—it was incredible.

Now, as Boston sat in Logan's Volvo on their drive home, she sighed—entirely satisfied with the way her second date with Logan had turned out. He'd asked her if they could do something together again soon, and she'd said yes, of course.

Still, as Logan turned into Boston's apartment complex, anxiety washed over her. Steph. It was only nine o'clock, and Boston knew Steph was home—knew she'd continue to be a brat, the way she had the night before when Boston had told her she was moving out. Oh, it wasn't like Steph gave Boston the silent treatment or anything—though Boston wished she would. Instead it had been incessant whining and self-absorbed pity parties from the minute she'd returned from Danielle's until Steph finally let Boston get to bed at two a.m. At that moment, Boston realized just why she was so tired so early in the evening. Five hours of sleep, followed by eighteen holes, lunch, a movie, and dinner—it was a miracle she had any energy left at all. What little she did have would be immediately drained when she entered the apartment and Steph started in on her again. There was nothing on earth more certain than that.

"You okay, Boston?" Logan asked. He pulled into a parking spot, shifted into park, and turned off the engine.

Boston glanced over to him—smiled at the sight of his handsome face, his soft, tawny hair, and his dazzling eyes.

"Yeah," she said. "I'm probably just tired. It's been a long day, and I was already pretty sleep-deprived when it started."

"Well, I guess it was kind of selfish to keep you all to myself the entire day," he said.

"Oh no! I loved being out with you!" Boston said. "I could stay out all night if you wanted me to."

When Logan arched one amused, rather daring, eyebrow, however, Boston quickly added, "I mean, don't think I didn't enjoy every minute. I was just explaining why I probably look a little less than fresh."

"I knew what you meant," he said. "Let me get your door, and we can get you to your apartment and into bed." He got out of the car and walked around to her side of it.

Boston knew he was only speaking metaphorically—that he meant he knew she was tired and wanted to turn in. However, the fact that the last four guys she'd dated always wanted to go much, much further than merely dating and kissing had left her a little suspicious. Still, Logan West wasn't like the other guys she'd dated— he was a gentleman. He hadn't even kissed her yet. Therefore, it seemed very doubtful he'd try to push her into anything more intimate.

Boston shook her head to rattle such thoughts from her mind as Logan opened her car door.

"Your roommate seems nice," he said as they walked toward Boston's apartment. Boston glanced at him quickly. Was he kidding? Sure, he'd only met Steph for a few minutes when he'd picked Boston up the week before for their zoo date—only spoken with her for another few minutes that morning when he'd picked her up for golf. But surely he hadn't bought her act; surely he'd seen through her sweet little façade of perfection. Even Danielle's brother had read Steph for what she really was, and he'd hardly even seen her. Still, most people bought Steph's act—at least initially. Therefore, knowing she was tired and probably a little too sensitive, Boston just cut Logan some slack.

"Yeah," she said.

They were at her apartment door then. Logan gripped Boston's upper arms in his strong hands, smiling at her.

"Thanks for spending the day with me," he said. "I had a great time."

"Me too," Boston said. He was going to kiss her good night! She could tell by the way his gaze lingered on her mouth. All at once, such a mess of conflicting emotions erupted in her stomach and chest that she wasn't sure she could remain calm. She wanted him to kiss her—she really did! Yet she was way nervous too. Boston had kissed a few boys when she was a teenager and had a couple of steady boyfriends as an adult. But the first kiss always freaked her out—always! Before every first kiss, she would panic, start to wonder if she was a good enough kisser, if a guy would be disgusted with her once he'd kissed her for the first time. It was a weird, obsessive-compulsive behavior of sorts—a strange anxiety she couldn't seem to beat.

As Logan moved closer to her—began to pull her to him, saying, "Good night, Boston"—her heart pounded like a kangaroo pent up in a barrel. She studied his face as he moved toward her. Surely the drop-dead gorgeous guy standing in front of her didn't really mean to kiss *her*—not Boston Rhodes, the boring, auburn-haired girl who worked at Channel 7.

"Oh! You're home!" Steph exclaimed, opening the apartment door at that very, very, very inopportune moment. Logan sighed with veiled exasperation, dropping his hands from Boston and stepping back.

Boston was furious, entirely vexed—she couldn't even look at Steph! She wondered how long Steph had been standing at the window, waiting for Logan to bring Boston home so she could muff the whole thing up.

"Yep. I'm home," Boston said. She was fuming, livid that Steph had managed to ruin the moment between her and Logan.

"Well, it's a good thing," Steph said. "You left your cell here, and Danny's been calling like crazy."

"Danny?" Logan asked.

"My friend, Danielle," Boston explained. Oh, she was so angry! She knew exactly what Steph was trying to do—trying to make it look like Boston had another man on the line.

"You better get in here and call her back," Steph said. "It must really be important." Steph then leaned against the doorframe and waited. She had no intention of retreating back into the apartment so that Logan and Boston could finish saying good night.

"I had so much fun today, Logan," Boston said.

Logan glanced to Steph, and Boston saw understanding wash over him.

"Me too," he told her. "I'll call you, and we'll do something next weekend, okay?"

"Okay!" Boston smiled at him, hoping her stupid roommate hadn't reflected too badly on her.

"Well," Logan began, shoving his hands into the pockets of his plaid shorts. "Good night."

"Good night," Boston said.

She watched him walk away, astounded that Steph had managed to ruin the moment—again. Boston had lost track of the fun, tender, or private moments Steph had ruined for her. Yep—she'd put up with Stephanie Crittendon for far too long.

"You're a real piece of work," Boston grumbled as she pushed past Steph to enter the apartment.

"It's not my fault that he's too shy to kiss you in front of me," Steph said.

Boston went to the coffee table to retrieve her phone. She'd intentionally left it home. She'd been afraid Steph would spend the entire day texting or calling her, just to attempt to interrupt her time with Logan.

"Danielle called once, Steph," Boston said. She held up her cell, displaying the missed call on its screen. "Once! And it was only twenty minutes ago!"

Steph shrugged. "Once, twice, or forty times…it was still irritating."

Boston gritted her teeth. She wouldn't be provoked further—wouldn't let Steph engage her in the contentious argument she knew Steph Crittendon wanted to have.

"Well, Logan's gone home, and I've got my cell if you need me for anything," Boston said, heading back toward the door. She grimaced, irritated with herself for giving Steph the upper hand by telling her she had her cell if she needed anything.

"Where are you going?" Steph asked. "To Danielle's, I suppose. I swear, I don't know why you didn't just move in with her in the first place. You've always liked her better than me. That's been clear from the very beginning!"

How true that was! Still, Boston wouldn't drop to Steph's level—she just wouldn't.

"But I'm guessing it's not just Danielle you're running off to see anymore, is it?" Steph continued as Boston grabbed her purse. "Remember, Boston…I saw Vance first! You can dream about him if you want to…but I'll get him. You just watch me."

Boston drew in a deep breath, attempting to calm her infuriated temper. She had to make it—endure a couple more weeks of Steph's junk while she worked out a place to stay until Vance moved out and she could move in with Danielle.

"I'll see you later, Steph," Boston said through tightly clinched teeth.

With Steph angrily babbling on about how Boston was such a terrible friend and roommate, Boston hurried toward her car. It was late, and she was tired, but she just couldn't endure Steph's berating.

She started her car, grabbed a chocolate Tootsie Pop from the glove compartment, unwrapped it, and popped it in her mouth. The moment the flavor of the sucker flooded her mouth with the soothing taste of sweet confection, Boston sighed. As both her hands rested on the steering wheel, she leaned forward and rested her forehead against it too.

What a weekend! Boston tried to calm her frazzled nerves as she thought about what a chaotic whirlwind she'd endured at work the day before—how an evening at Danielle's that was supposed to be her respite after a long week ended up with her and Stephanie at odds—with Danielle's brother, a complete stranger, reading her like an open book. Sleep-deprived and anxious, she'd somehow managed to have a great time in Logan's company. But now—now Steph had vamped her again. Boston felt tears begin to well in her eyes. Why had she waited so long to move out? There was being nice, and there was being used—and Boston had certainly been used. She felt stupid and embarrassed and experienced a self-loathing and disgust she'd never known before.

As she inhaled a deep breath and backed out of her parking space, a tear escaped her eye and traveled over one cheek. Boston was "too nice"—Stephanie herself had always told her that. But how could someone be too nice? And what was wrong with being nice? Nothing! But why did it seem—of late, anyway—that nice people always finished last?

Yet as Boston drove toward Danielle's—hoping Danielle wouldn't mind her hanging out until late again—she shook her head. No! Stephanie was just mean, that was all. Danielle's brother was right: Stephanie Crittendon was a poisonous friend, a poisonous person in many ways. She liked the term—poisonous friend. It was so perfectly descriptive. Poison was often something that killed people slowly. Sure, it could be quick and painless, but most of the time, being poisoned was a slow, tedious process—a process the victim was often unaware of until it was too late. That's exactly what Stephanie had been to Boston—she could see it clearly. As, in an instant, her entire experience and friendship with Stephanie flashed through her mind, Boston could see that the relationship had been poisonous.

"She ought to have one of those yuck-face poison stickers glued to her forehead," Boston grumbled. Of course, being too nice as Boston was, she immediately scolded herself for even thinking such a thing. Stephanie had baggage and issues just like everyone else on the face of the earth. It's just that Boston had begun to realize Steph's baggage and issues weren't the kind she could healthily deal with any longer.

"But I've got a plan now," she said, pulling the sucker out of her mouth for a moment. "Or, at least, I've got part of a plan."

She could move in with Danielle in a month. It was like being lost in the desert and seeing a waiting oasis just ahead in the distance. Yet Steph had demanded Boston be out of the apartment in two weeks. Compound that with the fact Boston wasn't sure she could even last two weeks in the apartment with Steph—she'd had to escape two nights in a row already—and her plan hit a brick wall.

She was sure Halle would let her bunk in with her until Danielle's brother was in his own place, but Halle had three other roommates. Though Halle would welcome Boston with open arms, Boston wasn't sure Halle's roommates would. Kara would probably beg her to move in with her family too—she still lived at home. Kara's parents would be hospitable enough, but Kara's six other siblings were still living there. It would be a profound imposition on Kara's family. Boston briefly wondered if Max had proposed to Kara while she'd been out golfing with Logan. Still, there had been no text or missed call from Kara on her cell, so she guessed not.

Other than Dempsey—and that was totally inappropriate and thus out of the question—Boston couldn't think of one person she could impose on for two weeks to a month. As she often did, but for different reasons than she did now, Boston wished her parents hadn't moved to Kansas. She wished they still lived in Oklahoma City, and not just because she needed a place to live for a while. She hadn't told her mom about how awful Stephanie was. Boston's mom got so wound up and worrisome when she knew one of her children was unhappy, but Boston still wished her mom was closer. She could really use her mom's nurturing comfort and advice.

Pulling into Danielle's apartment complex, Boston put the Tootsie Pop back in her mouth and parked her car. It was only ten p.m., and Boston was glad Danielle's lights were still on. It would be a couple of hours before Steph settled down and went to bed. In that moment, Boston was more grateful than ever for Danielle's unconditional friendship.

Oh sure, Danielle would say she still had never given enough to Boston to make up for what Boston had helped her through that first summer they'd met while working at the North Pole. But to this day, Boston didn't even know what she'd helped Danielle through that summer. She just remembered Danielle crying every night—sobbing as she struggled to overcome the deep, emotional pain she was dealing with. She'd explained to Boston that it was something she couldn't talk about—not specifically anyway—just that she was dealing with a terrible pain, the worst of her life. Boston had sat up with Danielle many, many nights that summer, simply to cry with her or encourage her that life was good and would brighten again someday.

Of course, Boston's wild imagination had been on overdrive where the mystery of Danielle's pain was concerned. At first she'd wondered if Danielle had broken up with a boyfriend. But it soon became apparent that whatever was causing her such misery was much more serious. Thus, Boston began to wonder if Danielle was terminally ill—or if she'd had a baby without being married and had to give it up for adoption—or if there were some sort of problem between her parents. All these things proved not to be the reason for Danielle's pain, and Boston had quickly decided just to be Danielle's friend, no matter what. The summer together, the shared emotions, had solidified their friendship, and Boston knew they would always be close—always.

Still, as she knocked on Danielle's apartment door, she hoped she wasn't asking too much of her friend.

Danielle opened the door and smiled. Giggling, she said, "Did you have another fight with Medusa?"

Boston sighed with relief, feeling as if she'd just returned home from some long misadventure. "There's no way I'm going to last two more weeks with her," Boston sighed.

"Well, quit dating hot guys, have somebody beat you with the ugly stick, and she might make it endurable for you," Danielle teased as Boston entered the apartment.

"You won't believe what she did tonight," Boston began, plopping down on the sofa.

Danielle giggled and sat down too.

"Oh, yes I will," Danielle assured her. "Spill it!"

"Well," Boston began. She paused, however, glancing around the room. "Is your brother awake?"

"He's out for a run," Danielle said. "I swear that's all he does— work and run, work and run. He won't be back for a while…so feel free to tell me anything and everything!"

"So," Boston began, "Logan drives me home…and, of course, walks me to the door."

"Ooo! Smooching stories! I love it!" Danielle exclaimed.

"Nope! No smooching stories…thanks to Stephanie Crittendon."

"You have got to be kidding me," Danielle whined, rolling her eyes. "Tell me!"

"So, Logan walks me to the door. He takes hold of my arms…thanks me for spending the day with him—"

"So you're ready to vomit, as you always are just before a first kiss," Danielle interjected.

"Exactly!" Boston admitted. "So, he moves in…and…"

"And?" Danielle prodded.

"And Steph opens the door and says, 'Oh! You're home,' all innocent…and then proceeds to tell me that 'Danny' has been ringing my cell phone all day long!"

"You have to be lying, Bost!"

Boston shook her head. "Nope! So…of course I have to explain to Logan that 'Danny' is really 'Danielle' and all. But by then, Steph has planted herself in the doorway…with no intention of leaving."

"So what happened?"

Boston shrugged. "He said goodnight, asked me if we could do something next weekend, and left."

Danielle shook her head, disgusted. "Why have you put up with this for so long, Boston? I would've clawed her eyes out!"

"I don't know. I guess I'm just stupid," Boston sighed.

"No, you're just nicer than any of the rest of us…and that's a good thing. Kindness is a vanishing virtue in this world, and you're the kindest person I know. I'm just afraid that all this junk with Steph will harden you up too much. That's why I want you out of there. I just want her to quit making your life so miserable."

"Well, it won't be long now. I just wish I hadn't waited so long. I should've moved in here when you first asked me to. But I admit…I was too chicken. I didn't feel like dealing with the emotional upheaval I knew it would cause."

The apartment door opened, and Vance entered, stripping off his T-shirt as he closed the door behind him.

"Did you have good run?" Danielle asked.

Vance nodded, wiping the perspiration from his face with the T-shirt. "Yep," he said. Then, looking to Boston, he added, "Hi, Brooklyn."

"Hi," Boston said. She smiled, amused he hadn't remembered her name—yet a little disappointed too.

"It's Boston, Vance," Danielle corrected. She nudged Boston's leg with her foot. "You should've corrected him."

Boston shrugged. She didn't like correcting people—ever.

Vance grinned and winked at Boston. "I knew it was some big city with a girly name. Sorry about that, Savannah."

"Oh, now you're being an idiot," Danielle scolded.

But Boston giggled. He'd known her name all along—she was certain he had.

"Well, I may be an idiot," he said. He raised his arms, flexing massive biceps. "But you better get a Band-Aid, little sister…'cause I'm ripped!" He raised one bulking bicep to his face and kissed it with pride.

"Oh my heck," Danielle moaned with disgust. "Just ignore my brother, Boston. He can be so stupid sometimes."

"Stupid maybe…but ripped," he teased. He sauntered over to the sofa, tucked the sweaty T-shirt in the waist of the back of his shorts, and asked, "So, you get driven out by that venomous she-serpent you call a roommate again?"

"Yeah," Boston admitted. She blushed, embarrassed, for she could only imagine how spineless she must seem to Danielle's brother.

"Well, it's probably safer for you to be here," he said. "They make slasher movies about chicks like her, you know."

"Vance!" Danielle scolded. "What the heck? Don't scare her! She's still gotta sleep there for a while…you dork!"

But Boston was amused. He was right, after all.

"Sorry, Boston," he said. He grinned—a totally mischievous grin, a handsome, alluring sort of grin. "But if she tries to get you to eat, like, soup or something…don't do it. Or if you notice certain large knives are missing out of the utensil drawer…"

"Vance!" Danielle said, tossing one of the sofa throw pillows at him. "Go take a shower! You're all sweaty."

"All right, all right, I'm going," he chuckled. He turned to leave the room but paused. His eyes narrowed, and he lowered his voice as he said, "Boston…count the knives before you go to bed. That way, in the morning, you'll know if—"

"Shut up, Vance!" Danielle interrupted, tossing another pillow at him.

He smiled, chuckled, and headed for the bathroom.

Danielle sighed, shaking her head with exasperation. But Boston giggled. Vance was funny and had managed to lighten her mood a bit.

"Oh my heck, I swear, he's such a dork!" Danielle laughed.

"But he's a totally ripped dork," Boston offered.

Danielle nodded. "And he made you laugh…so I guess I'll let him slide."

"Thanks for letting me hang out, Danielle," Boston said. Vance's amusing antics had lightened her heart and mind a bit—but she still felt guilty for being such a parasite on Danielle's time and space.

"Don't start that, Bost!" Danielle said, smiling. "You're going to live here in a month. You might as well start spending the bulk of your free time here now…just to make sure you're gonna like the apartment and everything."

"Yeah," Boston teased. "I might not like living in a nice apartment with a nice roommate."

Danielle smiled. "Hey! Wanna watch a movie? I figure it'll be couple of hours before you can go back, right? We never got to watch one last night."

"Okay," Boston giggled. She and Danielle loved watching movies late at night, especially romantic comedies or scary old black-and-whites. "What were you thinking?"

"I don't know. Let's make popcorn and then decide." Danielle paused and looked at Boston with an almost timid expression. "Will it be okay with you if Vance watches it with us?"

Boston smiled. "Why wouldn't it be?"

Danielle shrugged. "I don't know. I just thought you might not want him around."

"Danielle," Boston began, "what woman in her right mind wouldn't want Mr. I'm-so-ripped-I-need-a-Band-Aid around?"

"Come on then," Danielle said. She hopped up off the couch and headed for the kitchen. "Let's get the popcorn going, and then Vance can help us decide what movie to watch."

Half an hour later, Boston found herself sitting on the sofa between Danielle and a freshly showered Vance, sharing a bowl of popcorn, and laughing at John Candy as he tried to flip a giant pancake with a snow shovel.

The movie was great—*Uncle Buck* was one of her favorite silly comedies. The company was even better! Boston was amazed at how comfortable she felt. Again she was reminded that she'd never felt like she could relax in her own apartment—not since the day she and

Stephanie decided to share one. Even with Vance sitting next to her—the solid muscles of his forearm bumping her now and again as he plunged his hand into the bowl of popcorn sitting on her lap—she felt more at home. Certainly Vance's presence spun the dynamic a little differently than had it just been her and Danielle there. Boston found she was constantly aware of him; warmth radiated from his muscular body. He smelled like Old Spice bodywash, mint toothpaste, and popcorn. He was quite the dominating presence—distracting—in a delightful, thrill-inducing kind of way. He chuckled at something John Candy said, and Boston smiled. It seemed Vance only added to her sense of comfort and welcome in Danielle's apartment.

"Pause!" Danielle exclaimed suddenly. "I have to go to the bathroom!" Danielle fumbled with the remote, pausing the movie and fairly leaping off the sofa.

Boston smiled, and Vance shook his head. "She can never make it through a whole movie," he said. "She never could."

"I know," Boston giggled. She loved that about Danielle—how she could go hours and hours and hours without having to go to the bathroom, until someone put on a movie.

"So…Boston," Vance began.

Boston looked over to him. He was lounging back on the sofa, looking dangerously handsome and entirely comfortable.

"Yes?" she asked.

"You're kind of like that little goldfish, I guess, huh?" he asked.

Boston giggled and frowned at the same time, perplexed.

"What little goldfish?" she asked.

"That little goldfish. There he was, swimming along, just enjoying life…then bam! He swims right into a solid wall of cement," Vance said. "And do you know what that little goldfish said as he swam into the solid wall of cement?"

"No…" Boston admitted.

"Dam!" Vance said.

Boston laughed out loud, caught her breath, and asked, "And why am I like that little goldfish?"

Vance smiled a dazzling smile and replied, "Because you know how he feels. You just swam right into that cement wall with that roommate of yours last night, and it rung your bell. But you know what? It'll all work out. It's good you're getting away from her. I'm sure she'll make it as hard on you as she can…but once you're out from under her bullsh…her crap…you'll be fine. You'll rub your little goldfish head that you knocked against the wall, and you'll swim on…a little bruised up maybe, but smarter too. And you'll be a little better at navigating around cement walls."

"Thank you, Dr. Laura," Boston teased.

"You're welcome, Charlotte." Vance winked, grabbed a handful of popcorn from the bowl on Boston's lap, and added, "That's in North Carolina…in case you're wondering."

"I know," she giggled. She sighed for a moment. "How is it that you know so much about navigationally challenged goldfish and poisonous friends?"

He shrugged broad shoulders. "Experience," he answered. He smiled. "Unfortunately, a lot of experience."

"Okay, I'm back," Danielle announced, hopping back into her spot on the couch. "Unpause," she told the remote as she picked it up and started the movie again.

Boston reached into the bowl in her lap to retrieve several kernels of popcorn, but Vance teasingly pushed at her hand, gathering a fistful himself. Boston nudged his arm with her elbow, and he playfully nudged back. She heard him chuckle and glanced up to him, but she couldn't tell if the chuckle was caused by their playfully fighting over the popcorn or because John Candy was involved in some comedic ritual on the TV.

Boston watched the movie, but her mind kept wandering. Vance Nathaniel was a pretty smart guy. She was rather amazed by his insight and fairly profound advice and encouragement. She'd been in his company exactly three times. How was it that he was so affecting to her in a mere twenty-four hours? She shrugged and tried to concentrate on the movie. Logan West flashed through her mind; she hoped Steph hadn't scared him off. She was sure she hadn't. He'd said they'd go out again. She hoped he'd call soon.

Vance and Danielle both laughed, and the sound caused Boston to giggle. She couldn't wait to permanently escape Stephanie's emotional manipulation. Life would be fun and exciting again once she was away from Steph—she could sense it all around her.

"If I wasn't here, your friend could move right in," Vance said.

Danielle waved to Boston as she walked toward her car. She felt the familiar pinching pain of empathy in her heart. She wouldn't let him start to slip into guilt—she wouldn't.

"Oh, don't go all melodramatic, martyr-heroic on me, Vance," she said. She turned to him, flinging her arms around his neck and kissing him soundly on one whiskery cheek. "You know how excited I am to finally have you here! Boston's got tons of friends to stay with until she moves in here."

"Yeah…but that Stephanie chick is gonna give her hell," Vance mumbled.

"She's tougher than she looks," Danielle said. "Do you want some ice cream before bed?"

"Sure."

Vance yawned. He was tired—physically worn out. Still, neither Danielle's reassurance nor his own fatigue eased his mind about Danielle's friend Boston. He knew what ~~witches~~ chicks could be to each other—especially ~~hags~~ like this Stephanie. He should've just rented his own apartment for a month. Instead, he'd let Danielle talk him into staying with her. He was all for it too—until he'd understood Boston's predicament.

He was far more familiar with Boston Rhodes than she knew. Boston had been the one to save Danielle. Not him—certainly not him! He suspected Boston had literally saved Danielle's life that summer after…

Thus, he hated to see his sister's rescuer in misery. He felt an incredible desire to liberate her—to somehow offer recompense for her service to his sister. But if he moved out now, Danielle would worry like a crazy woman.

"She's really pretty," Vance accidentally said out loud as he sat down at the table to start on the bowl of ice cream Danielle had dished up for him.

"You mean Boston?" Danielle asked.

Vance grimaced, disgusted with himself for having slipped up in revealing his thoughts.

"Yeah. Sort of in a throwback way, huh…like classically, naturally pretty. She's got great hair…kind of like copper…or cinnamon." Danielle looked at Vance and seemed to study him for a moment. "And the same color of eyes you do, I think."

"Really?" he mumbled, feigning ignorance. Of course he'd noticed her green eyes—like warm jade. He wished he hadn't moved in with Danielle so her friend could've found instant escape from her poisonous snake of a roommate.

"Rocky road," he said as he tasted the ice cream. "My favorite."

"I know," Danielle said, smiling at him.

Vance's heart nearly broke as he looked at her—thought of her pain. Her hidden pain caused him to feel sick for a moment. He had trouble keeping moisture from rising to his eyes.

Vance forced a smile. He didn't want her to see his barely withheld emotion—didn't want to cause her to think of the past, of pain again. So he ate his ice cream, talked with his sister concerning the details of his upcoming new job, and tried not to think about what a venomous reptile was waiting for Boston Rhodes back at the viper's lair.

CHAPTER FOUR

Monday seemed long—at least Boston's time at work seemed to drag. For one thing, she was tired. For three nights running, she'd been up well after midnight, and the late nights and early mornings were starting to catch up with her. Sunday with Steph had been just as intolerable as Friday and Saturday nights, and Boston had ended up seeking escape and respite at Danielle's again. She'd decided to wait to talk to any of her friends about staying with them for the two weeks from the time Steph wanted her out until Vance moved to his place and out of Danielle's. But the longer she was forced to deal with Steph, the more she realized she had to do something soon. She couldn't continue to endure Stephanie's hateful remarks—couldn't continue to be provoked and remain unresponsive.

It was probably one reason work seemed so long on Monday—the fact that Boston's mind was so preoccupied with her apartment situation. She'd nearly lost her temper when Mr. Mercer had whacked her on the rear end after lunch. Sure, he would've deserved it, and she shouldn't let him treat her that way, but she wanted that assistant news scriptwriter's job and knew she had to play her cards just so for a little longer. Therefore, somehow she'd managed not to scream at him, stopped herself from slapping him soundly across his arrogant face, and kept from running to HR to finally report him. A week or two more and she'd know if the promotion were hers—then she would no longer put up with Dominic Mercer's stupidity.

The good thing about the day was that Stephanie wasn't home when Boston arrived there after work. Boston knew Steph often worked out at the health club right after work on Mondays. She was so grateful for the short reprieve. It gave her some quiet time to relax before heading over to Danielle's to pick her up for cake decorating.

Boston and Danielle had signed up for a cake decorating class. It was quite a commitment—every Monday night for two months—and sometimes Boston wished they hadn't signed up. Still, there were fun things about it—and only three weeks left. Furthermore, she and Danielle were getting pretty good at decorating cakes! A new skill was always an asset, and it was fun to be with Danielle and do something a little off the regular schedule grid.

After a light dinner of a sliced apple and a few spoonfuls of peanut butter, Boston still had an hour or so before she was due to pick up Danielle. Glancing out the front window, however, she saw Steph step out of the city bus. Boston's anxiety rose. An all too familiar nausea of anxiety began to churn in her stomach. She had to figure something out—she had to escape! She didn't want to face Stephanie. Furthermore, she knew she couldn't wait two more weeks to move out. She had to do something.

Grabbing her purse, she hurried out of the apartment. Steph would see her—there was no avoiding it—unless…

Racing up hard concrete stairs that led to the floor above, Boston ducked down behind the railing and waited—listened until she heard Steph open their apartment door downstairs and close it behind her. Heaving a sigh of relief, Boston made her way along the second-floor balcony to the other staircase. Stephanie wouldn't be able to see her from the other staircase, and she hurried to her car. She just had to get to Danielle's. Once she was there, she'd settle down. Once she was at Danielle's, her anxieties and fears would settle. The thought passed through Boston's mind that Danielle's house seemed even more a haven—a safe harbor—than it ever had before. She wondered why it did, and an image of Danielle's brother popped into her mind. Alone—walking to her car without anyone around who might possess the talent to read her mind—Boston consciously admitted there was something strong and protective about Danielle's brother, something that calmed her and made her feel safe, even from Stephanie. Vance was rugged and handsome, muscular and flirtatious. She figured it was the fact Vance Nathaniel was an exemplar of the idealistic and nowadays very rare manly man that made her feel that way about him.

Actually, Boston had made a conscious effort not to think about Danielle's brother—even avoided thinking of him by name, letting her mind refer to him as "Danielle's brother." There was a certain sensation she experienced in his presence—a sense of impending, insatiable attraction—as if he were some wizard of seduction that might be able to lure her into some unbridled, impassioned, reckless abandon. This was by no means a comfortable sensation for Boston. It seemed dangerous—almost wicked—and therefore she suppressed it, ignored it, and refused to let her mind nest on thoughts of Vance Nathaniel. Any man who caused her to think such things—well, it was best not to think about him at all. And so, once again, Boston pushed Danielle's brother to the back of her mind—just as she'd been doing all weekend.

She unlocked her car and slid into the driver's seat. Reaching over to the glove compartment, she retrieved a chocolate Tootsie Pop, grimacing when she noticed there were only three Tootsie Pops left. It would be awhile before she would be able to get to the little candy shop in Mustang to load up on chocolate Tootsie Pops again. Sandy's Sweet Tooth Shop was the only place Boston knew that sold Tootsie Pops in bulk. Boston only liked chocolate Tootsie Pops. Thus, every three or four months, she and Danielle would head over to Mustang, Oklahoma, to pick through the bulk Tootsie Pop barrel at Sandy's Sweet Tooth Shop. She'd always limit herself to fifty chocolate Tootsie Pops because she figured it wasn't fair to the owner of the store or the other patrons to be too selfish. Sandy Sorenson owned the little candy store and always assured Boston she could take as many chocolate Tootsie Pops as she wanted. Still, Boston tried to imagine that there were others, like herself, who preferred the chocolate ones.

As she unwrapped her fourth-to-last chocolate sucker, Boston realized she'd probably been eating more Tootsie Pops than usual because of the added stress over Steph and moving. What a nightmare! Cake decorating class would be good for her. It would offer another night of escape and a much-needed diversion for her tired mind.

Boston knocked on Danielle's apartment door. She startled—actually gasped slightly—when Vance opened the door instead of Danielle.

"Hi," Boston greeted, trying not to notice how thoroughly attractive Vance looked in a clean, yet ratty, tight T-shirt and khaki shorts.

"What's up?" Vance asked, smiling at her and stepping aside so she could enter the apartment.

Boston moved past him and into the apartment, smiling as she noticed the fresh scent of Juicy Fruit gum. It was an inward and conscious battle, but she managed to suppress the worrisome attraction she felt toward Vance.

"I'm a little early," Boston explained. "I just thought I'd see if Danielle wanted to leave early or anything."

Vance grinned. "Snake woman's home, huh?"

Boston felt stupid. How weak he must think she was. Still, there was nothing to do but admit stupidity and weakness. She shrugged and answered, "Yeah. I'm a weenie."

"Naw," he said. "You're just like a lot of people who don't like to cohabitate with reptiles."

Boston smiled—even giggled a little. "Do you like reptiles, Mr. Zoo Curator Man?"

"Zoo *exhibits* curator man," he corrected with a smile and a wink. "And no…not particularly. I'm more a big cats kind of guy."

"Really?" Boston asked, delighted. "I used to collect lions when I was a little girl! I had lion stuffed animals and little porcelain figures, a lion lunchbox, a lion bedspread. It was a big lion surrounded by a leopard skin background, and I always thought it was kind of weird that the bedspread manufacturer used leopard print on a lion bedspread." She had begun to babble—bit her lip to stop herself short.

Vance chuckled. "You actually used the word 'manufacturer' when you were a little girl?"

Boston giggled. "No. I guess not. I just thought it was strange…because I was a lion purest at the time. No leopard print for me."

"You were prejudiced? What's wrong with leopards?"

Afraid she may have somehow offended him, Boston's babble resumed. "Oh, no! I love leopards too, really. Now, I even have a thing for leopard-skin underwear and pajamas. As long as they're not too expensive, I can never pass them up! It's like an OCD or something. Danielle can tell you…if I see a pair of leopard-skin panties, I just have to—" Boston gasped and clamped her hand over her mouth—mortified!

Vance's verdurous green eyes blazed with amusement. "Leopard-print underwear, huh?" he began. "Well, that puts a man's mind to wondering if you're wearing them now." He forced a puzzled frown. "Probably not the most appropriate place my mind could be lingering."

Boston couldn't speak—she was too horrified with embarrassment! She could only shake her head, astonished at herself for being so unguarded.

"Still, as a zoo exhibits curator and big cats fan," he continued, "I like it."

"Oh my heck!" Boston breathed. "I am so sorry, Vance. Sometimes I just babble on and on. How embarrassing!"

But Vance chuckled. "Naw…don't worry about it. Does it make you feel better if I tell you I'm wearing boxer briefs? Plain white…but still."

"No, it doesn't," Boston said, smiling. Though it did make her feel better—somehow.

"I see you like suckers too…along with lions and leopard-print panties," he said, nodding his head to indicate the Tootsie Pop still held in one hand. The hard candy was gone—she'd eaten it on the way over. But the Tootsie Roll center still remained.

"Oh!" she said, suddenly remembering she'd taken the lollipop out of her mouth when he'd answered the door. "Yeah…but only chocolate Tootsie Pops," she explained. She quickly put the little white stick with the rounded blob of Tootsie Roll in her mouth, stripping the candy off the stick. She tossed the white cardboard sucker stick into the nearby garbage can.

"Only chocolate Tootsie Pops?" he asked.

"Yeah. I don't seem to like any of the other flavors. Now…I occasionally enjoy a root beer–flavored Dum Dum. But let's be honest, what's the point of a Dum Dum? They're like the size of a dime…and there's nothing in the center…and they don't come in chocolate. But sometimes, like at the bank—you know how they give them out at the counter and stuff—sometimes I can eat a Dum Dum…but only the root beer ones."

"Got it," he said, smiling—obviously amused. "Lions, no leopards—just leopard-skin pajamas and underwear. Tootsie Pops, but only chocolate. And no Dum Dums, except maybe at the bank, and even then, only root beer–flavored."

"You should know I have a tendency to talk too much," Boston told him. She could feel the hot crimson of a blush on her cheeks. Actually, she felt too warm all over. She figured even her toes were blushing. For Pete's sake, he knew what color her underwear was!

"Not at all," he said. "This is important stuff to know."

"Oh yeah, details of profound value," Boston giggled.

"Do you want something to drink?" he said as he turned and sauntered toward the fridge.

"No, I'm fine." Boston glanced around the room. She smiled when she saw the TV was on, muted, but tuned to the Animal Planet channel. "*Animal Cops*, eh?" she asked, delighted with his programming choice. "I guess the real *COPS* isn't on yet?"

"Dude! This is *Animal Cops: Detroit*," he explained, retrieving a carton of orange juice from the refrigerator and returning to where Boston stood. "It's my favorite city for *Animal Cops*."

"Is that so?" Boston teased. He was so funny! Just his random choices of TV programming made her feel giggly inside.

"Oh yeah," he confirmed. "Though I will say this…I'm watching way too much TV here. Work just wears me out. Then until I'm ready for my evening run, I just feel like sitting on the couch and doing nothing. I'm a pig since I moved in here."

Boston bit her lip to keep from laughing as she watched him drain the orange juice carton by drinking straight from it. He wadded the carton up and eyed the garbage can in the kitchen. Boston watched and admired his perfect follow-through as he free-throw-shot the carton into the garbage can.

"Ooo, swish!" she said, nodding at him with admiration.

"That's right," he said, proud of his basketball—rather, basketcarton—skills. "Danielle's not home yet," he announced, taking a seat on the sofa.

Instantly, Boston was unsettled. Danielle wasn't home? She was alone with Vance in the apartment?

"I'm sure she'll be here soon," he continued. He must've sensed her discomfort because he smiled and added, "But don't worry…I only hit on girls who wear, like, pink, glittery underwear…so you're safe."

"Oh well…whew…I guess!" Boston teased.

"Here, sit down," he said, tossing a throw pillow off the sofa and patting the cushion next to him. "We can watch something else if you want."

"No, I wouldn't want you to miss the animal cops rescuing a litter of neglected kittens…being that you are a cat person," she said playfully.

"Big cat person," he corrected.

"Oh, sorry."

"I met your friend Dempsey," he stated. It was not only a very quick subject change but an odd one.

"Really?" Boston asked, taking a seat beside him. Again she was struck by his intoxicating allure. Still, she pushed the fact to the back of her mind—willed her body to fight off any goose bumps that might be threatening to appear on her arms. "And what did you think of him?"

"I think he's cool," he answered. He looked at her then, his eyes narrowing a bit as he said, "And you and I both know how important that is...don't we?"

"Important how?" Boston asked. What did he mean? Of course it was important that Dempsey was cool. He was their friend—at least hers and Danielle's. Surely he couldn't be implying what she thought he was—not when years had passed since...

"Important for my sister's sake," he said. The TV was still muted, but he glanced at it for a moment, as if giving Boston time to consider what he was saying.

"Important because he's her friend?" she fished. He knew something! She was certain he did.

Vance looked back to her, any sign of amusement or teasing entirely vanished from his expression. "Important because she's in love with him."

"What?" Boston breathed. "In love with him?"

"Come on, Boston," Vance began, "don't tell me you don't know it. You have to! You're her best friend."

Boston did know it, not because Danielle had confessed it—at least not in a couple of years—but because she could see it. Every time Dempsey entered a room, Danielle lit up like a Christmas tree. Boston hadn't questioned Danielle about it, however. For one thing, Danielle had nearly shriveled up and died two years ago for being so thoroughly in love with Dempsey—yet, for some reason, unable to tell him so. Life had meandered on. Danielle had dated other men, and Boston tried to imagine that Danielle had somehow gotten over Dempsey, though she suspected otherwise. Still, how did Vance know?

"I-I do know," Boston admitted. "But...but she hasn't mentioned in years...literally years! Did she talk to you about it?"

"Are you kidding?" he chuckled. "Danielle? Talk to me about her worries, concerns, or problems? Hell no! I mean, heck no. She doesn't like to talk to me about anything she thinks will cause me to worry about her."

"Then how did you know?" Boston couldn't help but ask. He was so intriguing—the way he'd read Steph—and Boston. Now, he'd obviously read Danielle.

He shrugged. "I don't know. I can just tell," he began. "Every time you guys mention his name, she goes pale as a ghost. And it's in the way she doesn't talk about him too. Furthermore, I think the feeling is mutual."

"You do?" Boston asked. He had her entirely intrigued. How could he possibly know if Dempsey had deeper feelings than mere friendship for Danielle?

"Yeah," he confirmed. "He came to the door about fifteen minutes before you did. He dropped off invitations to some party he's having in a couple of weeks. He shook my hand—looked at me like he was picking up some girl for prom and I was her dad." He raised a daring, very suspicious eyebrow. "Then he asked me if I wanted to hoop it up with his team Tuesday and Thursday nights." He paused, waiting for her response.

"Well…well, Dempsey's very nice…and way, way friendly. He probably just wants to be your friend," she said.

"Guys don't ask other guys to join their city league basketball teams without seeing what they'll bring to the court first," he explained. "Naw…we got us a case of secret love…on both sides of the fence."

"Do you have, like, ESP or something? Are you psychic?" Boston asked, and she was serious. In the short time she'd known him, Vance Nathaniel's ability to read people and situations was uncanny.

"No," he answered. "I just pay attention to people—their body language, their eyes, what's hidden behind the front everybody puts up." He looked at her and grinned. "Like right now, you're sitting there wondering if I'm for real…or if Danielle's just been talking to me a lot since I moved in. You're also wondering if every time I see you from now on…will I wonder if you're wearing leopard print underwear." He looked away from her and to the TV.

"Will you?" she asked. He'd been spot on with his guess as to what she was thinking—if it were actually just a good guess and not some weird psychic ability he possessed.

"Definitely," he answered.

Boston blushed and felt the need to change the subject back to Danielle and Dempsey. "Why does she keep talking about the Harrison Ford guy at work then? If she likes Dempsey, why does she still date other people?"

"My guess is she's given up," he answered. "For whatever reason—and you might know more about it than me—she just doesn't think it could ever be. So she's into the bow tie guy at work as a second choice."

"But then, why doesn't Dempsey do something? If you're right about them—"

"Oh, I'm right about them," he interrupted.

"Then why doesn't Dempsey do something? He's really, really outgoing, confident, successful."

"Same reason Danielle sits on her heels," he said, looking to her again. "Fear and lack of faith. I mean, how long have you all been friends? Since that summer you guys all worked for Santa or whatever, right?"

"Yeah…"

"Would you want to have an affair of the heart with Dempsey, have it go awry, and screw up all those years you guys have had together?" It was a very valid question.

"Probably not," she admitted. "But I'm not in love with Dempsey either. If I was in love with him…"

"You'd be just as afraid as Danielle is," he finished for her.

Boston nodded. "Probably more. I am the weenie of the group," she said.

"Not the weenie…just the kindest soul." He paused and smiled at her with inexplicable understanding. "I don't think you're an idiot just because your roommate is, you know. And I don't think you're weak for dealing with her for so long. It just shows your strength of character where tolerance and kindness are concerned."

"Okay, what do you want?" she giggled. "Such flattery. Surely you want something."

He smiled. "Nope. Just calling 'em like I seem 'em."

Boston's eyes narrowed as she studied him. He intrigued her thoroughly. She wondered how his mind worked—wished she had the gift of perceptiveness he seemed to possess so that she could better read him at that moment.

However, she remembered something about herself then—a gift of her own when it came to people. Holding out her hand, she asked, "Can I rummage through your wallet?"

"What?" he asked, smiling.

She wiggled her fingers, a gesture he should give her his wallet. "I can turn the tables a little on you if you let me rifle through your wallet," she explained. "Come on. Or do you keep stuff in there you don't want someone seeing?"

His eyes narrowed with amused daring as he reached into the right pocket at the knee of his khakis. Removing his wallet, he handed it to her.

"You're a wallet packrat, first of all," she began.

"How do you know that?" he asked.

She smiled. The tables were turning now. "Because you carry it in the pocket at the side of your shorts instead of in your back pocket." She bounced the wallet in her hand once or twice and added, "It's too bulky and crammed with stuff to fit against your butt comfortably."

He arched his eyebrows, his entire expression displaying the fact she was correct in her assessment and that he was impressed.

"A single-fold wallet," she said as she unfolded the well-worn, black cow leather. "Another sign of a wallet packrat."

Vance chuckled, leaned back on the sofa, and tucked his hands behind his head as if waiting to be entertained. The muscles in his biceps bulged ridiculously, but Boston endeavored not to notice.

"Hmm," she said, letting her fingers count the cash in the cash pocket of his wallet. "Five, ten, twenty…one, two, three. Thirty-eight dollars in small bills."

"Means I don't make a good income?" he prodded.

"Means you don't waste a lot of cash…that you're not self-indulgent." One by one, she lifted his cards out of the credit card section. "One debit card, a rewards card from Cinnabon, one American Express, and one Visa credit card."

"So?" he urged her.

"You're frugal. You keep the debit card in front of all the rest, then the Cinnabon rewards card, then the American Express, and the credit card last. It means you avoid debt, using first your liquid asset, cash…then the card that has to be paid off every month so you stay within your budget. Then the last line of defense, the credit card, is just for emergency." Boston giggled as she pulled out the Cinnabon rewards card and showed it to him, as if he didn't know it was there. "And you have a Cinnabon problem…because you only need one more punch to get a free cinnamon roll!"

"Very good!" Vance chuckled. "I don't know that I was even aware of the whole order of the cards in there. But now that you point it out…you're right."

"Of course I am," she teased.

Boston removed his driver's license. She studied it for a long time, thinking how great the photo of Vance was on it. Most people looked awful on their driver's license, but not Vance R. Nathaniel.

"Middle name begins with R, huh?" She asked. "What does it stand for?"

Vance grinned. "Romance."

"Vance Romance?" Boston asked. She rolled her eyes and breathed, "Oh, brother. What does it really stand for?"

"Rockwell," he answered. "It's a family name."

"Hmm." Boston replaced the license and returned her attention to something she'd seen in the cash pocket—several store receipts folded together. Carefully, she unfolded them. "A receipt for two pair of khaki cargo pants, two three-piece business suits, and two men's fashion ties." She looked at him and smiled. "You're getting ready to start your new job, but you want to make sure you're ready to look the part of business professional or Steve Irwin…in case you need to wrestle a croc."

Vance's smile faded a little, and he shook his head. "I loved that dude," he said.

Boston remembered how saddened she was by the sudden death of the charismatic crocodile hunter several years before. She thought someone with animal and zoo connections and interests probably felt the loss even more.

"Next receipt," she said, going to the next receipt. "Ooo! Sofa, loveseat, and reclining chair. Brown leather too. Delivered to 104 Gem Lane, Oklahoma City."

"And?"

"You have good taste in furniture," she giggled. "Samuel's is a good store, with well-made furniture at a good price. You're getting ready to move into your new house and figured you'd need some furniture. Still, it wasn't delivered here. Storage unit?"

Vance shook his head. "Nope. The people I bought the house from said I could store everything in the garage. That's where all my stuff is…including that furniture."

"That was nice," Boston said. "And you kept the receipt until you're sure it fits and looks nice and things." She went to the next receipt. "Hmm. Wal-Mart! Now *this* will be telling," she giggled.

Vance chuckled and continued to watch her.

"Milk, orange juice, ice cream, gum. I'll guess that would be Juicy Fruit gum and that it's in your pocket too."

He nodded, and his smile broadened.

"Tomatoes, bacon, bread, lettuce—dated last week—at which point you had yourself a BLT for dinner."

"Okay, now you're creeping me out," he laughed.

"Well, join the club, Vance Romance," she teased. "Now for photos." There were very few photos in Vance wallet. "You're not public with your wallet," she began.

"What?" he asked.

"It's yours, and you don't expect a lot of people to be looking through it. Therefore, the photos in here are for you only…important to only you." She pointed to a picture of a little girl about five or six. "This is Samantha…yours and Danielle's niece. Danielle has one too. I'm guessing little Samantha gave it to you herself."

Vance nodded.

Boston flipped to the next photo—a picture of Danielle and Vance no doubt at a football game. "You and Danielle, probably in high school…since I haven't heard of her cheerleading or you playing football of recent."

Again Vance nodded.

The next photo was of Danielle at perhaps fourteen or fifteen, a school photo Boston had seen before. "Danielle as a freshman or sophomore." She went to the next photo. "Danielle again, sophomore or freshman…though I've never seen this one. Hmmm." She went on. "And this is your mom and dad. Is this recent?" she asked. She looked to Vance to find he was no longer looking at her but had returned his attention to the TV. His smile had faded.

"Yep," was all he said. He'd lost interest in her tell-all game—or, more likely, just lost interest in her.

"Well," Boston said, closing the wallet.

"What? That's it?" he said, looking at her again. She noted he grinned at her, but the sparkle of mischief that had been in his eyes only moments before had dulled.

"What do you mean?" she asked.

He shook his head, clicking his tongue as if scolding her.

"You see," he began. "Your attention span is too short. You didn't finish your evaluation."

"You mean I missed something?" she asked.

"Exactly," he said, taking the wallet from her.

"But what?" she said, reaching for it again. She'd only stopped looking through his wallet because she thought he'd grown bored with her.

"Too late," he said, shoving the wallet into the side pocket of his cargo khakis again. "You can't let your focus wander, Boston. That's the trick to reading people."

"Hey, you guys!" Danielle asked as she pushed open the door and walked into the apartment.

"Hi, Danielle," Boston greeted.

"What are you guys up to?" Danielle asked, tossing her purse into the little chair near the front door.

"Oh, just making out and stuff," Vance said as his attention remained affixed to the two Humane Society officers removing a pit bull from an abandoned house in Detroit.

"Oh, okay...cool," Danielle said, rolling her eyes as Boston's mouth gaped open in astonishment. "I guess Vance is proving to be more fun than Steph, huh, Bost?"

"He's only kidding, Danielle," Boston said, fairly leaping off the couch and walking toward Danielle.

Danielle giggled. "Sure he is."

Boston smiled as she hugged her friend. "How was your day?" she asked.

"Don't ask," Danielle sighed.

"Same here."

"Your pal Dempsey brought over some stuff for you, Danny," Vance called from his seat on the couch. "I put it on the table."

"Oh, really?" Danielle said, nearly dashing to the table. She hurriedly flipped through the papers and envelopes Dempsey had left for her until she found the envelope with her name on it. Fairly ripping it open, Boston watched as a smile spread across Danielle's face—a resplendent, elated smile. In fact, her entire face seemed to radiate joy suddenly.

"A Dempsey party, Bost!" Danielle exclaimed. "Oh my heck, I'm so excited!"

"When is it?" Boston asked, delighted by Danielle's perfect glee.

"Not this Saturday but the next one. Oh my heck, Vance! Dempsey throws the best parties."

"Does he now?" Vance said. He turned and looked over his shoulder, winking at Boston conspiratorially. "Well, he invited me too. So I guess I'll have to see what all the excitement is about, now won't I?"

"A Dempsey party!" Danielle exclaimed again. Boston was astounded at the change in Danielle. One note from Dempsey had done all this? "Suddenly, I don't feel so worn out."

"Good," Boston said. "Because tonight's class is supposed to be pretty challenging."

"Oh, well. We're up for it," Danielle said. "I want to take a quick shower though." Danielle glanced at her brother and then back to Boston. "Would you mind making out with Vance just a little longer while I freshen up?"

Boston felt herself blush. She couldn't figure out why she was blushing. She knew the teasing about making out with Vance was just all in good fun. Still, as Vance patted the sofa cushion next to him and winked at her, she blushed all the same.

"Not at all," Boston said.

"Come on, leopard girl," Vance said. "You ought to like this. They're going into a house filled with feral cats next."

"Leopard girl?" Danielle asked.

"Don't ask," Boston whispered.

"I won't," Danielle giggled as she headed for her bedroom.

"Hey, your purse is buzzing," Vance said.

Boston hurried to her purse and retrieved her cell. The caller ID told her it was Logan. Unwittingly, Boston quickly looked to Vance. His attention seemed entirely arrested by the Detroit Humane Society, and she certainly needed something to arrest her attention from the butterflies that had somehow taken flight in her stomach at the sight of him.

She answered, "Hello?"

"Hey, Boston!" came Logan West's masculine voice. "What're you doing?"

"Um…my friend Danielle and I are getting ready to leave. We have a cake decorating class tonight."

"Sounds fun," Logan said. "What are you doing Friday night?"

"Uh…well…I usually…I sort of have other plans," Boston stammered. She couldn't believe she was putting him off! Sure, she and Danielle got together every Friday with their friends, but that wasn't something to miss a date with hottie Logan West for—was it?

"That's cool. How about Saturday then?" he asked.

"Saturday's great," she said. For a moment, however, she wondered—did she say Saturday was great because she really wanted to go out with Logan? Or did she say Saturday was great because she didn't want to make Logan feel bad?

"Fabulous!" he said. "I was thinking dinner and a movie Saturday night. What do you think?"

"I'd love it," Boston said. She looked away from Vance Nathaniel sitting on Danielle's sofa watching *Animal Cops*. Closing her eyes, she forced her mind to produce a vision of Logan West. It helped—it really did.

"Okay…then let's say I'll pick you up at five. How's that sound?" Logan asked.

"Sounds perfect!"

"I'll see you Saturday then."

"Okay. Thanks, Logan," Boston said.

"Anytime. Bye."

"Bye."

An odd feeling of confusion washed over Boston as she took a seat on the sofa next to Vance. She was elated that Logan had called and asked her out—at least, she thought she was. Yet, as Vance grimaced, wrinkling his nose as the narrator on the TV episode began describing the strong stench of ammonia permeating the house filled with feral cats, Boston experienced a moment of doubt.

Inhaling a deep breath, however, Boston consciously reminded herself of how long she'd liked Logan, of what a gentleman he was, of how he would never tease her about her leopard-print panties or making out while Danielle was gone. Logan West was a dream, and she couldn't let Vance's good looks and charming personality distract her. Boston inhaled deeply again—her resolve strengthened, her memory of just how wonderful Logan was refreshed.

"Dang, Boston!" Vance exclaimed, however. Boston looked over to him to see him still grimacing as he pulled his ratty white T-shirt up over his nose. "Don't inhale it like that. It's cat urine for crying out loud!"

But Boston giggled. "It's on TV, Vance," she said, pointing to the television set. "You can't inhale it."

"Even so," Vance said, still holding his T-shirt up over his nose.

"Correct me if I'm wrong," Boston began, "but you are a zoologist, right?"

"Well, yeah! But that's way different than this," he said, nodding toward the TV.

Boston smiled and shook her head with amusement. She hoped Danielle would hurry. The impending, insatiable attraction she was beginning to feel toward Vance was increasing again. She needed to get to the cake decorating class so her mind could clear and think more rationally.

At that moment, Steph's venomous voice popped into her head. *I saw him first. Just remember that, Boston.* As Steph's voice echoed through her mind, Boston wondered why Steph's ridiculous demand had even affected her in the first place. Boston certainly didn't have any interest in Vance, other than maybe as a friend. Furthermore, she knew Vance had read Steph too perfectly. Steph wasn't about to draw him into her sticky web, so there was no need to worry about his well-being in that regard.

She just needed to get to cake decorating. Then her mind would clear. Then she could focus again—focus on her job expectations, on the mystery that was Danielle and Dempsey, on moving out of Stephanie's apartment.

"Want some?"

Boston was startled from her thoughts by Vance's voice, his hand holding out a package of Juicy Fruit gum toward her.

"Um…sure. Thanks," Boston said, removing a stick of gum from the package.

"It should help with the smell," he said, nodding toward the TV.

Boston giggled. He was so funny. Yet her next thought was that maybe the feral cats episode had triggered a scent memory for Vance. No doubt animal scents were familiar to him.

"Don't tell her I know," he said, lowering his voice.

As Boston placed the gum on her tongue, her mouth flooded with happy moisture at the sweet, distinct taste. "Don't tell her you know about what?" she asked, though she wasn't quite sure why she whispered.

"About the Dempsey thing," he explained in a whisper.

"Oh, I wouldn't," she said. "We'll keep it just between us."

Vance nodded. "Agreed."

Something in Boston's bosom felt suddenly more alive. She and Vance shared a secret! The knowledge delighted her for some reason. For some reason, she liked knowing there was something she and Vance shared that no one else did.

"Logan West," Boston mumbled to herself then.

"What's that?" Vance asked, pulling his T-shirt up over his nose as the narrator began talking about the conditions of the feral cat house again.

"Oh, nothing," Boston said, as she continued to force images of Logan West to the forefront of her mind.

CHAPTER FIVE

Boston's eyes felt dry and heavy. She just wanted to sleep, to be comfortable in her own bed. But that wasn't going to be the case any time soon. She wondered if she would ever be able to get a good night's sleep again.

The past few days found Steph more and more angry, more hateful and cruel, more intolerant of Boston's very presence. Things had gotten so bad that by Thursday, Boston had taken to simply leaving work and heading straight for Danielle and Vance's apartment. She'd even thought about sleeping in her car, afraid Steph would prank her in the middle of the night while she was capturing a few hours of sleep.

Over and over Vance had offered to share his bed with her. Over and over Boston had smiled, thanked him, and politely refused—even though, by the time he offered the place next to him on Wednesday night, his face was so lacking in teasing expression, she wondered if he might be serious. Maybe he was tired of her hanging out in his space, of being there from the time he walked in from work at night until he went to bed after his evening run.

Tired, frustrated, and simply worn down, Boston had finally decided to ask Kara if her parents would mind if she threw a sleeping bag down on Kara's bedroom floor for the next three weeks. She didn't want to impose—she didn't want to inconvenience Kara's family—but she knew them all, and she knew they would be welcoming, even for the inconvenience. She'd decided she would talk to Kara about it Friday night while everyone was hanging out at Danielle's. Still, that was twenty-four more hours away, and at that moment—as Boston lay on Danielle's sofa waiting to go back to her apartment at midnight, when she was sure Stephanie would be in bed—twenty-four hours might as well have been twenty-four days.

Danielle had gone to the grocery store. Boston had never understood how Danielle could stand to shop at ten o'clock at night, but she did. Danielle said it wasn't as stressful. After all, the crowd was gone by then, and she could peruse the aisles as long as she wanted. Danielle never made a shopping list—simply meandered up and down each and every aisle until her eyes lit on something she needed.

Vance was gone too, out for his evening run. It seemed he'd picked up the frequency and length of his runs lately. Boston knew it was her fault. She figured Vance must be nearly as frustrated with his lack of privacy as Boston was with Steph's hateful attitude. Yet Boston didn't know what else to do.

She was so tired! Two more hours and she could go home. The apartment was quiet with Danielle and Vance gone, and Boston bathed in the calm quiet. The low hum of the refrigerator in the kitchen, the rhythmic ticking of the clock on the wall, and the steady droll of passing traffic on the street beyond served as a soothing white noise, and Boston drifted into a deep, rather hard sleep.

Boston heard the apartment door open but couldn't seem to force herself to full waking. She tried to open her eyes, to force her body to alertness, to sit up. She wondered for a moment if Danielle had returned from grocery shopping or if it were Vance coming in after his evening run. Yet even the foggy, semiconscious knowledge it might indeed be Vance did not rouse Boston thoroughly.

In the next moment, she could sense someone standing over her. *Wake up*, her mind demanded. Yet great emotional and physical fatigue was weighing her down.

She did manage to mumble, "Just give me a minute. I'll be up in a minute."

"This is just bull…" Vance said, his voice trailing off as he swore under his breath. "That chick's unreal!" he growled.

It was Vance standing over her! Boston forced dry, tired eyes open and gasped as she felt herself suddenly being lifted off the sofa, cradled in powerful arms.

Even startled as she was, Boston's drowsy state handicapped her. As her arms weakly encircled Vance's neck as he carried her, she argued, "What the heck, Vance? I'll leave in minute. Just let me wake up a little bit."

"How much stuff do you have over in your apartment?" he asked as he carried her toward the bedroom.

"Not a lot," Boston answered. She was quickly regaining her bearings. He smelled like Juicy Fruit and warm night air. The back of his neck was moist with perspiration, and Boston was astonished that she didn't mind. "Why?"

"Well, you're moving in here Saturday, and I just wanted to get an idea of how long it's going to take us to get your stuff out of there and over here."

"What are you talking about? And what are you doing?" Boston asked as Vance nudged the door to his bedroom open with one foot.

"I got a call today, and my house is ready," he explained as he walked toward the bed. "I can move in Saturday. All my stuff is already there because it's been stored in the garage. So I figure we've all had enough of this skank roommate of yours, so we'll just spend Saturday moving you in here. Meanwhile, you're gonna take a nap before you go home tonight. I've got some paperwork I've got to fill out for the zoo before I can go to bed. So you take a little nap. I'll only charge you ten bucks an hour to use my bed. So for twenty bucks, you ought to be a little better rested before you go back to that wench you've been sharing an apartment with…if you can call the fact that she won't hardly let you breathe the air there sharing an apartment."

Abruptly, yet somehow gently, Vance dropped Boston onto his bed.

Boston opened her mouth to argue, but he said, "In fact, because I'm such a nice guy, I'll knock off the bed rental fee…give you a cut-rate deal on a nap. How does free sound? I'll wake you up in an hour or so. Enjoy the witch-free-zone peace and quiet."

He turned to leave.

"Wait a minute," Boston said. "You're moving out Saturday? *This* Saturday?" she asked.

"Yeah," he said, grinning. "I'm stoked too! I worked hard to buy that house. It's about time I got to enjoy it, don't you think?"

"Well, yes…but…" she stammered.

"Shh. Catch some z's before you have to head back to snake lady." He smiled—a perfectly dazzling, mischievous smile—and added, "Or…my offer still stands. You and me…we could have a sleepover."

Boston rolled her very tired eyes and smiled at him. "I'll take the nap, thank you." She pulled a pillow beneath her head and punched it a couple of times.

"Man! It's a good thing I don't let continuous rejection mess with my head," Vance mumbled as he closed the door behind him.

Boston giggled and snuggled into the pillow and bed, sighing with sudden and unexpected contentment. The pillow smelled like Vance, and her smile broadened. She decided not to cover up with a blanket—that way she wouldn't sleep too deeply. She'd be sure and wake up easily when the time came.

She closed her eyes, smiling again as a vision of Vance dressed in the armor of some medieval knight and riding across a hillside on a white horse floated across her tired mind. She should've argued with him—insisted on going home right then rather than lingering to take a nap on his bed. But what woman could've resisted such a chivalrous gesture as being carried to bed by a handsome road-construction-worker–slash–zoo-exhibits-curator? Not to mention that Danielle's apartment was dreamily homey and comfortable, so void of contention and electric emotion. Surely an hour more wouldn't matter. Further, it appeared she'd only have to endure living with Steph for this night and one more. Vance's house was ready.

Hurray! The room Vance had carried her to would soon be her own. She couldn't wait. For now, however, she'd simply relax—bask in the knowledge she could sleep for an hour or so without worrying whether or not Steph would dump a bucket of water over her or something.

Boston sighed and drifted to sleep, comforted by the knowledge that Vance was in the next room, filling out his paperwork.

Danielle stepped into her apartment and dropped the grocery bags in her arms. Vance looked up from his place at the table. There were papers spread over nearly the entire surface, and he looked tired.

"Two bags?" he asked, looking up at her. "You were gone for two hours and you brought home two little bags of groceries?"

Danielle shrugged. "I couldn't think of what we needed," she lied. The truth was Danielle had left the apartment hoping Vance would return from his run before Boston left to go back to her own apartment. She'd seen the way Boston tried not to be delighted in Vance's company, the way Vance limited his time with Boston. She studied her brother for a moment—his tousled hair, the dark circles under his eyes. "Why are you still up?" she asked. "You look tired…and don't you have to be up early?"

"I had some paperwork to finish," he mumbled. "Not to mention the fact I was worried about you being gone so long this late at night."

Danielle smiled, kissed her brother on the top of the head, and began putting the groceries away. "Well, I'm home now…so you should turn in," she said.

"I will," he said. "Um…would you mind if I slept on the couch tonight?" Vance asked.

"No…not if you really want to." Danielle frowned. Her heart began to beat harder as worry and fear swept over her. "Are you having trouble sleeping again, Vance?" she asked. Silently she prayed that it wasn't that—that Vance's torturous insomnia hadn't returned after so many years.

"No," he began, "but I won't sleep a wink tonight if I try to sleep in my bed."

"Why is that?" Danielle asked, relieved yet simultaneously curious.

Vance continued to mull over his scattered papers as he simply said, "There's a woman in it."

"What?" Danielle exclaimed. Was he serious? What was he talking about? What woman was in is his bed? Yet, all at once, understanding washed over Danielle, and she nodded. "You finally coaxed Boston into your bed...didn't you?"

"Actually, I carried her there...told her to take a nap," he said without looking up from the papers he was now gathering into a neat pile. "Haven't heard a peep out of her since...and I'm certainly not going to wake her up now and send her back to that snake she lives with. I'm just glad my house opened up so she can move in here on Saturday. I told her we'd help move her stuff for her." He paused and looked to his sister. "I hope you don't mind that I made that commitment for you."

Danielle smiled. "Not at all. But when did you find out about the house? You didn't say anything."

"They called me while I was on my way home from work today," he explained. "But you and sleeping beauty in there were so busy babbling on about men and chocolate that I just figured I'd wait until things settled down."

"Vance," Danielle began, "you don't have to hurry about moving. You know that. Boston would die if she thought you were rushing to get into your house and out of here just for her sake."

"I'm not. Why wouldn't I want to move into my house? It's costing me a fortune. It would be stupid not to move in as soon as possible, right?" He looked to her and grinned.

Danielle smiled too. She was happy for her big brother. He *had* worked hard to get into his own house, especially at such a young age. She was happy for him. She could just imagine him sitting in the privacy and comfort of his own place again—watching cop shows on TV and eating ice cream right out of the carton.

"You've got a point," she said.

"Of course I do," he said. He finished gathering his papers, set them aside on one of the counters, and yawned. He stood from his seat at the table, stretched, yawned again, and headed for the sofa.

"Now if I can just make it until my job at the zoo kicks in," he mumbled. "This road construction stuff is killing me."

Danielle thought of Boston asleep in Vance's bedroom. Boy, would she be rattled when she woke up in the morning. Danielle giggled to herself, knowing full well Boston would be mortified she'd spent the night—whether or not it was contrived by Vance.

"You know, Vance," Danielle began, very tentatively. She was scared—worried that what she was about to say might set her brother back. "You should pursue Boston."

Vance chuckled as he stretched out on the sofa. He tucked a throw pillow under his head and pulled the quilt off the nearby chair, haphazardly covering himself with it. "Oh, sure," he chuckled.

"Why not?" Danielle prodded.

"She's a good girl. She deserves a good man."

"And you're not a good man? You don't deserve a good girl?" Danielle asked.

Vance didn't look at her—simply closed his eyes and exhaled a heavy sigh. "You said it…not me," he grumbled.

"Oh, don't pull that on me," Danielle scolded. "Move past it all, Vance. I have! Why won't you—"

He looked at her then—glared at her with the recognizable pain and anger blazing in his emerald eyes. "*You're* not past it, Danny," he growled. "You're not over it, and it wasn't even your fault."

"It wasn't your fault either, Vance," Danielle argued. "Please just—"

He raised a hand, the familiar gesture that he didn't want to continue conversing the subject. "She's not my type, Danielle. You know that…so just let it go," he mumbled.

"Whatever, Vance," Danielle grumbled. "Good night." Danielle shoved the carton of ice cream in the freezing compartment of the fridge, slamming the freezer door a little too hard.

Vance could be so irritating! Maybe he'd been right. Maybe she was glad he'd told her to back off from encouraging him to pursue Boston. After all, maybe Danielle didn't want her best friend to be shackled to Vance's sometimes-irritating temperament.

Stomping off to her bedroom, Danielle closed the door and exhaled a heavy sigh of frustration. Vance—what an idiot! She shook her head, determining she would do as he suggested and let it go—for now.

Vance inhaled a deep breath. He held the breath for a moment—counted to ten before exhaling. He was tired—every which way tired. He'd worked road construction off and on all through college, but knowing a good job was waiting for him at the zoo in less than a month was turning him into a weenie. In that moment, he simply wanted to be able to get up in the morning, drive to the zoo, and get to work on the plans for the new lion enclosure.

His body ached from intense physical exertion. His head ached from going through the zoo paperwork. His stomach twisted with anxiety at the thought of Danielle's suggesting he should pursue Boston. He thought of the pretty, auburn-haired girl in the next room—felt his anger flare at the thought of her viper-like roommate. Boston was a uniquely kind, nice girl—the kind of girl he would've liked to have won for himself in another life, in other circumstances. He'd overhead Boston and Danielle talking about this Logan West that Boston was dating. He hoped the guy was worthy of such a rare young woman—that he treated her well and didn't take advantage of her inability to say no.

He clenched his eyes more tightly shut—shook his head a little to try and dispel the vision of Boston in his mind—the soft, sweet fragrance of her hair against his face as he'd carried her to the bed. He started thinking about maybe moving Boston into Danielle's apartment tomorrow instead of waiting until Saturday. That way she could sleep in his bed tomorrow night as well and never have to spend another hateful evening with that Steph chick. He sighed, however. There just wasn't time. Everyone had work, and then there was the Friday night hangout planned at Danielle's. It would have to wait until Saturday. Still, the idea of sending Boston back into the den of venom ticked him off.

Vance inhaled another deep breath—held it to the count of ten—exhaled slowly. He was tired—weary—plain worn out. He had to turn off his brain, settle down, and get some sleep. He began to concentrate on the rhythmic ticking of the clock on the wall, the sound of the traffic outside. It worked—and he slept.

Boston seemed to drift in and out of sleep. She was comfortable—unusually so—warm and rested.

She heard voices. They seemed distant at first, but then she realized they were in another room—just beyond the one she slept in.

Instantly, she sat upright—rather, bolted upright.

"Oh my heck!" she exclaimed. She clutched the worn quilt to her chest as she looked around. The digital alarm clock on the nightstand said six a.m. At least she wouldn't be late for work—not if she raced home and managed to shower and get ready without a confrontation with Steph.

Leaping from the bed, Boston flung open the door and raced into the kitchen. Danielle was there, dressed in a nightgown and a light bathrobe. She was pouring juice from a pitcher into a glass on the table.

"Good morning, Boston," she greeted. "How did you sleep? Do you think that bed's gonna be okay? It's a queen…but you can bring the twin from your apartment over if you'd rather."

"Vance didn't wake me up!" Boston exclaimed.

"Sorry about that," came Vance's raspy morning voice.

Boston looked to the sofa where Vance was sprawled. He looked charmingly handsome! His dark, tousled hair and the way he was rubbing his eyes gave him an adorable, boyish appearance.

"I got tired and lay down out here and…" Vance shrugged his shoulders. "Did you sleep well though?"

Boston inhaled a calming breath and nodded. "Actually…yes."

Vance smiled and tossed aside the blanket he'd been covered with. He sat up, stretched, and rubbed his eyes again. Boston sighed, somehow delighted by his groggy appearance. She looked to Danielle, who stood staring at her, a knowing smile on her own sleepy-looking face.

"Oh my heck!" Boston exclaimed. "I've gotta hurry! Steph will chew a hole in me when I get home, and I have to be to work on time."

Danielle shrugged. "Just shower here. You can wear something of mine. You don't really need to go back to the apartment before work, do you?"

"I…I don't know," Boston stammered. Her attention was arrested by Vance—by his rather unsteady saunter toward them.

"Your purse is buzzing," he said, brushing past Boston and reaching for the orange juice pitcher.

He raised it to his mouth, and Boston smiled as Danielle slapped him on the top of the head and scolded, "Use a glass, moron!"

Boston's purse was still hanging from the back of one of the kitchen chairs. Quickly, she began rummaging for her cell.

"Who could be calling at six a.m.?" she mumbled.

"One guess," Danielle said, shaking her head.

Boston's stomach churned as she saw Steph's name on the caller ID. She looked to Danielle. "Are you sure you don't mind lending me some stuff?"

"Not at all," Danielle assured her.

"She's gonna quiz me on where I was," Boston said.

"Tell her the truth," Vance said. "Tell her you spent the night in my bed."

"You're such a dork!" Danielle teased, affectionately slapping the top of Vance's head again.

"Ow!" he said, taking a glass from the dishwasher and filling it with juice.

Boston inhaled a deep breath and pushed send.

"Hello?"

"Where were you?" Steph screeched. "I was up all night worrying about you!"

Boston put her thumb over the cell's mouthpiece and looked to Danielle. "That would explain why she didn't call until now, right?"

"You are so rude, Boston Rhodes!" Steph continued, so loudly both Danielle and Vance could hear her as Boston held the phone away from her ear. "Seriously, I can't wait for you to move out of here! I can't believe I gave you two weeks! I should've made you leave last Friday! I can't believe I've put up with your lack of consideration for this long! Where in the world were you? I can't believe you put me through this! I suppose you were at Danielle's. What'd you do, sleep with her brother?"

"Steph," Boston began, but she paused as Vance moved to her, placing his mouth close to her phone.

"See you after work, Boston," Vance began. "Thanks for keeping me warm last night." Boston gasped as Vance then made a quick kissing noise with his mouth. With a triumphant nod and grin, he said, "Let her put that in her pipe and smoke it," then sipped his orange juice.

"Oh…my…heck!" Stephanie growled over the phone. "I knew it, Boston! I knew you were a fake! Miss Goody Two-Shoes, my foot!"

"It's not what you think, Steph," Boston began, "I just fell asleep over here, and no one woke me up."

"Yeah, right!" Steph spat. "I told you to stay away from him, Boston. I warned you."

Vance frowned as Boston fought to calm Steph down.

"Look, Steph…I'm sorry," Boston apologized. "I should've called. I-I was just so tired."

"Whatever, Boston," Steph said. "Just get home before six. I need a ride over to Danielle's to hang out tonight."

Boston's mouth matched Danielle's in dropping open in astonishment.

"You gotta be kidding me!" Vance said. "You telling me she still thinks she's welcome over here?"

"Vance! Shh!" Danielle scolded.

Vance swore under his breath and sipped more juice.

"I'll be home by six, Steph," Boston said. "But…but I feel it's only right to tell you that I'll be moving out tomorrow…instead of next week."

There was silence for a moment. Then Steph said, "Well, good! I can't take your inconsiderate rudeness anymore, Boston. Get your stuff out by noon! I'll tell my new roommate she can move in at one. That'll give me time to clean up any mess you leave."

"I'll be out as soon as I can, Steph," Boston said.

The line went dead. Boston felt tears welling in her eyes. As miserable and mean as Steph was, Boston actually felt bad about it all.

"That chick's a psycho," Vance said, pouring more juice into his glass.

"We'll have you moved out by noon, Boston," Danielle said. "Don't worry."

"I am so sorry, Danielle," Boston said. "I am so sorry that you have to put up with all this because of me. I'll never be able to repay you. I am so sorry!"

Danielle shrugged and smiled. "I'm just glad we're finally going to be roommates. And I can't wait until Steph's completely out of the picture."

"We'll get up first thing in the morning and get your stuff out of there," Vance said, stripping his shirt off over his head. "You can stay here again tonight, and then you won't even have to sleep there again."

"I can't," Boston said.

Boston gasped as Vance reached out, taking her chin firmly in one strong hand.

"Yes, you can…and you will," he demanded. "If you're worried about appearances, I can throw an air mattress on the floor at my place. The previous owners are supposed to be out by five p.m. today."

Boston was breathless! Vance's gorgeous face was so close to her she could feel his breath on her lips.

"So," he said. Nodding toward Danielle's bedroom he continued, "Run in there and see if Danielle has some leopard-skin underwear you can borrow...and just get on with your day. Your days in hell with that psycho chick are almost at an end." He smiled, patted her soundly on one cheek, and moved past her.

"I'm getting a shower, Danny," he said. "See you after work."

Boston watched him saunter away—watched the way the muscles in his back moved as he walked.

"You told my brother about your leopard-skin underwear thing?" Danielle giggled with disbelief.

"It was an accident, Danielle," Boston said.

Boston buried her face in her hands for a moment. She wanted to weep—to sob! Vance was right; she felt as if Stephanie Crittendon had been administering poisonous injections to her soul! She could see it now, the necessity of escape, of not waiting another week to move out. She wondered in that moment how she would make it another day!

But she couldn't cry, not at only six in the morning and certainly not in front of Vance Nathaniel. Shaking her head and willing her tears to remain in her eyes, she looked up.

"Do you want to shower first?" she asked Danielle.

"No," Danielle said. "You go ahead." In the next moment, she was in Danielle's loving embrace. "I'll make us some breakfast." Danielle released her, smiling. "Then we'll sit down and have a nice quiet moment or two before we head out for the rat race."

"Danielle," Boston began, "why did I let myself get into this mess?"

"What matters is you're getting yourself out of it now."

Boston nodded. "I'll hurry," she said, heading for Danielle's bathroom.

"Just take whatever you want out of the closet," Danielle said. "Surely I've got something you'll like."

Boston paused and turned to Danielle. "You don't really think she'll show up tonight, do you?"

Danielle shrugged. "I can't imagine she really will. But if she does…I can't imagine Vance will put up with much from her. Dempsey either for that matter."

"So Dempsey's free to come over tonight?" Boston asked.

Danielle's face immediately brightened. "Yeah! He said he didn't have anything else going on…so he'll be here!"

Boston smiled. Already she felt better, simply because Danielle was so obviously excited in anticipating an evening in Dempsey's company. For a moment, she thought the room brightened. She figured it must be the fact that the sun had risen just a little, spilling light in through the front window.

As Boston passed the front bathroom on the way to the one in Danielle's bedroom, she smiled. She could hear the water running as Vance showered—could hear his low voice singing an Elvis song. She giggled. Though Vance did a mean Elvis impersonation, it struck her as funny, his singing in the shower.

She sighed. Life would be a bit brighter once she was moved— once Steph could no longer infuse the poisons of hatefulness, cruelty, envy, and angst into Boston's mind and soul.

As she stepped into the shower—as the warm water instantly began to soothe her rattled nerves—a vision of Vance talking trash to Steph through the cell phone entered her mind. She smiled and tried to scold herself for taking delight in Vance's implying to Steph that something was going on between him and Boston.

"Logan West," Boston spoke aloud then. "Tomorrow I get to see Logan." Closing her eyes, she pulled visions of Logan West to the forefront of her mind—tried to force images of Vance Nathaniel to the corners of her mind—tried and failed.

CHAPTER SIX

"So she asked this guy from work out for tonight…and he said yes," Boston explained. "It's as simple as that! You cannot believe how relieved I was to get home and find her note." Boston frowned, thoughtful. "When's the last time she missed a Friday night soiree?"

"Like, never," Danielle said.

"It's all my fault, you know," Dempsey said. He finished pouring his root beer from the can into the glass of ice on the table before explaining. "After all, I'm the one who met her first. That job at Shea's Café was the worst one I ever had…and Stephanie Crittendon is a big part of the reason."

"You guys," Kara began, "I'm sorry…but I just have to say this. There's a whole different atmosphere here tonight without Steph. I know it's mean, but I was always waiting for something awful to happen whenever she was here. It seems like she was always mad about something or at somebody."

"I know," Boston said, guilt expanding so rapidly in her chest she thought she might explode. "I'm so sorry, you guys. I should've developed some backbone a long time ago."

"Hey, baby," Dempsey said, putting a strong arm around Boston's shoulders and hugging her with reassurance. "First of all, it wasn't your fault. We all thought maybe we could soften her up a little. You just have more compassion and endurance than the rest of us." Dempsey released Boston and picked up his glass of foaming root beer. "If I'd have been the one living with her, I would have beat the...the snot out of her by now."

"Me too," Danielle agreed.

Boston smiled as she saw Dempsey wink at Danielle in agreement. Danielle's cheeks pinked up, and Boston wished the two of them would pull their heads out of the sand and each see the other one liked them.

"How's work going, Max?" Halle asked, heaping chili on the hot dog in a bun on her plate.

Max, Kara's should-be fiancé, was a tall, slender, quiet young man. He sort of reminded Boston of a friendly old scarecrow, only more handsome.

Max ran fingers through his tousled blond hair and said, "It's all right. I feel a little cooped up being in an office all day. But...it's good. I like the work. It keeps my mind busy."

"Well, I may as well tell you guys," Halle began, sprinkling grated cheese over her chili dog. "I didn't get that job with Winfield and Roux." Halle sighed with obvious disappointment.

"Sorry, Halle," Danielle said.

Halle shrugged. "It's okay. But sometimes...sometimes I just wish life was as easy as it was when we were all working at the North Pole. You know?"

Dempsey laughed. "Easy for you maybe...but my self-esteem took a big hit that summer." He shook his head, chuckling at the memory.

"Oh, but you made such a cute elf," Kara teased.

"Yeah. You did," Max said, fighting back a smile. "I've seen photos."

"Dude!" Dempsey countered. "It takes a real man to dress up in green knickers, red-and-white striped socks, curly pointed shoes, and an elf cap and still pull off manly man."

Everyone laughed, and Max nodded. "You're right about that, man. You're right about that."

"What's so funny?"

Everyone turned and looked at Vance. He stood before them, fresh out of the shower, wearing only a towel wrapped around his waist, wet hair, and an innocent expression of curiosity.

When no one responded to his question, he rubbed his hands together and said, "Ooo! The chili dogs are ready?"

"Vance!" Danielle immediately scolded. "Sheesh! Can you at least put on a bathrobe?"

Boston smiled when Vance, Dempsey, and Max simultaneously exclaimed, "A bathrobe?" The men looked at each other as if Danielle had suggested the most asinine thing she possibly could have suggested.

"Danielle," Vance began, "guys don't wear bathrobes." He looked to Dempsey, then to Max, and asked, "Am I right?"

"Totally, dude," Dempsey agreed. "Bathrobes are for dudes who are too chicken to show a little pectoral flesh."

"Are you telling us that you never wear a bathrobe…Mr. Green Knickers and Curly Toed Shoes?" Danielle teased.

"Heck no!" Dempsey exclaimed. The girls giggled as Dempsey proceeded to strip off his shirt. "I ain't ashamed of my perfectly sculpted torso." He flexed and everyone laughed.

"How about you, Max?" Dempsey asked.

Max, who was normally quite reserved, stripped off his shirt, saying, "I don't even own a bathrobe, dude!"

Kara was so astonished by Max's brazen act of displaying a well-toned physique that she gasped, blushed, and placed her hands over her eyes.

"Oh my heck!" Danielle scolded. "You guys are ridiculous."

"Ridiculously ripped," Vance said, flexing massive biceps, sculpted pectorals, and chiseled abs.

"That's right!" Dempsey said, flexing his own well-molded musculature.

Max flexed as well, though his tall, slender look was more that of an athletic distance runner—yet still very impressive.

"Wait a minute," Dempsey said, looking to Vance. "You're still all wet." Dempsey looked to Max. "We need some water, dude. He's showing us up."

Instantly, Dempsey and Max raced to the sink. Dempsey turned on the faucet and began splashing water at his chest. Max, always the thinker, grabbed the spray bottle Danielle used to mist her ferns from on top of the fridge.

"Dude," Max said to Dempsey as he began to spray his chest.

"Exactly!" Dempsey laughed. Quickly, they returned to stand on either side of Vance, spraying their chests, arms, and stomachs.

"Here, man," Max said to Vance, squirting him a couple of times. "You're beginning to dry off."

Boston laughed so hard she thought she might never catch her breath!

Halle crossed her legs and, through her laughter, begged, "Stop! Stop you guys!" Halle had a bladder the size of baby toad, and the sight of her only caused Boston to laugh harder.

Danielle was overcome with such complete gut-busting that she'd sat down on the floor, wiping tears from her eyes as she tried to control her laughter. Even Kara, who was normally the most guarded of Boston's friends, was laughing so hard she appeared to be in pain.

And then—just when Boston didn't think she could laugh any harder—Vance said something to Dempsey and Max. They smiled, and in the next moment, all three men began to march in place in unison, singing the opening verse of "Macho Man."

Danielle was immediately on her feet. "Stop! Stop!" she begged breathlessly. Racing forward, she clamped a hand over Dempsey's mouth. Dempsey, however, simply shook his head, liberating his face from her grasp. His arms encircled Danielle's waist as he continued to march in rhythm and sing.

Halle was literally rolling on the floor, and tears of mirth were streaming down Kara's face.

"Stop!" Danielle begged, barely able to draw breath. "I can't breathe! I'll be sick! I swear it!" she panted between gasps for air.

Vance began to chuckle and broke into his own laughter, and the singing stopped, replaced by the deep resonance of masculine chuckles.

"Oh my heck!" Danielle breathed. "I haven't laughed that hard in years! I swear I haven't!"

Boston at last drew a deep breath—sighed with blessed relief—even as sporadic giggles continued to escape her throat. Never, never had they had this much fun when Steph was present—never! Stephanie wouldn't have approved of the guys being so silly—let alone so scantily clad. But it was all in good fun, and Boston was all the more thankful that Steph wasn't there.

Boston watched as Vance and Max wiped the moisture of mirth from their eyes. Vance was hysterical! After all, hadn't the whole hilarious scene been orchestrated by him? She liked that he'd unearthed Max's playful nature—that because of the whole incident, Danielle had ended up in Dempsey's arms for a time. Her heart swelled as she looked at him—but she quickly reminded herself of the date she had scheduled with Logan West the next day. Furthermore, Vance was Danielle's brother—Danielle's ridiculously ripped, lethally gorgeous brother maybe—but brother nonetheless. Boston knew nesting on the thought of "what if" where romance with Vance Nathaniel was concerned was out of the question—even if he had shown any kind of interest in her, which he hadn't.

"Look out!" Halle giggled, pushing past Vance and heading for the bathroom.

"Go put some clothes on, Vance," Danielle scolded, tousling his wet hair and smiling at him. "I'm sure you haven't eaten all day. Come get a chili dog."

Boston watched as Vance nodded, turned, and headed for his bedroom. Dempsey chuckled as he put his shirt back on—so did Max.

"Your brother's a scream, Danielle," Dempsey said.

"Yeah…I know," Danielle said. She was still blushing—still a little rattled at having been in Dempsey's arms. Boston loved it!

"You know what, Kara?" Max began then.

"What, baby?" Kara asked, still giggling now and again.

"I've got something for you." Boston held her breath as Max reached into the front right pocket of his pants.

Danielle looked to Boston, an expression of anticipation on her face.

"I've been trying to find a moment…or a way…to give this to you for three months," Max said. "I think it's time I quit messing around."

Boston and Danielle gasped in unison as Max dropped to one knee in front of Kara.

"No way!" Halle breathed, stepping from behind Dempsey.

As Max held out a red velvet jeweler's box, Kara's eyes filled with tears. She covered her gaping, gasping mouth with trembling hands.

"Will you marry me, Kara?" Max asked.

"M-Max!" Kara breathed through her tears. "Of course! Oh, Max!"

Boston felt her own tears trickling down her cheeks as Max stood, capturing Kara in a strong embrace as she threw herself into his arms.

Dempsey chuckled as Danielle, Halle, and Boston squealed, jumped up and down with delight, and began congratulating Kara.

"Good job, man," Dempsey said, patting Max on the back. "Congratulations."

"What did I miss?" Vance asked Boston as he returned. He pulled a black T-shirt on over his head.

Boston brushed a tear from her cheek and smiled at him. "Just a marriage proposal. That's all." She nodded toward Max and Kara, who stood kissing in the kitchen as chili and hot dogs simmered on the stove.

"That's all?" Vance exclaimed. He smiled and laughed. "I was only out of the room for sixty seconds. Dang! You people move fast around here."

"He's had the ring for, like, three months," Boston whispered. "It's taken him this long to get up the nerve."

"I can understand that," Vance said, nodding.

"You can?" Boston asked.

"Sure," Vance told her. "He's a quiet guy, probably scared to death of rejection…not that all guys aren't. But Max, he seems like a guy who likes things organized and in control most of the time. Proposing marriage…that's something that can sometimes have an unpredictable outcome."

Boston's mouth gaped open as she looked at Vance.

"What?" he asked when he glanced over and saw her expression.

"Correct me if I'm wrong," she began, "but isn't tonight the first time you've met Max?"

"Well…yeah. So what?"

Boston simply shook her head. The guy was incredible! She wondered if Vance's ability to read people at first sight would ever cease to amaze her. She thought not.

As the Friday night soiree at Danielle's wore down, it seemed the lighthearted moments of shared friendship only grew. Kara and Max were in la-la land, overjoyed and content in their new official engagement. Dempsey was as hilarious as always, forever dropping the funniest answers to game questions or going on about the most bizarre things. Halle was her typical energetic and giggly self. And Danielle's eyes never stopped sparkling, especially if she were looking at or listening to Dempsey.

Several times during the evening, Boston found Vance's elbow nudging her ribs as he drew her attention to Danielle and Dempsey's rather uncharacteristic flirting. Boston tried to ignore the fact she liked feeling Vance's elbow at her ribcage. As everyone was sitting on the floor in a circle playing a game of cards, she tried to ignore that the magnetism he radiated was pouring over her like hot syrup.

Vance leaned over and whispered, "Maybe we're starting to get somewhere," as Danielle and Dempsey laughed over a shared amusement.

At the sense of Vance's warm breath on her neck and ear—the pure fact he was so close to her—Boston found her entire body suddenly riddled with goose bumps.

"Let's hope," she whispered in return.

"I'm out!" Halle announced, tossing her last card onto the floor in the middle of the circle of friends.

"No way!" Dempsey exclaimed. "I got stuck with, like, three hundred points in this hand."

"Too bad, Dempsey!" Halle giggled.

Boston smiled and began to count the points of the remaining cards in her hand.

"You know," Dempsey began, "I've just got to say this...though I know you guys are all too nice to. I know you're probably all thinking the same thing...but I've gotta say it out loud."

"We never have this much fun when Steph is here," Danielle stated.

"Way to be brutal, Danielle!" Dempsey exclaimed.

"It's what you were thinking...wasn't it?" Danielle asked him.

"Unfortunately...yes," Dempsey admitted. "Though I feel like a dirty dog about it."

"But it's true!" Kara said. "I feel so free...like I can be myself tonight. And I haven't felt that way when Steph is around...ever!"

"I know!" Halle added. "I'm feeling guilty about feeling so carefree and happy...but I can't help it."

Boston frowned, a tidal wave of conflicting emotions snapping around within her. It was obvious—more obvious than ever! Stephanie Crittendon was a mean person who caused everyone around her to feel intimidated, frightened, nervous, and unhappy. She seemed to poison self-esteem the way rotting flesh poisoned water. Yet Boston felt guilty—guilty for consciously thinking such things. After all, Steph was a human being; she deserved to be treated kindly, even if she was mean.

"Right about now, old Boston Rhodes here is whipping herself," Vance said. "Am I right?"

Boston looked to him, frowning. "Maybe," she admitted.

"It's not your fault, Boston," Dempsey said. "We all tried to help her...tried to be her friends. In the end, sometimes you just have to cut out the infection before it spreads."

"Kind of like gangrene in a wound," Vance offered. "If you leave it there, it spreads, destroys everything, and you're dead." He looked to Boston. "Same goes for your mental health…for your soul."

"That's right," Max said. He tossed his cards to the pile in the center of the floor. "Wanna know why it took me so long to propose to Kara?" he asked.

"Of course," Dempsey said.

Max nodded. "About six months ago, Steph pulled me aside one Friday night…and told me that she'd overheard Kara talking to Boston about how scrawny I was…about how I'd never amount to anything."

"What?" Kara exclaimed.

Max nodded again. "It's true. She told me that. I figured she was making stuff up…but then, she also told me that I was too tall and skinny…that I'd be lucky to find a woman who would be able to look beyond my weak exterior."

"You're kidding, man!" Dempsey exclaimed. "Are you serious?"

"Oh, yeah," Max admitted. "I knew she was full of it…but you know how people can get into your head."

"Baby, you're gorgeous!" Kara said, snuggling against him. "That's why she tried to pull us apart. She was jealous."

Boston wiped a tear from the corner of her eye. She felt sick—literally sick! She wondered what else Steph had pulled behind her back. She wondered what other kinds of cruelty her true friends had endured because Boston Rhodes was too weak to pull herself out of the trap Steph had tripped her into.

"Remember the time we were supposed to go to Rayvon's for dinner for Boston's birthday?" Halle asked.

"Yeah?" Danielle prodded.

"Remember how we ended up going to that little truck stop dive instead?" Halle continued. "It's because I was in charge of planning it, and I gave Steph the assignment of making the reservations. She claimed Rayvon's wasn't taking any more reservations for that night. But I found out later…they had plenty of tables available."

"Sounds like your ex-roommate spewed a little more vinegar than it appeared," Vance said to Boston.

"Why didn't you guys tell me this stuff?" Boston asked. Her eyes were still brimming with tears. To think she'd caused her friends to have to endure such atrocious treatment! She was heartbroken.

"She was your roommate, Bost," Danielle said. "We didn't want to make your situation any more miserable than it already was."

"I am too nice," Boston mumbled, shaking her head.

"There's no such thing," Vance said. "You just need to be a better self-advocate…that's all."

"You wouldn't be you if you weren't so caring and nice to people, Boston," Halle said, putting a comforting arm of friendship around Boston's shoulders.

"Logan West wouldn't be hot after you if you weren't the Boston we all know and love," Danielle teased.

Boston shook her head, very little comforted.

Vance exclaimed—swore under his breath. "I got stuck with almost four hundred!" He tossed his cards to the middle of the circle. "I'll never catch up now." He reached over, taking Boston's cards from her hand. "Boston only had fifty points! How can you only have fifty points?" He tossed Boston's cards into the middle of the circle too. "Well, there's only one thing to be done when I'm losing this bad."

"And what's that, Vance?" Danielle asked.

Vance didn't answer—simply stood up, went to the freezer, and removed a carton of ice cream. Boston looked up and watched Vance count out seven spoons and return to the circle.

Setting the now-open carton of ice cream in the center of the circle, he tossed everyone else a spoon, handing the last one to Boston.

"Ice cream always makes me feel better," he said. "You?"

Boston took the spoon from him and smiled as Dempsey plunged his spoon into the center of the carton, moaning with satisfaction as he took his first bite.

Boston wiped a tear from her cheek and couldn't help but giggle at his sweet attempt to cheer her up.

"Man, I got so much to do on Monday," Dempsey said.

"You're coming over to help with moving Boston's stuff though, right?" Danielle asked.

"Of course!" Dempsey said. "We'll get you all settled in tomorrow, Boston." He wrinkled his nose, "And then I can worry about Monday."

"Are you stoked about your house, Vance?" Max asked, scooping some ice cream out of the carton with his spoon. "Danielle says you got a good deal on it."

"I did," Vance said, nodding and eating a bite of ice cream. "It's a fixer-upper...but not too much of a fixer-upper. It's about a hundred years old. The previous owners did a lot of work on it, so it's in really great shape. But...I'm sure I'll find a few surprises."

Danielle nudged Boston with an elbow. "Dig in," she said, nodding toward the carton of ice cream. "Apparently it'll make all your worries go away. Poof!"

Boston smiled, sighed, and plunged her spoon into the carton of ice cream.

"When can we come see it?" Halle asked.

"Oh, maybe a couple of weeks," Vance said. "Let me get a few of the minor repairs done and stuff, and then we'll have one of these little...what do you call them?"

"Soirees," Boston answered.

"Yeah," Vance chuckled. "Then we'll have a little soiree at my place. Sound good?"

"Oh, yeah!" Dempsey said. "Meanwhile...don't nobody make no plans for next Saturday. The fun's at Dempsey's! Remember?"

"'Don't nobody make no'?" Danielle asked, mimicking Dempsey's terrible grammar.

"That's right!" Dempsey chuckled. "This week we liberate Boston. Next week we party at my house!"

Everyone laughed, began talking to one another, and continued to enjoy ice cream. Boston thought how truly perfect Dempsey's word choice was—*liberate*. She was beginning to feel liberated, to see the hope of her daily existence seeming brighter. In her soul, she still felt sorry for Steph—even after everything. Yet her heart and mind knew she was to the point where she had to stop the poison, had to cut out the gangrenous ulcer and preserve herself. It felt wrong in some regard—selfish. But the longer she was in the company of good, positive individuals—of people who tried to be kind, who didn't envy and attempt to cause trouble—the longer she was in the company of loyal, true friends, Boston accepted that it was okay to remove herself from a poisonous situation. It was okay to put her own well-being first.

She glanced at Vance—caught him studying her with understanding. She smiled at him, a thankful smile. After all, it had been Vance who had finally managed to make Boston see the path of liberation.

"Rocky road, baby!" he said, winking at her and plunging his spoon back into the fast-emptying carton.

"Have you got everything you need?" Danielle asked.

Boston stood in the doorway watching Danielle and Vance strip the sheets and blankets off the bed—off her bed.

"Yeah," Vance said. "Everything I own is at the house. I'll just stick this stuff somewhere until I get the washer and dryer hooked up."

Boston smiled as Vance simply wadded up the sheets and blankets and shoved them in a duffle bag.

"You ready to sleep all comfy and cozy in my old bed?" Vance asked her.

"Thanks, Vance," Boston said. "Really. I know it probably would've been easier for you to—"

"None of that," he said, lifting the two duffle bags at his feet and swinging them over one shoulder. "It's late, and we've got to be over at your old place to salvage your stuff in the morning."

"Are you sure you've got everything you need?" Danielle asked again.

Vance sighed, shaking his head. "Danny, I've been living alone for, like, three years. I'm fine." He leaned forward, affectionately kissing her on the forehead. "Now, I'll see you girls at eight," he said. "Sleep tight, Boston."

"Good night," Boston said as he moved past her on his way out.

He was out of the apartment quickly, leaving Boston feeling somehow lonesome.

Danielle sighed. "I guess he'll be all right. Do you think?"

"I guess," Boston said. "Though I feel awful. I think he liked staying here with you…whether he needed to or not."

"I hope so." Danielle looked at the clock. "One a.m.! We are so going to regret staying up this late." She looked at Boston. "Want me to help you make the bed? There's extra bedding in the top of the closet."

"No. I'm fine," Boston assured her. "Let's just get to bed. I'm sure Steph will make my exodus as painful as possible tomorrow."

"Probably." Danielle rolled her eyes. She looked at Boston and smiled. "Oh my heck, Boston, I'm so excited. We are going to have so much fun!"

"I know!" Boston squealed.

The young women hugged and then retired to their bedrooms.

Boston sighed as she surveyed her new bedroom. It was bright and fresh and Stephanie-free! Furthermore, the lingering scents of Juicy Fruit gum, Old Spice bodywash, and clean cotton T-shirts still hung in the air. In that moment, the soon-to-be liberated Boston Rhodes thought heaven itself couldn't seem more inviting.

Vance pushed the driver's side door of his old pickup closed. Reaching into the bed of the truck, he retrieved the two duffle bags he'd brought from Danielle's. It was late, and he was tired, so he sauntered to the door of the cheap motel, unlocked it, and stepped in.

He wrinkled his nose as the smell of old carpet, dust, and grime filled his nostrils. Still, the room had a bed, a TV, and a bathroom.

What more did he need? After all, it was only for a few weeks—only until the previous owners of the house really did move out.

He dumped the two duffle bags on the wobbly little table under the front window and walked to the bed. Flicking a cockroach off the faded bedspread, he stripped off the motel's questionable bedding. He'd been glad Danielle had let him take the bedding from her place. He couldn't have slept in the bedding provided by the motel. He wondered how long it had been since it had really been washed.

As Vance made the bed with the bedding he'd used at Danielle's apartment, he silently wished that buying the house hadn't so completely wiped out his savings. In that moment, he silently admitted he would've liked to have holed up in a nicer place for the next three weeks. Yet he couldn't see wasting the money now. Furthermore, he'd only be there to sleep. He figured he could hang out at Danielle's on the weekend. Thus, maybe it wouldn't be so bad. He'd have to pick up some air fresheners though. The place did smell pretty closed up and rank.

Stretching out on the bed, he set the electric alarm clock on the nightstand. The old quilt he'd brought from Danielle's still smelled like fabric softener, and he pulled it up under his nose. At least Boston wouldn't have to spend another night with that psycho chick. At least he'd done one good deed lately—though he prayed his sister never found out. He chuckled, imagining the fit Danielle would throw if she knew he was staying in a dive like this.

Vance closed his eyes, breathed in the scent of fabric softener, and tried not to breathe in any other scents that might remind him of where he really was. He frowned—breathed deeper—pressed the hem of the quilt against his nose. Something else was there, something mingling with the fragrance of fabric softener. He realized then what the sweet scent was, wishing it was stronger, more perfectly discernable. Lotion, maybe? Perfume? Hairspray? The old quilt smelled like fabric softener all right—fabric softener and Boston Rhodes. Vance inhaled the lingering fragrance of Boston Rhodes again and—in the next breath—slept.

CHAPTER SEVEN

"Masculine hands are *so* important on a guy," Halle said as she placed the box of books she'd been carrying into the bed of Vance's pickup.

"Oh, totally!" Boston agreed. "Men's hands need a few calluses." Boston put the box she'd been carrying into the pickup bed as well.

"And I kind of prefer it when their fingernails aren't perfectly manicured," Danielle said, placing her box with the others.

"Max's hands are perfect!" Kara said. Kara was in the pickup bed. She stacked the boxes the other girls had just put in. "Callused…but not too rough. Strong too."

Vance and Dempsey arrived, carrying the only piece of furniture Boston was bringing with her—the lounge chair Boston's dad had given her for Christmas the year before.

Boston smiled and watched as the two men worked to lift the chair into the pickup bed. Vance leapt up into the truck bed and secured the chair with bungee straps.

"There," Vance said. "This has gotta be the easiest move I've ever done."

"You didn't have much in there, Boston," Dempsey said. "Are you sure none of that other furniture is yours?"

Boston shook her head. "Nope. Books, clothes, pictures, bedding…just stuff like that. Oh! And most of the framed stuff on the walls is mine." Anxiety began to rise in Boston's chest. "Once we start taking the artwork and pictures…that's when Steph's going to get upset."

Vance jumped down out of the pickup and dusted his hands on his jeans. "Well, she'll just have to deal with it."

"Let me see your hands, Vance," Halle said.

Vance frowned, puzzled. Yet he held out his hands, and Boston watched as Halle studied them.

"Very nice!" she said at last, sort of handing Vance's hands to Kara.

Kara turned Vance's hands this way and that. "Yep! Good ones," Kara said.

"What's going on?" Vance asked as Danielle looked at his hands next.

"Well, I've got to admit," Danielle began, "they're a pretty good example of what we were talking about. What do you think, Bost?"

Danielle nodded to Boston, and Boston took Vance's hands in hers. Instantly, a weird electric sensation traveled through Boston's body. Vance's hands were warm, callused, and obviously very strong.

Boston studied Vance's hands for a long moment. They certainly did not own manicured fingernails. Yet his nails were nice—no length at all to them. He had calluses on his palms, below each finger. Though his skin wasn't dry, it wasn't baby-soft either. In short, Vance's hands were the perfect blend of scuffed up, rugged masculinity.

"I concur," Boston said, releasing Vance's hands—for holding them was making her nervous.

The girls all giggled conspiratorially, and Dempsey—never one to be able to handle being left out of a secret—said, "What? What's so funny?"

By this time, Vance was looking at his own hands, his puzzled frown deepening.

"We were talking about men's hands," Halle explained. "Kara says Max's are very masculine…so we were just checking out Vance's to make sure his were too."

"I have masculine hands," Dempsey said. He looked at his hands, frowning with sudden doubt.

"Let me see," Boston giggled.

She took Dempsey's hands in her owns and investigated their masculinity. Slowly she began to nod.

"Yep," she said. "You pass the masculine hands test too, Demps."

Dempsey smiled and mumbled, "That's right!"

"See what you think, Danielle," Boston said, handing Dempsey's hands to Danielle.

Boston couldn't help but grin when she saw the way Danielle's breath caught in her throat, the way her own hands trembled as she studied Dempsey's.

"The masculine hands test?" Max asked as he approached carrying three boxes.

"Yeah, baby," Kara said, tiptoeing and kissing Max on one cheek. "You set the standard. We're just seeing if Dempsey and Vance can hang with you where masculinity is concerned."

Max smiled. "Well, very few guys can hang with me there," he teased.

"Check it out," Vance said. "Don't look, but your pal Stephanie is watching us out the window."

Boston's innards began to tremble with heightening anxiety as she thought of having to return to the apartment to begin taking the stuff off the walls. In truth, Steph could have a very violent temper. Boston was glad her friends were with her—especially the guys. She hoped the old "safety in numbers" thing would keep Steph in control. Surely she wouldn't lose her cool in front of the guys.

"She's in there muttering about how ungrateful you are, Boston," Max said. "I think she expected you to leave that chair."

"She likes it," Boston said. "And I actually thought about leaving it…but it was a gift from my dad." She frowned, irritation and anger causing her to clinch her teeth. "And besides…it's the principle of the thing. It's my chair!"

"It is yours, Bost," Danielle reminded. "Just like the stuff on the walls. So let's get back in there and finish this."

Boston shook her head, still worried. "She's gonna be mad."

"Then she'll just have to be mad. Come on," Vance said, patting Boston soundly on the back in offering reassurance. "I'll go first."

Boston couldn't help but smile as Vance then began using military hand signals to direct everyone as to where to go, as if they were all Navy SEALs sneaking up on the enemy.

"Well, all your junk is out then," Steph said as Boston stepped into the apartment behind Vance.

"I just need to get the stuff off the walls, and I'll be done," Boston said.

"You're not taking anything off my walls!" Steph shouted then. "You've already taken stuff that belonged to me! I'm not letting you steal stuff right off my walls!"

Instantly, fear borne of intimidation welled in Boston's stomach, and she began to tremble.

"I was with Boston when she bought most of this stuff, Steph," Danielle said.

"I don't care!" Steph growled. "She's not taking any more of my stuff!"

"Show me what belongs to Boston," Vance said to Danielle.

"With pleasure," Danielle said. Danielle glared at Steph, stepped past her, and began pointing to three custom-framed black-and-white photographs of trees.

"I'll call the cops, Boston!" Steph threatened. "I swear if you take one more thing out of this apartment, I'll call the cops!"

Boston started to cower, but she made the mistake of glancing to Vance. Rather, she made the good choice of glancing to Vance. His eyes narrowed and he nodded to her; he was encouraging her to self-advocate, she knew he was.

"Stephanie Crittendon," Boston began, "as hard as this is for me, I have to say something to you." She swallowed the lump in her throat and tried to fortify her courage as she looked to Steph to see her defiantly fold her arms across her chest.

"For a long time now, I've been trying to help you to understand that you need to soften up. You need to quit being so mean to everyone and start treating people more kindly. I've let you bully me and bring me down. I've let you treat the people around me like they were slaves…and I can't take it anymore. I *shouldn't* take it anymore. You're poisonous, Steph! Anyone who is ever around you feels horrible in your presence. And unless you want to spend your life all alone…miserable…feeling the way you make other people feel…you've gotta stop being so mean!" There! She'd said it. Not all of it, of course, but it was more than she'd ever said before—and suddenly, there was more.

"This is hard for me, Stephanie! It's, like, the meanest thing I've ever said to anyone in my whole life, but I don't know what else to do. I don't know how else to help you! All I know is, I can't be around you anymore. I can't let you poison my soul with your unhappiness, anger, and cruelty. The artwork in this apartment is mine. I found it all, I paid for it all…I even hung it on the walls! There's no reason I shouldn't take it with me. And no matter how much you threaten me or yell at me…I'm leaving and I'm taking the things I worked hard to earn with me. Is that okay?"

Boston sighed with disappointment in herself. After all that— after finally being honest with Steph—she'd still managed to ask her permission to take her own things.

Stephanie's eyes narrowed. She glared at Boston—hatefulness, envy, and resentment pulsating from her countenance.

"Fine," Stephanie said. "Take your stupid pictures! They make me sick! You make me sick! Take your stuff and get out of my apartment!"

Boston gasped as she felt Vance take hold of her arm—yank her out of the way as Steph picked up a large glass vase, hurling it across the room in her direction. Thanks to Vance, the vase missed Boston and hit the wall behind her—shattering into a thousand slivered pieces. But it wasn't over. Steph proceeded to grab another vase and hurl it across the room at Boston too. This vase grazed Vance's shoulder as he stepped in front of Boston to protect her. It shattered against the wall, and Boston covered her face to protect it from the flying shards.

"Hey!" Vance shouted at Steph. "Knock it off! I'm not afraid to call the cops on you, chick!"

Steph glared at Boston, her chest rising and falling with the labored breath of fury.

"You need help, Steph," Dempsey growled. "Seriously, you need some help."

Boston watched as Halle, Kara, and Danielle went about the apartment, retrieving every print and picture belonging to Boston. Vance didn't move—simply stood between Boston and Stephanie.

Dempsey stood near the door. Each time one of the girls left carryings something, he'd nod at Steph and say, "Stay chilled, Steph."

Stephanie folded her arms across her chest, still glaring at each person who left the apartment carrying Boston's things. When the other girls had left, Vance took hold of Boston's arm and began pushing her toward the door.

"Steph," Boston began, "I-I'm sorry. I'm really sorry…but I just can't…"

She was abruptly silenced as Vance's hand appeared from behind her, covering her mouth.

"Don't provoke her any further," he growled in her ear. "Come on, Dempsey."

Vance dropped his hand from Boston's mouth but continued to direct her out through the open doorway. She heard Dempsey say something to Stephanie—heard Steph slam the apartment door. It was over.

Boston looked ahead to where her friends stood leaning up against Vance's pickup waiting. As she approached, smiles spread across each loyal and beloved face.

"And it's done!" Dempsey exclaimed. "As simple as that, and you're out of there!"

"Simple?" Boston asked.

Taking hold of Boston's arm, Dempsey pulled her into a warm embrace.

"I feel like we've just liberated somebody from prison!" Max chuckled, hugging Boston once Dempsey had released her.

"You know, Boston," Halle began as she hugged Boston too, "you've freed us all!"

"That's right," Kara affirmed, embracing Boston.

"That's not true," Boston said, however. "You guys are the ones who did it. I was always too weak to do it on my own."

"All of us were too weak to do it on our own, Bost!" Danielle laughed. "What a bunch of weenies we are…letting one girl bully us around like that for so long!"

Boston hugged Danielle. She couldn't believe it. She was free! After so long—so much emotional baggage. She felt more lighthearted than she could remember feeling in years.

"Let's get home!" Danielle said. "We'll unload your stuff and then…then you can get ready for your date with Logan without having to worry about Steph pulling some kind of mess to screw it all up!"

Boston nodded, for it was true. She couldn't remember the last time she'd been able to get ready to go somewhere—anywhere, let alone on a date—without having to worry about Steph's interference. Yet there was one person she hadn't thanked yet—the one person who had finally managed to make Boston see how truly bad Stephanie was for her emotional well-being.

Turning to Vance, Boston smiled. "Thank you, Vance," she said.

"For what?" he asked. He shrugged broad shoulders. "I didn't carry any more than the other guys."

"No…thank you for helping me to finally wise up…to finally self-advocate for once."

But Vance shrugged again, feigning ignorance. "Well, I don't really see that I did anything out of the ordinary…but…you're welcome."

He quickly moved past her, sauntering around to the driver's side of his truck.

"Let's get back and get this stuff unloaded," he said. "It shouldn't take us too long."

Max and Dempsey hopped in the back of the pickup as the engine roared to life. The girls waved as the men drove off and then headed to Danielle's car. They'd all ridden over from Danielle's house together.

"He's not one to be comfortable with legitimate compliments or thanks," Danielle said as Kara and Halle got into the backseat.

"So I gather," Boston said.

"Oh, I just think Vance is too cute…too sweet…and way too hot for his own good!" Halle exclaimed. "Why isn't he married already? Or at least spoken for?"

Danielle shrugged. "I guess he's just been focusing on getting his career in line and stuff," she said. Yet Boston glanced to her. There was something in Danielle's voice, something she couldn't identify. Still, the breath of sweet liberation was too invigorating to deny, and Boston smiled.

"He is sweet…and hot," she said.

"Way hot!" even Kara admitted.

"You guys! He's my brother," Danielle giggled. "Please!"

Everyone giggled, and Halle asked, "So…Logan West tonight, eh, Boston?"

Instantly, Boston's nerves began to twitch. She'd sort of been keeping her date with Logan in the background of her thoughts, having known that moving out of Steph's apartment would probably be dramatic. Still, other than the flying vase incident, the exodus had been fairly uneventful. Now she allowed her mind to turn to Logan, and it unnerved her.

"Yeah," Boston finally confirmed. "It's our third time going out."

"Ooo! The third time's usually the deal maker or breaker," Kara said. "You either want to press forward or not. Has he kissed you yet? Is he a good kisser?"

Boston shook her head. "No…not yet." Instantly her stomach was churning with anxiety, for Kara was right—there seemed to be so many things about the third date with someone that were telling.

"He sounds like he'll be a good kisser," Halle said.

Danielle laughed as she turned onto Main Street. "How can someone *sound* like a good kisser, Halle?"

Halle shrugged. "Just his name. Logan West. How can he not be a good kisser with a name like that?"

"It is a good name," Kara noted.

"Kind of like Max Ironside?" Boston teased. Boston had always liked Max's name. It was kind of brutal sounding, whether or not it fit Max's appearance.

"Exactly!" Kara laughed.

"Logan West," Halle mumbled. "Logan West. Yep…he'll be a good kisser, Boston."

Boston shook her head. Oh, how she loved her friends! Oh, how glad she was she had them. Her heart pinched, however—sympathy for Steph. Even after everything, Boston still felt sorry for her.

Boston closed her eyes and inhaled a deep breath, exhaling slowly in an attempt to calm her nerves. Everyone had returned to the apartment and helped unload Vance's pickup. Dempsey, Halle, Kara, and Max left after unloading the truck, but Vance had stayed to help Boston and Danielle find a place for everything. Thus, the day had waned, and it was nearly time for Logan to arrive.

Boston had phoned him the night before, informing him of her new address. He would be arriving any minute, and Boston's anxieties were making themselves known by churning her stomach like mad.

Something was wrong. Boston couldn't quite put her finger on the problem—but something was wrong. Something was wrong because her anxiety and nervous state weren't caused so much because Logan was taking her out but because she wasn't sure she actually still wanted to go out with him. All afternoon she'd agonized over her feelings—feelings of uncertainty, even disappointment. Was she simply so nervous about the fact that this was her third date with Logan—the numbered date that often saw a couple born or two people deciding they weren't interested in each other? Was she nervous because she knew Logan may try to kiss her goodnight again, and with Stephanie nowhere to be found, he might actually be successful?

Boston knew her emotions were chaotic merely because of what had happened earlier in the day with Steph. She still couldn't believe Steph had thrown a vase at her! Perhaps just residual stress was causing her uncertainty and trepidation. Still, there was something else—something Boston didn't want to consciously admit.

Standing before the mirror in the bathroom, she looked at her reflection—studied herself long and hard. Then, taking another deep breath, she whispered, "It's Vance!" There! She'd said it! Vance was what, or rather who, was keeping her so wound up in regard to Logan West. There in the bathroom, Boston finally confessed to her conscious mind that, ever since Vance Nathaniel had appeared, Logan West had lost his luster.

She argued with her inner self as she brushed her hair once more. "You've known him a week, Boston Rhodes!" she whispered. "Furthermore, he's not interested…not one hint that he might be interested…in anybody…but especially you. What a drama queen he must think I am! All this mess with Steph?"

Boston shook her head, determined to purge any daydreams of knowing Vance Nathaniel as anything more than a friend. Inhaling a deep breath of courage and attempted calm, Boston left the bathroom.

Vance was sitting on the sofa watching some show with fast cars and lots of explosions. At the mere sight of him, Boston's resolve to purge him from her fantasies was vanquished. Quickly, she turned her attention to Danielle.

"Well?" she began. "How do I look?"

Danielle smiled and pretended to study Boston from head to toe. "I like the green shirt—it brings out your eyes. And that skirt is perfect! He won't be able to keep his hands off you."

Instantly, Boston felt nauseated.

"What?" she squeaked. "Danielle! You know how I get about things like this!"

"Things like what?" Danielle teased. "Things like going out with the hottest guy to ever work at Channel 7? Things like you look gorgeous?"

"You know what I mean, Danielle," Boston said. "Halle's right. It's the third date…the make-or-break-it date…the first-kiss date."

"He tried to kiss you last time—on the second date, if I remember correctly," Danielle reminded her.

"I know! That's what I mean! What if he's like a guy who wants to…you know…" Boston glanced to Vance sitting on the sofa. He seemed completely unaware of what was going on.

"You mean a loose guy?" Danielle offered.

"Yeah! What if he is? What if he's a guy who expects a girl to…you know…expects more out of a third date than a kiss?"

"What if he's a guy who doesn't?"

Boston sighed, "Well, that's almost as bad! What if he hates me? What if I sicken him? What if I'm a terrible kisser? Oh my heck! Just today the girls said Logan looks like he'll be a good kisser! What if I'm not?"

"Boston, you're wigging out over nothing," Danielle said, lowering her voice. Danielle glanced to where Vance sat watching Mike Rowe perform some nasty task on *Dirty Jobs*. Boston glanced at Vance again too. He still appeared to be completely unaware of the conversation she was having with Danielle. He even exclaimed, "Oh, man! That is sick!"

"You do this every time you're dating a new guy," Danielle said. "You're always worried about this…and the first kiss…and I'm sure you kiss fine! How many guys have tried to get you to do way more than kissing? Am I right? Then you know you must kiss well…so quit worrying about it."

"But this guy is different, Danielle," Boston said. "He makes me nervous all over." She glanced at Vance, still intrigued by whatever was on the TV screen. "But I can't decide if it's because I like him or because I don't. I mean, you've seen him. He's totally handsome. You've seen how together he has everything. How would you feel?"

Danielle nodded. "Nervous, I admit. But not as whacked as you're getting right now."

Vance strained his ears to continue eavesdropping. He felt kind of bad for Boston, owning such anxiety over anticipating a first kiss. What was the big deal? The guy would kiss her, and that would be that. He tried not to glean too much amusement at her predicament; he was certain it was very serious to her.

Mike Rowe vomited over the side of a ship and coughed. Vance winced and groaned, "Ooo!" His attention was immediately arrested again, however, by the conversation going on behind him. He smiled as he realized Boston was breaking into one of her characteristic babbling marathons. For some odd reason, he really enjoyed when she got on a roll.

"This is Logan West, Danielle!" he heard Boston exclaim. "Logan West! Do you understand how long I've had a crush on him? He's, like, totally perfect, totally gorgeous, totally smooth! And you're right—he was actually going to kiss me last week, but good ol' Steph interrupted it. And you know, that's another reason I'm glad to be out of an apartment with her. I mean, like today, while Vance and Dempsey and everyone were moving my stuff, there she was…eating my Fruit Loops! Just last week she was chewing a hole in me for borrowing one of her eggs. But no! She can eat three bowls of my Fruit Loops and not even blink? And what if Logan goes to kiss me tonight and I'm not ready? What then? What if I decide I don't want him to kiss me? What if I do want him to kiss me and I chicken out? Oh my heck! I don't think I'm going to be able to look at him when he gets here. And that still doesn't solve the problem of how am I ever going to find the nerve to kiss him back if he kisses me. What if he sicks me out? What if, after all this time of liking him, he turns out to be a womanizer? Or a crazy man? I can't even think about it without feeling like I'm going to throw up! It's the anticipation that kills me! You know I'll never be able to settle down and enjoy the date!"

"You'll never make the date if you hyperventilate from talking and pass out," Danielle said.

In the reflection on the glass of the front window, he could see Boston moving toward the door. He glanced over his shoulder to see her raise herself on tiptoes and look through the peephole.

"He'll be here any minute, and I'm gonna throw up," Boston said. "I'll throw up all over him. That's what will happen...and then where will I be?"

"I'm pretty sure if you do that, you won't have to worry about him kissing you," Danielle teased.

Vance turned off the TV. He got off the sofa and walked to where Boston stood with her hand poised on the doorknob, waiting for her hot date.

"Seriously, Danielle," Boston began again. "I don't know what I'm going to do. Maybe I should cancel...say I'm sick or something. I just know I'll botch this up...I just know I will! One way or the other. Whether it's the kissing or simply deciding he's not—"

"Boston," Vance mumbled.

"I mean...Logan...he's like the man of my dreams! Why would I blow it? What if—" Boston continued to babble.

"Boston," Vance said. The commanding sound of his voice caused Boston to cease in her prattling and look to him.

"What?" she asked, somewhat grateful he'd interrupted her panic attack.

Vance frowned and shook his head.

"Shut up," he said. "You're all worked up about nothing." He reached out, slipping one hand beneath her hair to the back of her neck.

Boston was so startled by his touch, she couldn't speak. She could only stare up into his mesmerizing green eyes. His hand was strong and warm, powerful and reassuring.

"If it freaks you out so much...just kiss in the dark," he said.

Boston watched as Vance put the heel of his free hand to the light switch. In an instant, the room went black. Boston gasped slightly as she felt Vance's mouth press to hers in a soft, lingering kiss. Rendered entirely breathless with astonishment, she did not move as he kissed her again, coaxing her lips to part a little.

"Kiss me back," he mumbled against her mouth, kissing her a third time. "Just let nature take its course, and you'll be fine," he said. His mouth was warm and moist against hers. "Instinct is all you need."

Again he kissed her, one hand still supporting her at the back of her neck, the other powerful arm going around her waist—pulling her body against his—and Boston thought she must be dreaming. Vance was kissing her? It couldn't be! She had to be dreaming. Yet she wasn't, and as he continued to kiss her, Boston placed one hand on his cheek, intending to push him away—for she couldn't possibly allow herself to kiss a man she'd only known a week, a man who was only kissing her to prove a point, whatever it was. Yet she found her hand would not obey her mental command to push him away. Instead, she began to revel in the feel of his strong, whiskery jaw against her palm, awash with a warm sensation of blissful intoxication, unable to deny herself the opportunity to live a dream.

Slowly, alluringly, he kissed her—tutored her in meeting the pleasant demands of his mouth. His skill at toying with her mouth—at drawing a desire from her so thoroughgoing it was nearly frightening—was ethereal! And his kiss—his kiss itself was indescribably wonderful—invigorating—captivating—delicious!

"Vance Nathaniel!" Danielle scolded. "You are going to totally wig her out!"

Vance broke the seal of their lips and released her. Boston opened her eyes as glaring light vanquished the rich, delicious darkness.

"Oh, she's okay," he said. He grinned and rather slap-patted her on one cheek. "You see? You'll do just fine. If you can kiss me, you can kiss anybody. Right?"

Boston nodded—managed to say, "Thanks for the tip."

"Anytime," Vance said, winking at her. "They don't call me Vance Romance for nothing." He sighed as he reached beyond Boston and opened the apartment door.

"Well, ladies…gotta get home and get my run in before it gets too late."

In the next instant, he was gone.

"Vance Romance," Danielle said, shaking her head. "More like Dr. Perve. I am so sorry, Boston! He can be such a brat sometimes."

"It's fine," Boston said. "Really. He cracks me up." In truth, however, the good doctor, Vance Romance, had entirely freaked her out! She still had goose bumps on her arms and legs—still couldn't catch her breath! What a kiss! What a kisser! The thought traveled through her mind that Logan West would have to be pretty awesome to push the memory of Vance Nathaniel's kiss from her mind any time soon.

"Well, when he has a point to prove…he's gonna prove it no matter what it takes," Danielle giggled. "I guess he thought you were too worked up over nothing, huh?"

"I guess," Boston said as she sat down on the arm of the chair nearest the door. She rolled her eyes with self-disgust at the realization that her knees were actually Jell-O—weakened from Vance Nathaniel's tutoring kiss!

"He's right, though," Danielle said. "Now that I think about it, it is easier to kiss someone for the first time when it's dark." She frowned, pensive. "That's weird, isn't it? Why is that? It's not like you kiss with your eyes open anyway. So why is it easier when it's in the dark?"

Boston shrugged. "I don't know…but he is right."

"I swear, Vance is, like, totally way smart about things like that. Stuff I would never even think about, he just seems to naturally know."

"I guess he's had a lot of…experience…being that he's Mr. Romance and all," Boston said. She wondered then if Danielle's brother held the same high standards where intimacy was concerned as Danielle did. Most likely not, being that he was so hot and gorgeous and attractive and virile. In Boston's experience, guys like Vance were always promiscuous. Still, she wouldn't settle on that sure judgment yet. After all, he was Danielle's brother—she'd just pretend his fiber was of the same stuff as Danielle's.

Danielle shrugged. "I don't know. He's always been pretty picky." Danielle went to the table, putting the remains of the rotisserie chicken they'd had for dinner in a plastic container. "He used to talk to me about his relationships and stuff…but he's pretty tight-lipped anymore." She giggled. "Though…my friend in high school, Trisha Coleman…she once told me Vance completely ruined her! She said nobody ever curled her toes the way Vance did. She swore kissing anyone else was pointless. Of course, she's married now…so I guess she got over it in the end." Danielle giggled again. "Vance Romance. What an idiot! I haven't heard anyone call him that for years."

The doorbell rang, and Boston nearly jumped out of her skin.

Danielle looked at her expectantly. "Well? Are you gonna answer it or not?"

Boston nodded. At last her knees felt less gelatinous, and she stood.

She looked through the peephole. Logan West was standing on the doorstep—handsome, charming Logan West. Yet residual Vance Nathaniel goose bumps still covered her arms, the taste of Vance's kiss causing her mouth to water.

Opening the door, Boston said, "Hi, Logan!"

"Hi," he greeted with a smile. To her surprise, Logan leaned forward, kissing her on the cheek.

Boston forced a happy expression as Logan said, "You look great. Are you ready?"

Boston nodded and kept the forced smile plastered on her face. "You bet," she answered.

Still, as she walked with Logan to his car, a swarm of butterflies took flight in her stomach when her peripheral vision caught sight of Vance's pickup pulling out of the parking lot. At the mere thought of Vance's kiss—the memory of the rapturous sensations he'd rained over her in the dark—Boston Rhodes began to wonder. Had Vance Romance and his euphoric kiss in the dark ruined her the same way he'd completely ruined Danielle's friend so long ago?

Boston smiled at Logan as he buckled her seatbelt for her and winked. She sighed as he slid into the driver's seat and started the car. She guessed she'd find out soon enough.

CHAPTER EIGHT

"So…in the end…there's only one conclusion," Boston told Danielle as they sat at the kitchen table later that night.

"And what's that, Bost?" Danielle giggled.

Boston shrugged, shook her head, and said, "I'm a tramp. That's it. That's all it can be."

Danielle couldn't help but giggle. Boston could be so dramatic.

"So Logan West kissed you, and it fell flat," Danielle began. "That doesn't make you a tramp. That just means it wasn't meant to be—that Logan West, as hot as he looks, as nice and charming and gentlemanly as he is…he's just not the one."

Boston sighed. "But…but I had a crush on him forever, Danielle! I encouraged him to ask me out again…and again…and a third time. But all this week, all I wanted was to find an excuse not to go. All week I was wound up because I knew he would try to kiss me again. And I wanted him to kiss me last time, the time Steph ruined it, but by the time tonight came around, I didn't. So, I'm a tramp. That's what tramps do…lead men on."

Again Danielle laughed. "Boston! Tramps do a lot more than lead men on. And where did you come up with the word tramp anyway? Just settle down. Logan West is a nice guy, and he'll make some girl a nice boyfriend…just not you." Danielle paused. She wasn't certain whether she should actually say what she was thinking about saying. An idea had begun to form in her mind—it had been forming for some time. Yet if she were wrong about what she thought she'd read in Boston, the ramifications could be devastating.

Danielle inhaled a deep breath of courage, however, and—feigning a casual demeanor—asked, "You don't think my brother has anything to do with the fact that you sort of lost interest in Logan, do you?"

"What?" Boston exclaimed. "Pfff," she breathed, rolling her eyes. "Are you kidding me? Don't be ridiculous, Danielle. Vance is your brother! That would be…well…just weird."

Danielle smiled, however. Boston's reaction—the bright blush on her cheeks—was far too betraying. Vance had more to do with Boston's sudden disinterest in Logan West than perhaps even Boston realized.

"Well, I had to ask," Danielle said. "I thought maybe that kiss he laid on you just before you left might have had something to do with it."

"Danielle Nathaniel!" Boston exclaimed. "What are you trying to do? One minute you're talking me out of thinking of myself as tramp-ish, and the next minute you're implying that I am! I mean, it was harmless, that kissing in the dark thing…harmless! Not to say it wasn't a great kiss…not to say it wasn't probably the best kiss I've ever had…but Vance is your brother, and there's just something not right about implying I might have lost interest in Logan simply because Vance kissed me! I mean, obviously Vance has a way with women—which on one hand, makes me very suspicious…but on the other hand it was the best kiss I've ever had. And what else would anybody expect from a guy like Vance? Right? I mean he's totally gorgeous…and not just his physicalness. He's, like, smart too! I don't know if I've ever met someone who can read people the way Vance does—right off he reads them. And he's very gallant and protective. Look at the way he helped me with Stephanie…even pulled me out of the way before the vase hit me this morning. And of course he's got a great sense of humor. It's obvious he and Dempsey will be fast friends for, like, ever. But that doesn't mean he turned my head from Logan. I probably subconsciously knew Logan wasn't for me after our first date! Knowing me, I just felt too bad about encouraging him to ask me out…didn't know how to stop dating him. I mean, even tonight, after Logan kissed me—which was a pretty benign kiss, actually, but made me want to never kiss him again for some reason—even after, when he said he'd call, did I tell him not to? No! Of course not! I said, sure! What an idiot! So now I'll have to figure out how to put him off or tell him I'm not interested or something, and you know how hard that is for me. And it's not because of Vance…because, as I said, he's your brother and that would just be too weird…no matter how handsome and smart and protective and funny and just plain perfect Vance might be. Besides, I'm sure that every woman he comes in contact with feels that way about him. Look at Steph, for instance!" Boston paused—drew a breath at last.

Danielle was still smiling when Boston finally finished her rambling attempt to convince herself that Vance wasn't the reason Logan West had lost his appeal.

"He's haunted too," Boston continued then.

"Logan?" Danielle asked. Yet she already knew Boston wasn't talking about Logan. Her insides began to tremble with anxiety. Boston was very perceptive—too nice and often a pushover perhaps—but her perceptions concerning people and what pained them was exactly why she was a pushover—too much true empathy.

"Vance," Boston corrected. "I'm not quite sure what it is. But I think that's why he runs so much…almost like he's running from something." Boston studied Danielle for a moment, and Danielle began to perspire beneath her gaze.

Danielle knew. Boston was convinced that Danielle knew what Vance was running from. She wondered if it was connected with whatever deep, destructive pain Danielle had struggled with the summer they were working at the North Pole.

Still, it wasn't any of her business. When she'd mentioned it, Danielle's eyes had lost their merriment, their amused twinkle replaced by trepidation—and Boston wouldn't press her. To do so would be plain nosy, not to mention disloyal and wrong.

"Anyway," Boston sighed, "Logan West…he's not for me." She giggled. "If for no other reason than his kiss didn't goose bump me the way Vance's did. Not that I'm saying I have a thing for Vance or anything…just that he's a great kisser. I mean, I've only known him, like, a week. How pitiful would that be…to let someone you've known only a week get into your head like that. Nope, in the end…I'm just a tramp."

Danielle's expression brightened, an obvious relief lighting her eyes.

"You're not a tramp," Danielle reassured.

"Well, maybe not…but I am tired," Boston said. "What a weekend, huh? Drama, drama, drama with Steph…nearly killed by a flying vase…"

"Having your toes curled by your best friend's brother," Danielle interjected.

"Figuring out I'm so stupid that I'm giving up a guy like Logan West," Boston added.

"You've had quite a weekend!" Danielle pointed out.

Boston nodded. "And to top it all off, I only have one Tootsie Pop left. I don't know when I'll get over to Mustang to drop in at Sandy's. I swear I'm going to go through withdrawal."

Danielle smiled—a mischievous smile that caused Boston to recognize just how much she looked like her brother at times.

"What?" Boston asked. "You're thinking something you shouldn't be thinking. I can tell. Say it."

"You might get mad," Danielle warned.

"Is it funny?"

"Hysterical!"

"Then say it," Boston demanded.

"Well," Danielle began, "I was just thinking that maybe you could give up your Tootsie Pop habit. You know…replace it with something else."

"Like what?" Boston asked, smiling. "Name one thing more delicious than a chocolate Tootsie Pop."

"Whenever you get the urge for a sucker, maybe you could just douse the lights and kiss Vance instead!"

Boston giggled, sighed, and said, "That just might do it! Kind of like those nicotine patches people use to quit smoking, huh?"

"Exactly!"

"Oh, you're hilarious, Danielle," Boston said, shaking her head and thinking it would be a nice trade—being able to kiss Vance Nathaniel as often as her mouth watered for a chocolate Tootsie Pop.

As she lay in her bed that night, however—actually, as she tossed and turned in her bed that night—Boston couldn't purge the sense of Vance's kiss from her memory. She'd tried—all night she'd tried. Following Vance's seductive kiss in the dark, Boston had attempted to keep her mind from lingering on the incident—yet she couldn't. Vance's kiss had haunted her all through dinner with Logan, all through the movie he'd taken her to. Then, finally, when Logan walked her to her door, told her what a wonderful time he'd had in her company (which she found hard to believe, considering she'd been preoccupied with thoughts of Vance all night), and kissed her— she'd known. Logan West's kiss hadn't curled her toes. Logan's kiss hadn't even curled her interest! And she knew why. Danielle had been right: Logan West wasn't "the one." Logan West wasn't even "the maybe." Furthermore, Boston suspected—no, Boston knew—it was all Vance Nathaniel's fault. Vance Nathaniel and his bad-boy kiss—his delicious, sensual, ethereal bad-boy's kiss.

Stephanie Crittendon was out of the picture. Sharing an apartment with Danielle would bring more relief and joy than Boston could even imagine. Furthermore, Boston suspected the assistant news scriptwriter's job would be hers. All should be right with the world. But no—now there was Vance Nathaniel. Beautiful, ridiculously ripped, wise, insightful, funny, heroic Vance Nathaniel.

With a heavy sigh, Boston closed her eyes and attempted to sleep. Why was it, just when everything in life seemed to be falling into a nice rhythm, why was it something always disrupted the harmony?

❧

"How much do you love me?" Vance asked Boston.

Danielle chuckled as Boston breathlessly exclaimed, "Wh-what?"

"How much do you love me?" he repeated. He frowned. "Actually, let me put it this way. What would you do for me if I was about to make you the happiest woman on the face of the earth?"

Boston blushed. No, Boston turned red as a sun-ripened tomato!

"W-well…how are you planning to make me the happiest woman on the face of the earth?" she asked. He was so affecting, so handsome standing there in his dirty, dusty work clothes!

"Guess where I worked today," he teased.

"Where?" Boston asked. She was still nervous. What he'd said had been so startling—so deliciously flirtatious!

He smiled. "Oh, on a little highway project out near Mustang."

Boston's nerves settled, and her smile broadened. "Oh, yeah?"

"Yep. And…a little bird text messaged me and told me a little something about a little chocolate Tootsie Pop fan I know."

Boston giggled, delighted with Vance's attention. She noticed then that he held one hand behind his back. She figured it was probably a bag of Tootsie Pops from Sandy's Sweet Tooth Shop.

"So, I'll ask you again. What would you do for me if I was about to make you the happiest woman on the face of the earth?" he teased.

"Well, what would you expect me to do for you?" Boston flirted, delighted in owning Vance's attention.

"Ooo! That's a brave response," Danielle warned.

Vance chuckled, pretending to think hard. "I'll tell you what. I'll accept an IOU for a comparable favor…but just this once." His smile broadened, and he said, "Write me out an IOU, and I'll make you the happiest woman in the world."

Boston giggled and hurried to the fridge, grabbing a pen off the counter and ripping a piece of paper from the magnetic notepad on the freezer compartment door.

IOU one comparable favor, she quickly wrote. *Sincerely, Boston Rhodes.* She folded the piece of paper and handed it to Vance. "Will that do?"

Vance nodded and shoved the note in the pocket of his ratty brown T-shirt.

But instead of holding out the hand he held behind his back, he turned and walked out of the apartment once more.

Boston frowned, puzzled.

"I was sure you sent him to Sandy's for me," she told Danielle.

"Well, I did," Danielle said, also frowning with puzzlement.

Boston gasped, however, as in the next moment, Vance returned—carrying a small wooden barrel—the same kind Sandy used to display candy in her store.

Vance set the barrel down on the kitchen floor and announced, "There you go, Miss Boston Rhodes. Two hundred eighty-three chocolate Tootsie Pops, compliments of yours truly and Sandy's Sweet Tooth Shop."

Boston squealed with delight and clapped her hands with excitement.

"It's like Christmas!" she exclaimed, plunging her hands into the barrel to feel the seemingly endless supply of her favorite lollipop. "You must've cleaned Sandy out!"

"Pretty much," Vance admitted. "But she said she didn't mind…once I told her who they were for."

Oddly enough, Boston herself would've never felt okay about cleaning out Sandy's supply of chocolate Tootsie Pops—but she didn't feel bad at all about Vance's having done so.

Boston gasped and looked to Vance, horrified as sudden realization washed over her. "Oh my heck!" she said. "How much do I owe you? These are, like, fifty cents apiece…plus tax!"

But Vance reached into his ratty T-shirt pocket, producing the IOU Boston had written.

"Oh, don't you worry, Tootsie Pop girl. I've got this IOU signed and delivered by your own little hand. You'll pay me back one way or the other," he said, winking at her.

"I cannot let you spend, like, a hundred and forty dollars on my stupid habit and not—"

"Hey! I said we'd find a way to call it good," Vance interrupted. "After all, Danny told me to pick up, like, thirty. I'm the one who decided to buy the whole barrel."

"But—" Boston started to argue.

"Are you going to stay for dinner?" Danielle asked Vance.

Vance looked down at his pants and shirt. "I'm kind of grimy," he said.

"So? What, you can't eat when you're grimy? Just go wash up a bit in the bathroom."

Vance chuckled and nodded. "Okay. If you're sure you have enough."

Boston could not resist. She took a sucker from the barrel, unwrapped it, and popped it in her mouth.

She sighed and moaned, "Mm! These are fresh ones."

"Fresh ones? It's not produce, Boston," Danielle giggled.

Boston sighed again, twirling the Tootsie Pop around in her mouth and savoring the sweet flavor.

"Hey!" she exclaimed as Vance suddenly reached out and pulled the sucker from her mouth, however. Boston's mouth dropped open as Vance then popped the Tootsie Pop in his own mouth, saying, "You don't want to spoil your dinner, do you? Anyway, you're gonna rot your teeth out eating all these, you know." He winked at her and headed for the bathroom.

"Ew! Vance!" Danielle scolded. "Eating after someone is one thing…but sucking on a lollipop? Sick!"

Boston stood somewhat startled. In her whole life she wasn't sure she'd ever known anyone she'd share a lollipop with—at least, not before knowing Vance.

"Thanks, Danielle," Boston said, digging into the barrel of Tootsie Pops.

"Don't thank me!" Danielle laughed. "I just texted him and asked him to pick up ten or twenty if he had time. It's Mr. Overachiever that bought the barrel. Sandy must've been having a fit!"

"Yeah," Boston said. She stared at the barrel, still unable to believe Vance had taken the time, not only to go to Sandy's Sweet

Tooth Shop but to rummage around and pick out so many chocolate Tootsie Pops. And the cost! Even if Sandy cut Vance a deal—and Boston could well see Sandy falling prey to Vance's gorgeous appearance and rogue-like charms—she must have charged him for the barrel too. There was no way Vance paid less than a hundred and forty dollars for the Tootsie Pops and barrel.

"Now stop right there, Boston Rhodes," Danielle suddenly scolded.

"What do you mean?" Boston asked, as guilt over Vance's expense of time, effort, and money on her behalf began to thicken.

"I know you! You're starting to worry about this," Danielle said. "Well, don't. For once just let someone enjoy doing something fun without slathering yourself with guilt. Besides, you gave Vance a handwritten IOU. And believe me, you're treading dangerous waters there."

"But this must've cost easily over a hundred bucks," Boston began.

"Boston," Danielle said, lowering her voice, "I haven't seen my brother that delighted in something crazy he's done for a long time. I'm begging you—for my sake if nothing else—just let him know how much it meant. Let him enjoy his moment. Okay?"

Boston frowned and felt her eyes narrow as she stared at Danielle. Danielle was so sincere. She truly was begging Boston to enjoy the gift—for Vance's sake. Again Boston had the sense of being ignorant of something, something she may never gain a knowledge of. And that was okay because she loved Danielle—and she feared she was beginning to love her brother.

"Okay," Boston agreed.

"Thank you," Danielle said. She forced a smile—a rather melancholy smile—and said, "Let's finish dinner. Vance is probably starving!"

Boston smiled and nodded. It would be nice to have Vance over for dinner. Who was she kidding? It would be fantastic! She'd be able to look at him for maybe half an hour—and what wasn't delightful about that?

"I still can't believe he took that sucker out of your mouth and stuck it in his. Bleck!" Danielle grimaced. "You should be very flattered."

"I am," Boston said, looking at the barrel of chocolate Tootsie Pops once more. "I really am."

Vance chuckled as he washed his face, neck, and arms with a washcloth from the bathroom's linen closet. The look on Boston's face—the pure delight and joy—had been worth a hundred and sixty bucks. Still, he shook his head, worried for a moment that maybe Boston Rhodes was getting into his head—or worse, his heart. He wouldn't pay for nicer accommodations—was staying in the dive of a motel—but he'd blow a hundred and sixty bucks on a barrel load of candy just to see Boston smile?

Vance's smile faded a little. He couldn't let her get in his head, though he admitted she already was. There was just something so vulnerable about Boston—yet something strong too. He'd never really met anyone who owned as much empathy—owned as much guilt over not being able to fix everyone's problems and save the world—as Boston did. It was admirable. Sure, it made her the perfect target of idiots, users, and jerks, but it also made her sort of ethereal, something the world had lost—a genuinely nice, caring, compassionate person. He shook his head, hoping she never got wind of what kind of a loser he really was. No doubt her empathy would take quite a beating, and he didn't want that.

He swallowed, excess moisture having flooded his mouth as he thought of Boston. He couldn't believe he'd kissed her the night before! Furthermore, it'd had nothing to do with her being nervous about kissing the dude she had a date with. Vance reprimanded himself—bathed in self-loathing—knowing kissing Boston just before her date had everything to do with planting himself in her mind so that the other guy wouldn't get anywhere close to first base with her. He was a jerk, and he knew it. Still, he couldn't stand the thought of this other guy kissing her—even being with her. She deserved better. Sure, he'd never met the dude, but Vance was sure

Boston deserved better. There was no sparkle in her eyes when she talked about this Logan West—no fire in her cheeks. Naw, the Logan West guy needed to be history. So Vance had kissed Boston before her date. It was mean maybe—but if she'd had a sparkle when she talked about the guy, Vance would've left well enough alone. At least, that's what he told himself.

His mouth watered again, and he shook his head. She'd tasted like pure sugar when he'd kissed her! Furthermore, in the short time he'd had her in his arms and known the moist warmth of her mouth, she'd put his mind to traveling down all sorts of inappropriate and unrealistic venues. He'd even wondered if he'd be able to let her go. Wondered if, when the lights went back on, he might not just tie her up and keep her from going out with the guy at all.

Vance bent down to the sink and splashed cold water on his face. Too much thinking—it was never a good thing. Not for Vance Nathaniel. He'd learned long ago not to let his mind nest too much on certain subjects. He decided then and there that his sister's roommate was one of them.

Still, he chuckled again as he tossed the empty lollipop stick into the wastebasket. Boston's face when he'd brought the barrel of Tootsie Pops in—priceless!

"What did Dempsey ask you to bring to the party Saturday?" Danielle asked.

"That bean salsa stuff I make that he likes," Boston answered, cutting her pork chop with her knife and fork.

"I'm bringing chips," Vance said, smearing cinnamon-flavored applesauce over his. "Do you think he means, like, potato chips or, like, corn chips?"

Boston and Danielle both giggled.

"Well, what exactly did he say when he asked you to bring them, Vance?" Danielle asked. Boston looked when Vance paused in smearing the applesauce.

"He said, 'Dude…you should bring, like, three bags of chips,'" Vance said. "Those were his exact words."

Boston smiled, shaking her head at Vance's perfect impersonation of Dempsey.

"Then I think you should bring three bags of, like, potato chips," Danielle told him. She shook her head, still smiling. Leaning toward Boston, she said, "Guys totally crack me up."

"Danielle, 'bring chips' doesn't mean what it used to thirty years ago," Vance explained. "Bring chips used to mean bring chips— potato chips. But now days, it can mean bring unflavored tortilla chips in case there's salsa, nacho-cheese-flavored or ranch-flavored tortilla chips, corn chips, baked chips, fried chips. It's totally a new world where chips are concerned. So quit making fun of me for being confused."

Danielle bit her lip to keep from laughing. "Okay, Vance. I'm sorry."

"That's right," Vance said, cutting a piece of applesauce-slathered pork chop and putting it into his mouth. He looked to Boston, grinned, and winked. "Dempsey could've meant to bring buffalo chips for all I know."

"Oh, yeah, Vance," Danielle said, rolling her eyes with exasperation. "I'm sure Dempsey would've asked someone to bring buffalo manure."

Vance shrugged broad shoulders. "You never know. You've always said he's a prankster."

"Do you have a satellite dish hooked up at your place yet?" Danielle asked.

"No," Vance answered. "Why?"

Danielle smiled. "'Cause if Boston doesn't mind, you can stay awhile longer…because they've started running *Mr. Bean* reruns on the BBC channel at six thirty."

Boston giggled as Vance's eyes lit up with excitement. "I love that dude!" he exclaimed. He looked to Boston. "Do you mind, Boston? If I stay a little longer and check it out?"

"Why would I mind?" Boston said, watching Vance slather more applesauce on his pork chop. "When a hottie with a naughty body brings me a barrel of my favorite candy…it's the least I can do. Right?"

Vance's eyebrows arched with astonishment, and he choked a little on the bite of food he was swallowing.

"Am I a hottie with a naughty body?" he asked.

Boston smiled—delighted, yet simultaneously surprised, by her own brazen flirting. "Well, I'm sure Sandy Sorenson must've thought so…or else you never would've gotten out of her store with two hundred and eighty-two chocolate Tootsie Pops."

"Two hundred and eighty-*three*," Vance corrected, pointing his fork at her for dramatic effect. "And you're forgetting the barrel."

"No…I'm not," Boston said.

Vance laughed. "Boston, flattery will get you everywhere," he began, "except out of fulfilling this IOU I have in my pocket."

Boston shrugged. "Can't blame a girl for trying."

Danielle watched, determined not to say a word—not one word that might break the flow of Boston and Vance's flirtatious exchange. Oh, Boston could say all she wanted—go on and on and on (as she often did) about how Vance hadn't turned her head from Logan West. In truth, Danielle was surprised Boston wasn't wearing a neck brace— the result of the whiplash she must've endured when Vance caught her attention.

And what about Vance? Danielle could not remember a time— not in all their lives—when her brother had dropped so much money on something as frivolous as a barrel full of suckers. Nope, they were both stupid—blind to what was happening—but Danielle wasn't, and she was hopeful. She couldn't think of two people with the potential to be happier together than Vance and Boston. Still, things could interfere—the past—and she knew it. But she would try to be hopeful, patient, and as nurturing as she could of the potential romance she saw blossoming before her.

Danielle sighed, wishing Dempsey would show as much individual interest in her as Vance was showing to Boston. Yet she buried her own broken heart—tried to ignore her own unrequited love. Vance was on the brink of true happiness, she was certain of it. And that was all that mattered—for now.

CHAPTER NINE

As always, Dempsey's party was beyond compare when it came to fun. Food, music, conversation—everything at Dempsey's party Saturday night was incredible. Nearly twenty people had joined Dempsey for the evening, and it was obvious everyone was having a good time. Best of all, Dempsey was so unusually attentive to Danielle that Danielle fairly beamed the whole night.

"Maybe he's finally decided to just man up and go for it," Vance whispered as he and Boston sat on one of Dempsey's sofas watching Dempsey and Danielle sitting on the floor in front of the massive fireplace, laughing together over pictures in a photo album.

"Maybe," Boston said. Dempsey pointed to one photo, and he and Danielle both broke into pealing laughter. "It's the photos of when we were all working at the North Pole…that first summer we met."

"Well, whatever it is, they're loving it," Vance chuckled. Vance looked around the room. "Looks like your pal Dempsey has done well enough financially."

"Yeah," Boston said. "But…but Dempsey's not usually so into stuff. It surprised us all when he bought this big house…all the furniture. It was almost as if he was trying to…"

"Fill a void?" Vance finished.

Boston looked to him, frowning and smiling at the same time. "Yes…Mr. Mind Reader."

Vance nodded. "He wants my sister," he whispered. "He's wanted her for a long time. For whatever reason, he thinks, or thought, she was unobtainable...so he bought a big house and filled it with stuff. A lot of people do that."

"Is your house big?" Boston asked. She'd been curious all week—curious as to why Vance seemed to put off Danielle every time she offered to come over and help him settle in.

"Nothing like this one...and it's older," Vance said. "I kind of like older homes. They seem more...more..."

"Cozy? Lived in? Inviting?" Boston suggested.

Vance smiled, and Boston's heart swelled at knowing she was the cause of it. "All of the above, Miss Mind Reader." He smiled, adding, "And more. It's almost like you can feel the history in an older house, sense a time when things were more defined, when people's priorities were better organized."

Boston smiled, even though inside she was beginning to feel nervous once more. Vance was too attractive—so tuned to what was important! She shouldn't have sat down next to him. She should've known it would mess with her mind. Still, what woman in her right mind could've resisted settling into a free space next to him? What woman out of her right mind? Certainly every woman at the party was affected by him. She'd never seen so many flirtatious, giddy girls in one place. Well, maybe at the Backstreet Boys concert she'd gone to when she was twelve, but certainly never under normal circumstances. Vance, however, seemed completely unaware of the fact. Whether he was truly unaware of his affect on the women at the party or whether he only pretended to be unaware of it, he was all the more attractive for it.

Boston was rattled from her contemplation of the fabulous man next to her when Dempsey stood up and cleared his throat.

"Okay, everybody, settle down," he said. "Now...those of you who've been to a Dempsey Mattice party before know exactly why my parties are like nobody else's, right?"

Everyone applauded, whistled, and called out their approval.

"Oh, no," Boston mumbled, the familiar mixture of excitement and anxiety stirring in her stomach.

"What?" Vance asked.

"It's okay…it's okay…I usually win," Boston said. "So it's okay."

"What?" Vance asked, rising concern in his voice.

"You'll see," Boston said. She smiled as she watched Dempsey get ready to make his big announcement. It was all in good fun, after all—all in good fun.

"Ladies and gentlemen," Dempsey began, "it's time for the highlight of the evening. Get ready for Dempsey Mattice's kissing games!"

"Kissing games?" Vance exclaimed. Boston giggled at the mortified, nearly terrified expression on his face. "What is he talking about?"

"It's fairly harmless," Boston said, patting him on the knee with reassurance. "Dempsey always has to have his kissing games, but I'm pretty good at them all…so I do all right in avoiding. The trick in Kissing Rugby is to pay attention and try to learn everyone's letter or number. That way you can sort of pad your competition. If not…you just have to be wiry."

"Wiry?" Vance exclaimed. "Do I look wiry to you?"

Boston studied him for a moment, giggled, and said, "No. You look more like fresh meat…chick bait." She laughed when the color drained from his face, and he swore under his breath. "Oh, come on, Vance Romance. Where's your sense of adventure?"

Vance looked at her, one eyebrow arching daringly.

"Are you calling me a chicken, Boston Rhodes?" he asked.

Almost instantly, Boston regretted egging him on. What had she done? Opened the door for any woman in the room to kiss the man she…the man she wanted! It was Boston's first conscious moment of admitting to herself that she wanted Vance Nathaniel—wanted to kiss him, wanted to date him, wanted to win him over for good!

"No," she said.

"Do you play them all?" he asked. She thought the mirth in his expression lessened a little.

"Yeah," she confessed. "But they're not like you might be thinking. They're pretty benign."

"Okay," he said, nodding. "Then, if you're in...so am I."

Boston felt sick. She wanted to throw up. She didn't want anyone else kissing Vance! Especially if Dempsey decided to throw Spin the Bottle or I Love You, Baby—Smile in the mix. Kissing Rugby wasn't so bad; it usually only resulted in kisses on the face, not the lips. Even Dempsey's version of Post Office was endurable. Yet Boston didn't even like the idea of another woman's lips touching Vance's cheek.

"Then form a circle, girls and boys!" Dempsey announced. "We'll play Kissing Rugby first."

Everyone was excited and delighted by the prospect of the silly game. Everyone save Boston—and Danielle. When Boston glanced across the room to Danielle, it was to see her friend gazing regretfully at Dempsey the same way Boston felt like gazing at Vance.

"Max and Kara!" Dempsey shouted as everyone nosily formed a circle. "You guys are officially engaged—thereby off the market—so you can be the referees. Okay?"

Max and Kara wholeheartedly agreed.

"Well, let's go," Vance said, standing up from the couch and heading toward the circle. Boston watched all the women watch him approach. With her luck, every girl in the circle would have their number called with Vance—every girl but her.

"How do you play?" Vance asked Dempsey as he sat down.

"Oh, that's right! You're new to this, Vance," Dempsey said. Dempsey hunkered down in front of Vance. "It's easy. The girls count off in numbers, the guys in letters. Then one person starts...stands in the middle and calls out a number and a letter. Pretend you're in the middle and you call out B-5. The girl who is 5 will race into the circle and try to kiss you somewhere on the face...or lips," Dempsey added with a wink, "and the guy who is B will try to kiss her before she can kiss you. You have to chase around in the circle. Whoever gets kissed first loses and has to stand in the middle and start the next round. I broke Kara's arm once a couple of years ago…so we try not to get too rough. Got it?"

Vance smiled. "Yep. I've got it."

"Cool!" Dempsey said, patting Vance on the back. "Have fun, man."

"Oh, I will."

And he did. Boston tried to bury her jealousy every time Vance would get called into the ring to try and kiss whatever girl was in the middle. Every time his letter was called, he managed to kiss whomever was in the middle before the girl whose number was called had the chance to kiss him. Even though Vance only kissed the girls on the cheeks, Boston was nearly wrathful inside. She played the game, put on a happy face, and had as much fun as she could, but watching Vance chase other girls nearly caused her to explode! She was relieved when the game finally ended—delighted by the way it ended. Halle was in the middle and called Dempsey's letter and Danielle's number. Max yelled go, and Dempsey leapt into the ring. Instead of trying to chase Halle, however, he simply turned around and spread his arms, taunting Danielle to try and catch him. Danielle lunged at Dempsey, and when she did, he didn't move out of her way—simply caught her in his arms and took her mouth with his in what Boston suspected was the most voracious, ravenous kiss Danielle had ever known.

Everyone clapped and cheered, delighted at the display. Vance whistled and clapped, and Boston could almost forgive him for kissing so many female cheeks—not one of which was hers.

The games continued. Boston managed to make it through the games on wit or skill without taking too many pecks on the cheek. Even the times she did lose, it was to guys she'd known for years—friends.

Vance likewise showed amazing intellect and quickness. He made it through both rounds of Kissing Clue and Kiss Your Neighbor without once being kissed. Boston's temper and jealousy settled after a while, once she realized Vance was quite dexterous at winning kissing games—or losing them, whichever way one looked at it.

❧

"You want me to rig it?" Dempsey asked in a whisper.

"Heck yeah!" Danielle exclaimed in a lowered voice. "There's no way Vance will break a smile for anybody else. He knows this game, and he's, like, unbeatable at it. Even Boston might not crack him," she said. "But if any girl in this room can do it…it's her. You're offering a hundred bucks to the winner. That's motivation for anybody. So I figure she'll give it her best." Danielle shrugged. "If she can't crack him…they end up in the pantry making out. So either way, it works out. It's a win-win."

"Your big brother will have your head on a platter for dinner if he finds out," Dempsey whispered.

Danielle giggled and whispered, "Not if he can keep a straight face and ends up in the pantry with her."

"Okay then," Dempsey said, dumping the shoe box filled with folded, numbered papers into the shoe box Danielle was holding.

"Here," she said, taking a sandwich bag filled with folded papers out of her pocket. "Put these in."

Dempsey shook his head. "If he finds out—"

"He won't."

Setting the box aside, Danielle held the bowl as Dempsey dumped the bogus papers into it.

"So they all have Boston's number on them?" he asked.

"Exactly," Danielle whispered with delighted anticipation. "Good ol' lucky number seven."

Dempsey laughed. It was a great little prank. He had to give the woman he was secretly in love with credit for her wit and effort.

"Ladies and gentlemen," Dempsey announced as he entered the room holding the bowl of secretly tampered-with numbers. "It's time for the pièce de résistance: I Love You, Baby—Smile! Tonight, the grand kissing challenge—the winner of which will, if the lady wins, take home a lovely, crisp one hundred dollar bill, thanks to everybody putting a five spot in the bowl earlier. However, if one of my brothers in kissing games here tonight wins, then, ladies, he'll see you in my kitchen pantry for exactly eleven minutes of making out!"

"Oh, no!" Boston breathed.

"Hey, wait!" Vance said. "I know this one. I'm great at it!"

"Me too…but you never know," Boston muttered.

The pretense of the game was simply this: again the men were given letters and the women numbers. Dempsey would call out a letter, and the guy owning it would then draw a number out of the bowl. Then the fun—or horror, depending on how one looked at it and with whom one was paired—began. The girl would have two minutes to try and flirt, toy, and coax the guy into smiling by using her feminine wiles and only the words *I love you, baby—smile.* If the girl could make the guy crack—get him to smile in the very least—she won and received the hundred dollars. But if she couldn't manage to get the guy to smile, he won eleven minutes of kissing in the pantry. Either way, it was a crapshoot. Boston had only been chosen to play the game once and won. But the year before, Max had drawn Kara's name out of the bowl. Kara had lost, and Max had cashed in on some pretty serious kissing. That was all well and good for Kara; after all, the outcome had been too divinely romantic. Yet as Boston glanced around the room, she silently begged that her number—the number seven, assigned to her at the beginning of Kissing Rugby— was at the way bottom of the bowl. Even if it were Vance whose letter Dempsey randomly called—what if she lost? What if he didn't smile and she ended up locked in the pantry for eleven minutes with him? In truth, the idea thrilled her. But there were nine other men in the room, eight without Max. What if one of the other guys' letters were called? She wanted to chicken out, to turncoat and tell Dempsey she was sitting out.

"I call…wait…wait…it's coming to me…it's coming to me," Dempsey said, closing his eyes and pretending to be telepathic. "I see the letter R!" he said. "Who's letter R?"

"Me," Vance said. He raised his hand, and an audible sigh emanated from the women in the room.

"Vance, my man!" Dempsey said. "Are you worried?"

"Nope. Nobody's ever cracked me yet," Vance said.

"Ooo! Strong words from our boy Vance here," Dempsey said. "And now…if my lovely assistant will draw a number from the bowl. Hold your breath, ladies. Wouldn't you each love to spend eleven minutes in this guy's arms?" The girls all giggled with elated eagerness as Vance plunged his hand into the bowl. "And the winner…or loser…is…lucky number seven!"

Boston was both relieved and totally freaked out. She was relieved that some other girl in the room wouldn't have the chance to make out with Vance in the pantry—freaked out at the thought that if she couldn't get him to crack a smile, *she* would be making out with him!

"I think that's Boston!" Halle squealed. "Boston! Girl, you rally for us. Don't you let that boy have his way with you!"

"Let him! Let him!" three of the other girls called out.

"Boston? Really? All right!" Dempsey laughed. "Get going, girl! Your two minutes starts when Vance says he's ready."

Boston looked to Vance. He settled himself comfortably on the sofa. He held a hand out to her and said, "Come on, baby. Come to Vance Romance."

Everyone laughed, and even Boston smiled. Surely he wouldn't be able to keep a straight face for two minutes—surely. Still, as his smile faded—as his expression went totally stoic—she wondered.

"Ready," Vance said. Dempsey produced a stopwatch from his pocket and said, "Okay, Boston…go!"

Boston went to Vance. Reaching out, she wove her fingers through his soft, dark hair. The sensation of his hair between her fingers and beneath her palms caused goose bumps to prickle her arms. She was glad she was wearing a long-sleeved shirt.

"Vance," Boston began, taking a seat on Vance's lap. "You'll smile for me…won't you?"

"Maybe later," he said. There was no hint of a smile on his face. Not even a hint he might smile.

"No talking! Except for the line," Dempsey ordered.

Boston swallowed the lump of nervous energy in her throat. Part of her wanted to lose—wanted Vance to somehow keep from smiling so that he'd win and she could be locked in the pantry with him and know the sense and taste of his kiss again. Yet, the other part of her—the logical, reasonable part—knew she had to win, had to get him to smile! She didn't even care about the hundred bucks; she just wasn't sure she could endure the bliss of kissing him again. She'd, no doubt, come out of the pantry red-faced, and then everyone would tease them. Even worse, everyone might see how she felt about him.

Boston drew a deep breath. She reached up, slowly running her fingers through Vance's hair again—through his soft, sable hair. She willed her arms to keep more goose bumps at bay, but it was impossible.

"I love you, baby," she said, drawing out the words with a vulnerable yet seductive tone. "Smile?"

Vance Nathaniel gritted his teeth—hard. He didn't smile, even though he figured having Boston Rhodes sitting on his lap and running her fingers through his hair was just about the most affecting experience he could be having. But he wouldn't smile—he couldn't—not if he wanted to find himself locked in the dark pantry with her. Oh, he didn't care one ounce about winning for the sake of competition, but he'd sure like to kiss Boston Rhodes again—even though he knew he shouldn't.

He frowned as she whispered in his ear, "I love you, baby...smile?" The warmth of her breath on his neck sent goose bumps rippling over his legs. He clinched his jaw tighter—still didn't smile. Everyone laughed and teased Boston, telling her she might as well give it up and head straight for the pantry.

How did he find himself in this mess anyway? Vance should've known better. Dempsey and his mischief—his asinine kissing games. As Boston breathed the now-familiar words in his ear, Vance feared it might be the end of his reputation of having an impenetrable resolve where the game was concerned.

He made the mistake of looking into Boston's eyes—found himself momentarily mesmerized by the jade and diamond twinkle in them. Their gemmy sparkle caused his heart to leap, and he felt the corners of his mouth threaten to curl. Purposefully, he frowned and strengthened his resolve to find himself locked in the pantry with Boston, and he did not smile, even when she took his face between her small, soft hands, caressing the whiskers over his upper lip with her thumbs.

There couldn't be much time left. Surely he could resist giving in to her charms for just a few more seconds. Still, as she smiled at him—as her pretty pink lips curved invitingly—Vance wondered if his strength might well abandon him.

"I love you, baby...smile," she whispered. Her breath was sweet where it caressed his cheek. He wished he could taste it. He had to hold out! A few more seconds, and he would taste her breath—taste her!

Boston could sense the delighted yet nervous trembling bubbling inside her. She couldn't believe she was sitting on Vance Nathaniel's lap! She couldn't believe she was running her fingers through his hair, caressing his face. It was entirely surreal! She loved the way his prickly, two- or three-days' beard growth felt against her palms, loved the faint scent about him—of some sports-scented deodorant and Juicy Fruit gum.

"Boston Rhodes...you lose!" Dempsey called.

"I win?" Vance asked, nodding to Dempsey as Boston removed herself from his lap and stood in desperately nervous anticipation.

"Yes, you do, Vance my man," Dempsey chuckled.

Boston's mouth gaped open a little in astonishment as she saw a dazzling, triumphant smile spread across Vance's handsome face. He chuckled as he stood, taking hold of her arm and pulling her toward the kitchen—toward the pantry.

Everyone laughed, whistled, and clapped—called out, egging Vance on.

"Hold up! Hold up!" Dempsey said. Vance paused, and Boston followed his gaze to Dempsey as their friend raced over to the controls of the sound system. As the sappy, breathy blast-from-the-past band Air Supply began crooning "Lost in Love" over Dempsey's sound system, as the saying goes, the crowd went wild! Everyone began whistling, laughing, calling out encouragements, and egging them on.

"Come on, sugar lips," Vance teased as he took her hand again and nearly dragged her into the kitchen.

Boston thought she might faint from the overwhelming and mixed sensations the situation afforded. There was nothing more she wanted in that moment than to have Vance Nathaniel take her in his arms and kiss her the way he'd kissed her in the dark the week before. Yet did he want to kiss her? He'd won the game, and she knew how guys were. They had to act all virile and manly in front of one another—take their woman by the hair and drag her into the cave sort of thing. Boston didn't want Vance to kiss her simply because he had to prove his masculinity in front of the other guys. She wanted him to kiss her because it was what he wanted to do! Yet to kiss him—no matter the reason—the thought caused a thrilling quiver to travel through Boston's body.

Dempsey ran ahead of them, opened the pantry door, and ushered them in. He reached inside and removed an old timer, winding it to exactly eleven minutes. Boston watched as Dempsey set the timer on a shelf and pulled the pantry door closed, shutting her and Vance inside.

A lightbulb hanging from an electrical wire overhead glowed bright, its pull-chain brushing over one of Vance's broad shoulders.

"Well, baby," Vance began, pushing the sleeves of his tight-fitting shirt up over his muscular forearms, "you ready?"

Boston smiled at him, attempting to appear unaffected by his proximity, his possibly legitimate preparation to kiss her.

"Vance," she began, "you don't have to pretend you want to—"

"Are you kidding me?" he interrupted, scowling and smiling at the same time. "Do you have any idea how hard it was for me to keep a straight face out there?"

"I'm sure I did look pretty ridiculous," Boston admitted, smiling—though she felt more like bursting into tears of humiliation.

"I'm sure you did not," he said. "I'm talking about me! Do you know what that kind of thing does to a man?" he asked, nodding toward the pantry door to indicate the room beyond. "Running your fingers through my hair…whispering in my ear…touching my face that way?" He shook his head as he continued to look at her. "Chicks have no idea the power they wield."

"Chicks?" Boston teasingly scolded.

"Girls, then," Vance said. "Girls have no idea the power they wield over guys." He quickly studied her from head to toe and added, "You're standing in here proving it right now."

Boston shook her head. "You're just trying to make me feel better…for making a fool of myself out there. Not to mention that I lost," she said, playfully slugging him on one solid arm. "Admit it."

He frowned, sarcastically pensive for a moment.

"Nope. That's not it," he said. "I just want to collect my winnings…what I deserve to collect for keeping a straight face while you were messing with me out there."

Boston's heart began to pound almost painfully within her chest as she felt Vance's strong hands settle at her waist—as he pulled her body flush with his. She had to put her hands somewhere, so she lightly gripped his arms at his biceps, thinking he really did need a Band-Aid! She was rendered breathless as his head descended toward hers.

"Now *you're* messing with *me*," she giggled.

"Oh, I'm gonna mess with you all right." He wrapped one arm around her, holding her firmly against his powerful body as he reached up and took hold of the pull-chain for the lightbulb. "But I know you'd rather kiss in the dark, so…"

Boston gasped slightly as she heard the click of the pull-chain— as darkness enveloped her.

"But…but I'm kind of…kind of dating somebody else…sort of," she stammered. Oh, she was lying all right. She had no intention of ever accepting another date invitation from Logan West. Yet she felt desperate to hang on to her resolve—the reality that Vance was Danielle's brother—out of reach.

"And how's that going for you?" Vance mumbled, taking her chin in one hand. The scent of Juicy Fruit gum wafted over her, warm and sweet, causing her mouth to water a little.

The warmth of his lips pressed her own, and she melted.

"I-I don't really know," Boston breathed as he paused in kissing her. She couldn't think clearly—couldn't focus on one thought other than she wished he would kiss her again. In the darkness of the pantry, she felt his thumb travel slowly over her lower lip.

"I won the game, you know," he said.

"I know," she breathed.

"Is it okay that I won?" he asked. Boston smiled, enchanted. She knew what he meant—he was asking permission to kiss her. Her heart swelled at his modernized attempt at chivalry.

"Yeah," she managed.

As Vance gathered her into his arms more snuggly, as he kissed her again a little less tentatively, Boston couldn't keep her hands from traveling over his shoulders—couldn't keep her arms from going around his neck.

Maybe it was the sappy Air Supply song echoing repeatedly through the other room—maybe it was the darkness enabling Boston to abandon her inhibitions—maybe it was the warm flavor of Juicy Fruit flooding her mouth. Whatever the reason, Boston's stomach leapt; her heart swelled to near bursting as she found herself fully and willingly accepting Vance's deepening kiss. Not only was she accepting it, she was returning it.

She thought for a moment that his mouth seemed made to fit to hers—wondered how he knew just how to kiss her so perfectly as to send her entire body to racing with swarms of butterflies and rippling goose bumps. She'd kissed other boys—other men—but kissing Vance was an entirely different experience, just as it had been the first time. As his moist, Juicy Fruit–flavored mouth melded with her own, she was conscious that kissing him would, no doubt, mess with her head again, but she didn't care. The experience was utterly and entirely euphoric!

Vance broke the seal of their mouths for a moment, changing the direction of the incline of his head and kissing her again. She felt his hand weave through her hair at the back of her head—gasped a little as he palmed her head, deepening the firm demands of his mouth.

Passion! Passion like Boston had never experienced was blazing voraciously inside Dempsey's pantry—unbridled passion! She couldn't seem to hold him close enough—couldn't seem to quench her thirst for his kiss. Vance's arms nearly crushed her as he held her to him, as his mouth endeavored to quench her thirst—or his.

"Boston," he breathed once, breaking the fastening of their mouths. She felt his embrace slacken, felt their bodies separate, but she could not give him up—not yet. When the timer sounded—when the light in the pantry was turned back on—his attention, his kiss would vanish. Reality would then return, and Vance Nathaniel would swagger away to a life that included Boston only in the most casual, nonintimate sense.

An odd, uncontrollable desperation gripped her. She would not lose a moment of his attention—of his kiss.

Allowing her hands to caress his face a moment, she whispered, "There's still time."

Raising herself on the tips of her toes, she boldly pressed her mouth to his once more, driving her own demanding kiss. At once his arms banded around her, pulling her body flush with his own as command of the affectionate exchanged fell to Vance once more.

"This is just all in fun," he mumbled against her mouth.

"I know," Boston whispered, breathless in his arms. One hand rested at his broad chest as it rose and fell with labored breathing.

"It was just a game," he said, kissing her again.

"I know," Boston breathed, returning his kiss.

"It's just that stupid song…and the way you were messing with me," he grumbled. Still, the moist heat of his mouth demanded she continue to kiss him—and she did.

"I-I know," she managed between kisses.

Boston knew she could never have kissed Vance Nathaniel with the light on. Never! If he hadn't pulled the chain to leave them in complete darkness, she never would've been able to make good on having lost the game. Vance Nathaniel! Danielle's brother, for Pete's sake. What was she doing? She was experiencing pure, rampant bliss—that's what she was doing!

She thought for a moment of all the women who surely would give anything to find themselves making out with Vance Nathaniel. How had she gotten so lucky? Dempsey could've pulled any number out of the number bowl—any girl's number at the party—but he hadn't. He'd pulled the number seven, and Boston was never so happy at random circumstance.

The timer buzzed, startling Boston, heaping mountains of disappointment over her. Vance immediately released her, broke the seal of their mouths, and gently pushed her away from his body.

"I need some comic relief, baby," he mumbled.

He tugged on the pull-chain, and Boston grimaced as the bright light stung her eyes.

"What?" she breathed as she watched him strip his shirt off over his head and wad it up in one hand.

He winked at her. Pushing the pantry door open, he stepped out of the pantry to the gasps and cheers of the company. Dempsey put two fingers in his mouth and whistled loudly as everyone else applauded.

"Boom, baby! That's right!" Vance chuckled, raising his arms and flexing triumphantly. "You boys go on. You keep wishing you were as good at that game as me!"

Everyone clapped and shouted and laughed with amusement—though Boston didn't miss the fact that a couple of the girls only glared at her.

"Dude! You're awesome, bro!" Dempsey laughed.

"No," Vance said. "Boston Rhodes is awesome!" He winked at her.

Boston smiled, still numb with the euphoric bliss of having been held and kissed by Vance Nathaniel.

"I have to tell you all…I have to. Boston's a good sport, kids," he said. "That's why she told me I could come out here and let you all think that she let me have my way with her."

Boston smiled—modern chivalry again. He was going to let everyone think they'd only pretended passion had heated up Dempsey's pantry.

"You mean…you mean you didn't make out?" someone asked.

"Nope," Vance said, winking at her.

"Is that true, Boston?" Dempsey asked. "'Cause to me that sure looks like whisker-burn around your mouth…and possibly the residue of pink lip gloss there on Vance's."

Vance gave the truth away when he guiltily reached up, running the back of his hand across his lips, and then looked at it as if expecting to find lip gloss residue there.

"Ah ha!" Dempsey laughed. "You, my friends, are busted!"

Everyone whistled and shouted again.

Vance shook his head, chuckled, and said, "Sorry, baby."

"It's okay," she told him, smiling.

He laughed and put a strong arm around her neck, pulling her against him. His skin was warm and soft—clean and fresh smelling—and as Boston's arms went around him to return his friendly embrace, she allowed her face to linger against the smooth warmth of his skin at his shoulder.

The sappy, old Air Supply song had begun again (Dempsey was famous for putting a song on repeat), and Boston smiled as Vance began to sway. He slipped an arm around her waist and began to dance with her.

"Dempsey," Max shouted. "Dog! Change that stupid song before Vance loses all sense of reason and starts crying or something!"

Everyone laughed, and Vance chuckled and released Boston. He pulled his shirt on, ran his fingers through his hair to straighten it, pushed up his sleeves, and sat down in a nearby chair.

"So?" he asked. "What next?"

Danielle smiled as she studied her brother. Vance was happy—truly happy! In that moment, there was something in her brother's countenance she hadn't seen in a very, very long time—joy.

Inhaling a deep breath of courage, she walked to Boston. She took her arm and led her toward the snack table. No one else was snacking now. It would allow them some privacy.

Boston worried. Danielle was smiling, but there was concern in her eyes. Was she angry with Boston for losing the game, for kissing Vance? Or had spending so much time with Stephanie Crittendon so thoroughly trained Boston to expect the worst that she was simply paranoid?

"I want to ask you a favor, Boston," Danielle began as she pulled a can of pop from the big ice-filled bowl in the center of the snack table.

"Yeah?" Boston prodded. She was rattled. Was Danielle about to ask Boston to quit kissing her brother?

"It's...it's about Vance," Danielle said.

Boston gulped down the lump in her throat, trembling with trepidation. Was Danielle truly that upset?

"Okay," Boston managed. "What's the favor?"

Boston held her breath a moment, afraid of Danielle's reprimand—afraid she might ask her to stay away from Vance or something.

Yet, in the next instant, she gasped as Danielle did not reprimand her or ask her to stay away from Vance. Instead, Danielle simply said, "I want you to seduce my brother."

CHAPTER TEN

"What?" Boston exclaimed.

Danielle glanced over her shoulder and whispered, "Shh!"

Boston lowered her voice and said, "I must've misunderstood you, Danielle. I thought you said you want me to—"

"Seduce my brother...yeah. That *is* what I said." Boston's mouth still hung agape with astonishment as Danielle shrugged and began to explain. "Maybe those weren't exactly the right words. I don't want you to, like, literally seduce him into...well...you know."

"Okay...then what?" Boston asked, somewhat relieved—but only somewhat.

"I want you to seduce him away from loneliness and self-contempt...away from the darkness and into the light."

Boston frowned. "Away from the darkness and into the light? Who do you think I am? The brother whisperer?"

Danielle smiled. "No...I don't think you're the brother whisperer. But I do think you like my brother...and I know that he likes you." She looked to Boston, her eyes pleading.

Instantly, Boston's heart leapt with hope, excitement, and the possibility that Danielle might be right. Still, it was dangerous to hope for the heart of a guy like Vance; it was even more dangerous to try and win it!

"Now, Danielle," Boston began, "don't mess with me like this. Just because I'm attracted to Vance—and I'll admit that I am because it would be stupid of me to try and lie to you about it—just because I like him doesn't mean that he likes me back! It doesn't mean something will come of it, and it doesn't mean I should…or even could…find the courage to—"

"He's got baggage, Bost," Danielle interrupted. "Big baggage." Danielle shrugged again. "I mean, everybody does. We all have baggage." She looked to Boston, her eyes pleading for Boston to understand something she knew Boston couldn't possibly understand. "But Vance…Vance is carrying a lot of luggage. I mean…they'd charge him extra at the airport for it."

"Okay," Boston accepted. "And I'm guessing it's baggage you shouldn't reveal to me…right?" Boston's insides had been trembling. It's why she thought it was strange that a sudden calmness should begin to expand within her—an odd, encouraging sort of calm.

"That's right," Danielle affirmed. "I won't hurt him by letting everybody search through his luggage without his permission…even you. I know you understand, Boston. No one knows you understand like I do."

Boston nodded. Danielle was referring to her own secret pain—the pain Boston's friendship had helped her to work through the summer they worked at the North Pole together. Though her imagination was running wild, Boston wouldn't press Danielle. She wondered if perhaps Vance had once been an addict of some sort. It might explain his near obsession with running and exercise. She wondered if he had a past where a woman was concerned—maybe a psycho girlfriend, which might explain why he had such vast experience with poisonous friends and had recognized Steph as one. Still, she wouldn't press Danielle. If Danielle held her brother's confidence, then she should well guard it.

"He likes you, Boston. You do something to him…bring something to him that I haven't seen in him in a long, long time. His heart is lightened when you're around," Danielle continued, "and I'll tell you something else. Vance would never, never, never make out with a girl he didn't absolutely want to…in the light or the dark. You're seeping into his soul, and I want you to save him." Danielle giggled. "I guess I do think you're the brother whisperer."

Boston drew a deep breath. "Danielle…have you ever looked at your brother from another woman's perspective?" she asked. "Do you know how gorgeous he is? How the fact that he is that gorgeous lends itself to intimidation and fear?"

"Fear?" Danielle asked, puzzled.

"Fear," Boston said. She swallowed the lump of nerves in her throat and said, "Fear…because Vance is the kind of guy that, once he's in your head and your heart, there's no tearing him out of them. He's the kind of guy who can wreck your life, Danielle…literally!"

"I know," Danielle admitted. "But I'm your best friend. I wouldn't ask you to let go of your fear and risk your heart…if I wasn't certain it was the right thing." Danielle studied Boston for a moment. She smiled and said, "He's already messed you up…hasn't he?"

Boston guiltily glanced away. It was true! Vance Nathaniel had started messing her up the moment she'd first seen him. She'd gotten more and more messed up with every passing minute she spent in his company. However, he'd completely wrecked her when he'd doused the lights and kissed her in the dark a week ago—had begun to possess her entirely at Dempsey's party and in the pantry.

"He has," Boston said. "Your friend…that Trisha Coleman you told me about."

"Yeah?" Danielle prodded.

"She was right," Boston whispered. "One kiss from Vance Nathaniel…and I was ruined!"

Danielle smiled again. "Why ruined? Why not found…spoken for? What if…by kissing you…why can't one kiss from Vance be the sign you needed that you've finally found the guy you were meant to be with?"

"Have you looked at him?" Boston asked. "Look at him now…right now!" Boston turned around and nodded to where Vance stood surrounded by women. "I swear, they'd start licking his face if we weren't in public."

"Well, that's because they know he's still on the market," Danielle said. "So…take him off the market."

"He's too perfect," Boston said, anxiety over the feelings she was trying to suppress for Vance twisting her stomach into knots.

"You know," Danielle began, "that is one of the things I hate about Stephanie more than anything. What she's done to you." She took Boston's arm and turned her away from Vance. "She's made you doubt yourself! She's made you think there are things you can't accomplish. She's taken so much of your energy that you sometimes don't see things the same way you used to."

Danielle was right. Boston knew she was right. Yet she didn't know how to overcome the self-doubt Steph had so perfectly planted in her mind.

"Remember that first summer, Boston?" Danielle asked. "You saved my life...and I'm not exaggerating. Just by letting me know you cared, by being my true friend, by not pressing me to reveal things I wasn't ready to, by just knowing me and loving me unconditionally...you saved my life. I wanted to die, Boston! I'd thought about how I would do it. I had it planned. I was going to take the job at the North Pole to get away from my parents and family so that I could kill myself and they wouldn't be the ones to find me."

Boston frowned and felt tears in her eyes. Danielle had never before told her of having thoughts of suicide. Never! She hadn't known. It was very hard to imagine—to hear—to absorb.

"Then I met you...that very first day I came into the café and you and Halle were there," Danielle explained. "It was going to be my last cup of hot chocolate. I'd decided that hot chocolate was the last thing I wanted to remember about being alive." She smiled. "But you were friendly...talked to me like you'd known me forever." She giggled a little. "You were babbling on and on and on about how excited you were because they were going to add hot spiced apple cider to the menu. I looked at you...and couldn't believe anyone would be so excited about apple cider. You said, 'Danielle! You *have* to come in tomorrow! The cider will be in, and you *have* to come in and taste some with us!' I couldn't believe it! You were so excited about apple cider...and I started to think that maybe, just maybe, apple cider was good enough to live for...that maybe I didn't want that mug of hot chocolate to be my last. So I didn't do it. I didn't go home and take the pills I'd stolen from my mom before I left home to go to work at the North Pole."

"Danielle," Boston began, brushing the tears from her cheeks. "I...I..."

"I started enjoying taking the pictures of the kids with Santa," Danielle continued, "really enjoying it...not just pasting on a smile and pretending. And then you and I started hanging out, going to movies, talking for hours. And I told you something was wrong with me, but you didn't push me...just kept telling me how great I was...how wonderful life is. You saved my life, Boston."

"*You* saved your life, Danielle," Boston mumbled. "Nobody saved it but you...except, of course, probably God. But in the end, you made the decision. I only listened and encouraged."

"You loved me," Danielle said. "Now I'm asking you to let yourself fall in love with my brother. He's strong enough to have made it through what he did without contemplating ending his life. Vance is too strong. The thought would never occur to him of simply wimping out on pain and struggle. But believe me when I tell you, his baggage...is maybe even heavier than mine was. But I'm still asking you to let go...let go of whatever Steph did to you that's keeping you from following your heart and chasing your dreams."

"Chasing my dreams?" Boston asked.

"You don't really want to be the assistant news scriptwriter at Channel 7," Danielle said. She turned and nodded toward Vance. "You just want what Vance can give you—love, happiness, a home, and babies."

"Danielle!" Boston scolded. She'd been through enough emotional drama in the past few minutes with what Danielle had revealed! She didn't want to have hope well up in her only to be crushed by cruel, cruel reality.

"Will you do it?" Danielle asked. "Will you let go of all the trash Steph injected into your brain and mind and soul? Will you let go of it and make my brother happy? Save him?"

"Danielle," Boston whispered. "He'll break my heart! He'll rip it out of my chest, take a bite, grimace, and throw it down the garbage disposal. I don't know…I don't know if I could ever recover from that!"

"He's not a cannibal, Boston," Danielle said. "He's just a man with a lot to offer…to the woman he was meant to offer it to."

Boston shook her head and brushed the tears from her cheeks as Danielle brushed the tears from her own. She smiled then.

"I know he's not a cannibal," she giggled.

Danielle giggled too. "No…he's a lot of things, but a cannibal isn't one of them."

Boston's fear returned then. She bit her trembling lip and said, "It's way scary, Danielle."

"I know," Danielle said. "But think how great it will be when the scary part is over." She grinned. "You can spend all the time you want locked in the pantry with Vance. According to poor Trisha Coleman, *that* would be worth any risk. Wouldn't it?"

Boston looked at her friend. Danielle was right. Too much time spent in Steph's company had not only poisoned Boston's confidence but had also dulled her senses—the senses that led her to helping others, to reading them, to staying on the path she knew she was meant to be on.

"Here," Danielle said. "Close your eyes for a minute, Bost. Close your eyes, and put aside all that poison Steph pumped into you."

Boston closed her eyes and inhaled deeply.

"Now keep them closed," Danielle whispered. She felt Danielle's hands on her shoulders. "Keep them closed…and turn around." Boston let Danielle turn her around. "Breathe…breathe…that's it. Now…Boston Rhodes…open your eyes."

Boston did as Danielle said.

"Tell me what you see," Danielle whispered.

Naturally, Boston's gaze fell to Vance. He was still surrounded by women, still talking with them, being his charming, enchanting self. He glanced up, smiled, and winked at her. Instantly, her heart soared. Vance Nathaniel was everything she'd always dreamed of finding in a friend, a boyfriend, a lover—and more. Everything! Even down to his imperfections, he fit the bill—Boston's bill. She could see it then—see her chance, perhaps her only chance, to find true happiness. She could see something else too; she glimpsed Vance Nathaniel's very soul. For only a breath, for a mere instant, Boston saw the goodness in him, saw the promise of faithfulness and heroism. She saw too that he did indeed yet endure some secret torture—some malicious, haunting thing. In that moment, she meant to vanquish it—to conquer whatever thing it was holding him so tormented. She meant to conquer it, free him, liberate his soul the way he had liberated hers by protecting her from further damage at Steph's hand.

Boston's confidence—her self-assurance—was short-lived. Yet the moment had offered her a glimpse of her past self—of who she really was. Boston Rhodes wasn't meant to be a pushover. She wasn't too nice either. She'd simply been poisoned and lost a measure of her strength. Yet it was returning—she was returning.

"Okay," she breathed. "Okay, Danielle...I'll seduce your brother," she said. She turned to her friend, and they embraced. She heard Danielle sniffle and knew more tears had escaped Danielle's eyes just as they had her own.

Danielle giggled, even for her tears. "I knew you would. I knew he had his hooks that deeply in you already. They didn't call him Vance Romance for nothing!"

Boston giggled too. "And you promise me, Danielle? You promise he's not a cannibal?"

The heavy roller coaster of emotions both Boston and Danielle had been riding over the past few minutes finally reached its peak. Boston and Danielle embraced, laughing and weeping simultaneously.

"Like I said, he's a lot of things, Bost...but a cannibal ain't one of them!" Danielle laughed.

"Who's not a cannibal?"

Boston gasped, looking up to see Vance standing behind her.

"What's so funny?" Dempsey asked, arriving at the snack table and dunking a stale tortilla chip in the bowl containing Boston's bean salsa.

"I don't know," Vance said as Boston and Danielle continued to snicker and wipe residual tears from their eyes. "Something about a cannibal...though I suspect we've just intruded on an estrogen surge."

"Ooo, dude! Scary!" Dempsey exclaimed.

Boston sighed and wiped a tear—a tear of laughter and mirth—from the corner of one eye. Danielle giggled too.

"Shut up, you guys," Danielle scolded. "We were just having a tender moment."

Vance's handsome brow puckered into a puzzled frown. "About cannibals?" he asked.

Instantly, Boston and Danielle burst into giggles.

"No, you idiot," Danielle said once she'd managed to control her giggles. "About...the past...and the future."

Boston smiled at her friend. What would she do without Danielle? Who would she be? In that moment, she realized just how much influence Danielle had on *her*—on who Boston Rhodes had been and was. Danielle had enriched her life immeasurably—still did—always would. Silently she prayed—offered thanks for such a wonderful friend and teacher.

"Definitely an estrogen spill," Dempsey said. "Call the coast guard!"

"Be nice," Danielle teased, slapping Dempsey playfully on the arm.

"I'm always nice," Dempsey said. He took her hand and held it for a long time.

Boston smiled as she watched the blush rise to Danielle's cheeks. Danielle was a great one for matchmaking, that was obvious. Still, Boston decided it was time Danielle stopped worrying about everybody else's future and started worrying about her own—and Boston determined she'd find a way to make that happen.

"While you girls were over here brewing estrogen, the party started breaking up," Dempsey said. "Everyone's leaving, and Vance—weenie that he is—says he's tired," Dempsey whined dramatically. "So, I was wondering if you would mind staying and helping me clean up a bit, Danielle. Boston can go, and I'll run you home afterward. Would that be okay?"

Boston felt her own eyebrows arch in astonishment. She glanced up at Vance to see him fighting a knowing grin.

Danielle looked like a deer caught in headlights. "Uh…um…" she stammered.

"That would be fine," Boston answered for her. "In fact, I'm tired too. So why don't you just bring my salsa bowl home with you when you come, okay, Danielle?"

"Um…sure," Danielle managed.

"Great!" Boston exclaimed. She reached out and quickly embraced Dempsey. "Fabulous party, Dempsey," she said. "As usual! Thanks for inviting me."

"Thank you, Boston," Dempsey said.

"Yeah, man," Vance said, offering a hand to Dempsey. "It was awesome."

Dempsey shook Vance's hand and nodded.

"Well, good night," Vance said. Boston smiled as he placed his hand at the small of her back and began pushing her toward the door. "I'll see you later, Danny."

"Good night," Boston called over her shoulder as Vance hurried her out the front door.

Vance closed the door behind them, smiling at Boston. "I think your pal Dempsey is finally manning up," he whispered.

Boston giggled. "Me too!"

Vance exhaled a heavy breath—as if he'd been holding it in for a long time. He shook his head and said, "I just want her to be happy, you know? Really happy."

"Me too," Boston whispered. She studied Vance for a moment, astounded at the realization only just beginning to wash over her. Vance and Danielle were each amazing! Not only in the obvious ways of Danielle's being beautiful and Vance's being gorgeous, but also that they both valued the other's happiness more than their own. It was a rare and admirable quality—perhaps especially in siblings.

"Come on," he said. "I'll walk you to your car."

"It's a little cooler than I expected," Boston said, rubbing her arms with her hands.

"Yeah," Vance mumbled as he looked up into the clear night sky. "There must be a little cold front moving in or something."

Boston shivered, and he said, "Hey! I've got all my laundry in my pickup...including a nice, clean, very warm sweatshirt. Let me get it for you."

"Oh, no! I'm fine," Boston assured him.

"No...let me get it," he insisted, pausing next to his pickup.

Boston watched as he took his keys from his pocket and unlocked the passenger's side door of the old pickup truck. He rummaged around through a couple of duffle bags for a moment, finally producing a pristine white sweatshirt.

"Here," he said, unzipping it and holding it out for her to put on. "We don't want you catching cold, now do we?"

Boston giggled at his parental tone, delighted as he proceeded to zip the front of the sweatshirt for her. She frowned, however, glancing past him to the duffle bags full of laundry sitting in the front seat of his pickup.

"Why are you dragging your clean laundry around?" she asked. "Don't you have a washer and dryer at your house? You can use the one in our apartment next time if you want."

"Um...uh...um...I just haven't had a chance to hook them up yet," he stammered. "I'll get to it this week. I just went to the laundry place today...'cause it was just easier. I knew you guys were getting stuff ready for Dempsey's party...so I just went to the laundry thing."

Boston's eyes narrowed. She studied him for a moment, noting the way he seemed to be having a hard time looking her in the eye. He was babbling, sort of like she babbled when she was wound up about something. The thought quickly passed through her mind that he was lying about his laundry, the Laundromat, and not having his appliances hooked up. Yet why would he lie about something like that?

"Come on," he said, taking her arm and fairly dragging her toward her car. "I want you to get home and get warmed up." They reached her car quickly, and he held a strong hand out to her, saying, "Keys?"

Boston reached into her pocket and retrieved her keys, handing them to him.

Vance opened her door and shoved the keys in the ignition.

"Thanks," Boston said.

"No, thank you, Boston Rhodes," Vance replied.

"For what?" she asked, entirely bewildered.

He grinned—the handsome, naughty grin Boston had begun to recognize as the precursor to mischief.

"Well, let's just say...I'll never think anyone's pantry is a boring waste of space again."

"Good night, Vance Nathaniel!" Boston giggled as he closed her car door.

He chuckled, and she started the car.

She heard Vance's pickup roar to life and glanced in her rearview mirror to see him pull out of Dempsey's driveway.

Suspicion rose in her bosom again. He'd been lying about his laundry situation—she was sure he'd been lying. But why?

Carefully, Boston backed her car around so that she could drive out of Dempsey's roundabout driveway the same way Vance had. She didn't know why, but she wanted to see him safely home— needed to see that he was tucked in his new house all nice and cozy.

Yet as she followed quite a distance behind him, she was surprised when he passed Gem Lane. Gem Lane had been the delivery address on the furniture receipt she'd found in his wallet. Why wasn't he going home?

Boston became more and more unsettled as Vance's pickup meandered down into the south section of town—a very undesirable section indeed.

"What the heck?" she asked aloud as his pickup turned into the parking lot of a seedy motel.

Boston drove past the first entrance into the parking lot. She didn't want Vance to see her—to figure out she was spying on him like some psycho ex-girlfriend. Slowly she pulled into the second entrance to the motel's parking lot and parked out a ways away from the nearest parking lot light.

Boston watched as Vance pulled into a parking spot in front of a room. He turned off his pickup, pulled the two duffle bags out of the front seat, locked the vehicle, and headed for the motel room door.

Boston shook her head. Surely Vance hadn't lied about more than his laundry? Surely he wasn't staying in this roach motel?

Then, as realization began to seep into her mind, Boston's stomach smoldered with a sick nausea. Surely Vance hadn't moved out of Danielle's nice, comfortable apartment and into this dive simply so Boston could escape from Steph. It couldn't possibly be the reason—he hardly knew her! Well, they spent a great deal of time talking whenever Boston was at Danielle's and Vance was home, and they had shared an intimate, delicious kiss the week before. But that had been after he'd already moved out. Certainly he hadn't known her—still didn't know her—well enough to make this sort of a sacrifice. And no guy left on earth was that chivalrous anymore.

Boston felt her eyes widen as something else occurred to her then. Perhaps Vance hadn't even bought the house! Perhaps he'd just told Danielle he had—hoped he'd be able to buy it in a month's time. Something had gone wrong with the sale. That was it—that had to be it!

Still, a tiny, nagging voice in Boston's head maintained Vance had indeed moved into this motel so that Boston could move in with Danielle. She had to know! She had to confront him and find out why he'd moved out, why he was living in a motel.

As Boston stepped out of her car, locked it, and looked around, half expecting to be mugged, she hoped there was some other logical reason for finding Vance at the shabby place. Her heart twisted with guilt as she again wondered if Vance was here because of her.

It was so dark in the parking lot. Only a handful of the streetlights had bulbs in them. As Boston passed Vance's pickup, she couldn't help but pause to peer in through the driver's side windshield. She grinned at the mess inside—Juicy Fruit wrappers strewn hither and yon, three empty sports drink bottles tossed on the passenger's side floor. A parking pass for the zoo hung from the rearview mirror, and the ashtray under the center panel radio and temperature controls was pulled open and heaping with discarded change.

The fleeting thought that she would love to ride in the old pickup breezed through Boston's mind, and she turned her attention to the door of Vance's motel room.

"Number fourteen," she mumbled out loud as she approached.

Reaching out, she tentatively rapped on the door.

"Hang on," Vance called from beyond the door with the number fourteen on it.

Boston's heart was pounding so violently within her chest she wondered if the entire motel complex could hear it. Naturally, the thought had never occurred to her—until that very moment—that Vance might be pretty ticked off when he found out she'd been spying on him, that she'd followed him home.

"Oh my heck!" Boston breathed. "I really have turned into Steph—a psycho, stalker type!"

She thought of turning, running, and hiding behind the nearby shrubbery and pretending that someone had only been ding-dong ditching. But it was too late—Vance opened the door.

He stood before her wearing only his jeans, having already stripped off his shirt in obvious preparation for retiring. He wore one other thing besides his jeans—an expression not so unlike that of a child having just been caught stealing cookies out of his mother's cookie jar.

"Boston? What are you doing here?" he greeted, guilty as sin.

Boston studied him quickly—as usual, entirely impressed by the well-defined muscles of his upper body—as usual, entirely bashful because of them.

"What are *you* doing here? I mean...I followed you," she flatly confessed. "I thought there was something fishy about the way you were acting at Dempsey's...so I followed you."

A purely mortifying thought drove its way into her tender brain then—a lewd, horrid, sickening thought that Boston hadn't considered before. Perhaps—perhaps Vance didn't live at the cheap motel. Perhaps he was only meeting someone there for one night! Though Boston's heart didn't want to even imagine that Vance Nathaniel was the kind of guy to meet a woman at a motel, her world-worn, Steph-poisoned mind began concocting all sorts of scenarios, including visions of exactly what kind of woman a man would meet at such a place and such a time.

Boston's stomach churned and threatened to heave out its contents.

"My...uh...my house wasn't quite ready...so I'm...I'm staying here until it is. Just...just for the next two weeks or so," he answered, drawing her thoughts from streetwalkers and a *Law and Order* episode she remembered and back to reality.

"So you lied," she said. "You lied to Danielle...and me. Please tell me you just couldn't stand the estrogen level at the apartment. Don't tell me you did this because you felt sorry for me."

He grinned a little, his eyes sort of twinkling with mischief. "I couldn't stand the estrogen level at the apartment," he said.

"I had no idea you were such a big, fat liar!" Boston exclaimed, relieved to know Vance wasn't meeting some tramp—yet guilt-ridden too, for she knew the truth now.

Vance glanced past Boston a moment. She looked over her shoulder to see a rather unsavory looking man staring at her—specifically, staring at her rear end.

"Get in here," Vance said, taking hold of her arm and pulling her into the room. He closed the door and twisted the deadbolt before turning to look at her once more.

"Now what are you doing here?" he asked. "Why did you follow me, and what does it matter if I'm not moved into my house yet?"

"You did this because of me," she accused.

"I did this because of your pal Stephanie," he corrected, folding strong arms across a chiseled, broad chest. He frowned and nearly growled, "Man, you had to get out from under that chick's…sh-stuff! I couldn't stand there and watch you take that any longer." He ran one hand through his thick, dark hair, shook his head, and chuckled. "I knew you wouldn't move in while I was still there…whether or not I slept on the couch. So I figured, what's a couple of weeks here?" he asked, looking around. "I'm at work most of the time anyway. Danielle was all wound up over you too. You might as well have been letting that Steph chick beat you over the head with a shovel. So what's sleeping here for a few weeks compared with all that?"

He was downplaying his own heroism—or he really didn't see it as anything too concerning. As Boston's heart swelled with appreciation, admiration, and delight, she smiled—and, unfortunately, spoke her thoughts aloud.

"Well, I'm not happy to find you living here. But I'm glad you're actually *living* here and not just meeting someone," she began, her tongue characteristically unleashed. "I mean, for a minute I had this horrible vision that you were meeting some hoochie here…you know…for…you know…for a reason I can't even begin to verbalize because it would make me sick to talk about it…and to find out you're living here instead of that…whew! I mean, I'm just so relieved about that…but I'm still mad at you for lying to us. You didn't have to do this. I would've been fine…I could've just bunked in with Halle or something until your house was ready. I feel awful about this! In fact, the more I think about it, the worse I feel…but I'm just so glad you're living here…you know…instead of…well, you know."

"You thought I'd driven down to Central Street and pick up a hoo—" he began.

Boston's hand clamping over his mouth silenced him, however—though it was obvious by the fury in his eyes that he was greatly offended.

"Don't even say it!" Boston scolded. "I just watch too much *Law and Order*. You know I would never really think that you would—"

"You did!" he growled, pushing her hand from his mouth. "You thought I picked up some streetwalker and came back here to...I can't believe you would think that of me!"

"I don't!" Boston assured him emphatically. She shrugged with admitted guilt and said, "Well, I sort of did...but just for a minute...and just because I've watched too much TV lately. I swear it! I know you're not that kind of guy."

"Really?" he asked, scowling so thoroughly Boston looked around in search of a hole to crawl into. "Then what kind of a guy do you think I am? Obviously you think I'm scummy enough to—"

"I think you're the kind of guy who lies to stupid girls who have stupid roommates and can't handle their own stupid problems so that they don't know he's doing something to help them out...probably because you don't like attention or some stupid thing like that," she blurted. She felt the tears in her eyes—the ache in her heart—an emotional eruption of disbelief and gratitude welling up inside her. "I can't believe you did this!" she said, her voice breaking as tears escaped her eyes and traveled over her cheeks. Boston brushed them away with the back of her hand, humiliated that she should show such weakness in front of him. However, her humiliation was not so great as to keep her tongue still, and she babbled on, glancing around the dim, shabby room.

"I mean...this cannot possibly be comfortable! And are there roaches? Oh my heck! I won't be able to sleep at night if I know there're roaches crawling all over you in here! Did you clean the bathroom before you used it the first time? Oh my heck! Did you wash the sheets? What are you doing here, Vance?" She bit the inside of her cheek and quit talking as he took hold of her shoulders.

"Hey, baby...dial it down a notch, okay?" he said, forcing her to look at him. He tweaked her nose as if she were a little girl and added, "It's cool. It's all good. First of all, it's only for a couple more weeks. Second, I haven't seen one roach...okay, maybe one. And I did clean the bathroom...and I'm even smart enough that I brought my own bedding. On the flip side, you've been liberated from that psycho chick you lived with...and Danielle can quit worrying." He shrugged broad shoulders and shook his head. "I'm working so much and am so tired when I do get home that I don't care where I crash."

Boston, however, was little soothed. She turned away from him, brushing more tears from her cheeks. She couldn't believe it! She couldn't believe a guy she'd known only two weeks would make such a gesture of impeccable character. Furthermore, she still didn't like the fact he was living in such ugly, frightening, and downright depressing circumstances—not to mention he was having to pay who knows how much to live there. Vance Nathaniel may have been working so hard that he didn't care where he crashed, but Boston did care—and she knew she wouldn't get a good night's sleep as long as Vance was in the ratty motel.

"I…I can't think of anything I can possibly do to thank you," Boston said. "Not one thing."

"Don't worry about it," he said. She heard him yawn and turned back around to look at him. He did look tired. His hair was tousled, his eyelids kind of droopy. She suspected Dempsey's party had worn him out. After all, Dempsey's parties always wore everyone out—and it was very late.

Boston knew Vance was probably anxious to get to bed, but she couldn't leave without somehow conveying her gratitude. The barrel of Tootsie Pops from Mustang was nothing compared with this! He had to know how she felt. She wanted to be sure he knew how truly heroic his behavior was.

"You have to let me do something for you," she said. "You can't do a thing like this—make this kind of sacrifice—and not let me thank you, Vance…offer some sort of service in return. There's got to be something I can do for you. Please…I won't be able to settle down or sleep or work well until you let me repay you somehow. I already owe you for the suckers."

He frowned a little, inhaled a deep breath, and exhaled slowly. He reached up, scratching the short whiskers on his chin.

"Well, I suppose asking you to sleep with me would be out of the question," he began.

"What?" Boston exclaimed. She thought of Danielle's request that she "seduce" her brother, and all Boston's deep-seated fears of there not being one moral man left on the face of the earth (even including Vance Nathaniel) washed over her like a natural disaster.

Vance shrugged. "I mean, obviously that's the kind of guy you think I am...the kind of guy who would meet a skank at a cheesy motel and—"

"I said I was sorry for that," Boston interrupted. She realized then he was teasing her—raking her over the coals as punishment for even daring to have one suspicious thought about his character. She admitted that she deserved it. Only fifteen minutes ago—after the conversation she'd had with Danielle—she was ready to nearly marry Vance on the spot. She deserved to be pestered for doubting him so quickly, for letting Steph's and the world's poisonous assumptions win her over so swiftly.

"And I wouldn't want to disappoint you by letting you find out that I really am an okay guy...so I guess that's it. You can sleep with me, and I'll count it as your thank you."

"Vance Nathaniel, you cannot be serious. I know you're just being a brat."

"So, as I was saying," he continued, "you can either sleep with me...because I *am* a depraved, wanton degenerate with an insatiable appetite for women...or...it's been a long time since I've had a really big, really good batch of homemade chocolate chip cookies. Danielle says you can bake like a bakery baker. So those are your options— sleep with me...or bake me cookies."

He smiled, pure delight and mischief burning in his eyes. Boston sighed with relief in realizing he was totally teasing her. She giggled, suddenly all the more enchanted with his sense of humor.

"And just what would you do if I chose not to bake the cookies?" she flirted.

"Wouldn't you like to know?" he chuckled.

"Well, I'll bake your stupid cookies for you, Mr. Nathaniel," Boston said, turning and unlocking the door. She had to leave—she wasn't even certain why—but she felt that if she didn't leave she might start thinking a little too much about how perfectly wonderful Vance Nathaniel was—how heroic. "But I'm still mad at you for lying to us…and I still won't be able to sleep well as long as you're here."

"Don't worry about it, Boston," he said. "It really isn't a big deal."

She turned to find him looming before her, close to her—so close she could smell his warm, suntanned skin and the residue of Juicy Fruit gum on his breath.

"It is to me," she whispered, gazing up into the deep green of his eyes. She made the mistake of letting her gaze fall to his lips—swallowed when the excess moisture of desire flooded her mouth. What was done was done—there was no changing it now. Vance was living in the motel; she was all moved in with Danielle. There was nothing left to do but to express her thanks—prove to him she was grateful for his chivalry.

Reaching over, she quickly flipped the light switch near the door. The room went black, and Boston stood on the tips of her toes, took Vance's whiskery face between her hands, and kissed him squarely on the mouth. She hadn't expected to suddenly find his hands at her waist, to find that he had kissed her after she'd kissed him, that they were now standing in the complete darkness of the shabby motel room kissing each other. She'd meant to kiss him once—to thank him for championing her. She'd turned off the light first because—as Vance himself had twice taught her—somehow it wasn't so intimidating to kiss someone in the dark. Yet now that he'd kissed her in return—now that his mouth was coaxing hers into a deeper, more intimate exchange like they'd shared in Dempsey's pantry—she began to tremble.

Passion erupted not so unlike Mount Vesuvius! Vance's arms banded around Boston like steel restraints, and she didn't care. The moments in the pantry were flinging themselves through her memory, causing her to thirst for more of them.

Again she was struck by his skill in kissing her, by the manner in which she feared she would never be able to leave him. It was even worse—or more wonderful, whichever way one viewed it—for now her mind and soul had decided to seduce Vance toward the light and away from whatever secret darkness imprisoned him. Therefore, in admitting to herself that she wanted him—wanted him forever— Boston realized the weakness he found in her, the desire he toyed with.

Yet she couldn't leave him—not yet—and so she kissed him— kissed him wildly, unbridled, and with insatiable thirst!

Abruptly, however, she pulled away from him, wiping the moisture from her still tingling lips as she flipped the light back on.

Vance grinned at her and teased, "I thought you'd changed your mind about baking the cookies there for a minute."

Boston blushed and shook her head. "No, you idiot. I just…I just want you to know that what you've done…that I appreciate it more than you can—"

"It's no big thing, Boston," he interrupted. He opened the door, took hold of her arm, and led her from the room. "Come on. I'll walk you to your car so you can get home and fire up the oven."

On the way to the car, however, Boston's emotions began to get the better of her once more, and she brushed new tears from her eyes.

"Really, Vance," she began, "you didn't have to do this."

"It's fine, Boston," he said. "Just bake me a big batch of chocolate chip cookies, and we'll call it even." She took her keys out of her pocket, and he put out his hand for them. She smiled and dropped her keys in his hand. He winked at her, unlocked her car door, and held it open.

"Admit it," he began. "Let logic dictate the truth of the fact that it's far less difficult for me to sleep here for a few nights than it would've been for you to deal with that psycho chick for one more day. Then just let it go and bake those cookies for me."

Boston slid into the seat of her car, and Vance pushed the key into the ignition.

"You…um…you're not gonna tell Danielle, are you?" he asked, his handsome brow puckering with concern.

"She'll find out sooner or later," Boston warned. "But…but I won't say anything if you don't want me to." The thought drifted through her mind that Vance and Danielle harbored a lot of secrets—even from each other.

"I'd appreciate it if you didn't," he said. "If she finds out, then she finds out…but I'd rather she didn't. She worries a lot about me…especially since…she just worries a lot. You know how she does. I won't ask you to lie if she flat out asks you. There's no reason to drag you to hell for lying too. But just don't offer the information for no reason. Okay?"

"Okay," Boston said. She smiled at the lethally handsome man standing half-naked outside her car in the parking lot of a shady motel. "This will be our little secret."

"Secret," he said. "That's always a scary word."

"Oh, it's a fun word, Vance," she said. "I like secrets."

He smiled and said, "Drive safe."

"I will."

Boston giggled, reached over to the glove compartment, and retrieved a chocolate Tootsie Pop. She quickly removed the wrapper and popped it in her mouth. She twisted the key and started her car.

Just before Vance closed her door, however, he reached out and pulled the sucker from her mouth, popping it into his own mouth and saying, "You're gonna rot your teeth out with these things." He closed the car door then and nodded at her, an indication he would wait for her to drive off before returning to his hovel.

Boston waved at him, and he nodded again as she drove away.

After retrieving a fresh Tootsie Pop from the glove compartment, Boston sighed and smiled. There was something rather intimate about the way he took her suckers out of her mouth and pressed them into his own without hesitation. She liked it! Her delight was quickly squelched, however, by the remembered knowledge that Vance would be spending the next however many nights in a nasty motel. Still, it was heroic in the true sense! Maybe guys didn't wear armor anymore and ride white steeds and slay dragons for a girl, but lying about his house, staying in a dive like that one—Boston figured it pretty much evened the field.

CHAPTER ELEVEN

"So," Danielle began, "how'd you manage to get a double batch of Boston's best chocolate chippers?"

Vance sat sprawled on Danielle's couch, watching *COPS*—a large rattan basket heaping with chocolate chip cookies sitting in his lap.

"Last night she refused to sleep with me, so I told her I'd take a batch of cookies instead," Vance nonchalantly answered.

"What?" Danielle exclaimed, looking to Boston, her mouth gaping open in astonishment.

"He's kidding, Danielle," Boston said, rolling her eyes.

Danielle sighed and shook her head. "Vance Nathaniel, you are so bad! Quit being so naughty all the time. Boston will think you're a…a…"

"A normal, red-blooded, American man?" Vance asked.

"Oh my heck!" Danielle breathed with exasperation. "Just watch your stupid show and eat your cookies!"

"That's what I was doing in the first place," Vance mumbled.

Danielle frowned and stared at Boston. "You never make cookies for boys anymore."

"That's right…but I'm a man," Vance interjected.

Boston giggled, and Danielle rolled her eyes again. Still, Danielle leaned forward and whispered, "Cookies…a great seduction tool! Good idea!"

Boston leaned forward to meet Danielle's conspiratorial stance. "He said you told him I can bake like a bakery baker…and I wanted to prove to him that I could," she explained. It wasn't really a lie—both statements were true. So she didn't tell Danielle that her brother was living in a dive. So she didn't tell her that he'd lied to them about moving into his house. It was still true that Danielle had told Vance Boston was a good baker, and she did want to prove it to him.

Danielle shook her head. "I knew when I'd told him that he'd eventually figure out a way to weasel cookies out of you. If there's one certainty in life...it's that Vance loves chocolate chip cookies." Danielle picked a cookie up from the plate on the table. Boston never made cookies to give away without making sure there were some left for friends.

"He's a piece of work, my brother," Danielle sighed, smiling.

"Oh, yeah," Boston agreed. "He sure is."

Boston looked past Danielle to the couch where Vance was sitting. Her stomach was suddenly attacked by wave after wave of butterflies. He was the one she wanted—and she'd started the journey of finding out if he could even want her.

She'd lain awake half the night, thinking over what had erupted between them in the pantry and then at his lousy motel room. Once she'd started to look at the situation from the viewpoint of the real Boston Rhodes instead of the Steph-tainted Boston, she could see a little clearer. She and Vance did gravitate to one another as Danielle had implied. He did smile at her, wink at her often. He went out of his way to please her, like bringing home the barrel of Tootsie Pops—not to mention his current living conditions. Surely he wouldn't have forced himself into such undesirable living circumstances for just anybody.

Thus, Boston had lain awake half the night mulling over the possibilities with Vance—and the other half of the night feeling simply mortified at what Danielle had revealed to her about the depth of her pain that first summer they'd met. All in all, Boston figured she'd left for work that morning on maybe two hours combined sleep at best.

Still, even for feeling so fatigued at work, she'd been happy, hopeful, and motivated. She felt more like herself than she had in a really long time—since moving in with Steph, in fact. She began to remember that Boston Rhodes was an optimist and liked to help people to feel better about life and living it. In short, the true Boston Rhodes—the one Steph had tried so hard to poison (and actually succeeded in poisoning to a point)—in her soul Boston Rhodes believed in sprinkling joy and sunshine through the world. In short, she preferred sifting sugar to spreading manure. Perhaps it was the baker in her that thought of the sifting idea. She had a vision of a little gingerbread town she and her mother had once made together when she was little. She remembered how her mother had put sugar in an old metal sifter and then let Boston sift it out over the tiny little gingerbread rooftops of the town to look like frost-kissed snow. What a vision it was in her mind—what a beautiful memory, a memory that caused her to feel warm and sweet and hopeful and happy inside. It was even how she'd finally managed to get to sleep— by closing her eyes and hearing "Silent Night" waft through her imagination as she laid in her comfortable bed remembering how beautiful the sifted sugar looked sprinkled over the little gingerbread town so long ago.

Vance sighed, stretched, and rose from his lounging position on the sofa. He picked up the remote and pressed the off button.

"Thanks for letting me hang out, girls," he said. He tucked the large basket Boston had filled with chocolate chip cookies under his arm and sauntered toward them. He set the basket on the table as he took a seat next to Boston. Frowning with an expression of sincere intent, he proceeded to pick through the basket of cookies until he appeared to find just the one he wanted.

He bit into it, closed his eyes, and moaned, "Mmm!"

Danielle rolled her eyes, yet her amusement was apparent.

"Boston," Vance began, "these are the best damn cookies I ever tasted!"

"Vance!" Danielle whined. "Quit swearing!"

But Boston giggled, reached out, poured milk into her glass from the carton sitting on the table, and then pushed the glass toward Vance.

"What's that for?" Vance asked. He immediately dunked a cookie into the glass of cold milk.

"For swearing," Boston said.

"Boston Rhodes! I am trying to refine my brother...not encourage him to further corruption."

But Boston shook her head. So much was coming back to her—so much of herself.

"It's just...it's just that it's one of the things that drove me crazy about Stephanie. Any time she heard someone swear—cuss even a little—she had to go off about it...like she was so perfect and without fault. I can't stand that about people—the hypocrisy. I mean, we all struggle with it in some regard. I know that. But Steph was just so judgmental...so intolerant of the fact that everybody does stuff...has faults and things they aren't perfect about. So Stephanie doesn't cuss—and that's a good thing, sure—but she can't say a nice thing about, or to, anyone. She can't find a compliment or a kind word or help someone in need. But, man oh man...she sure doesn't swear! And she thinks that gives her the right to sit pointing the finger at everyone who does drop a little curse word here and there. I'm not talking about huge, filthy-mouthed stuff...just the basics—what my grandma used to call 'farmers' colorful metaphors.' And not that I encourage tons of profanity...but a well-placed, basic cuss word now and then—"

"Like the time Steph chewed a hole in Dempsey for slipping up with the s-h bomb when he dropped that car battery on his foot," Danielle said. "Remember that? He was changing her car battery for her, dropped it on his foot, and swore. She ripped into him like no hell-fire-and-brimstone preacher ever would!"

"I remember. Didn't Dempsey even pay for the battery? Remember?" Boston added.

Danielle nodded. "He did...and he spent six weeks with his foot in a cast."

"Six weeks with Stephanie chewing a new hole in him each and every time she saw him...just because he swore when the battery broke his foot. Forget that she called him out of work to change it for her. Forget that he spent six weeks in a cast, all for her sake."

Danielle nodded, looked at her brother, leaned over, and kissed him.

"You're right, Vance," she said. "Boston does make the best cookies anybody ever tasted."

Vance nodded his agreement, dunked another cookie, and mumbled the cussing compliment again, smiling to himself.

Boston grinned at him. In truth, his swearing about her cookies was about the most flattering thing she'd ever been told. And she did feel liberated—liberated from Stephanie's manipulative hypocrisy, from her emotional manipulation, and she began to wonder why she'd put up with it for so long. So Stephanie didn't approve of the use of a farmer's colorful metaphor now and then. Well that was fine—even good. But in that moment, Boston consciously realized that, just as Stephanie Crittendon didn't like swearing, Boston Rhodes didn't like cruel, manipulative people. And which was the greater sin, in truth? An occasional cuss word uttered in pain, anger, or admiration—or prideful arrogance in one's own perfection, self-righteous superiority, and cruelty to others?

Boston felt tears well in her eyes as she studied Vance, watching him dunk his cookie in the glass of milk and then eat it in one bite. Again she was conscious of the fact he paved the venue for her liberation from Steph's intolerable manipulation and unkindness; he was the one to point out Stephanie as a poisonous friend in the first place. Boston owed Vance Nathaniel much more than even she thought, much more than one basket of cookies could ever recompense.

Vance glanced at his watch.

"Oh, man! I gotta get home and catch some z's!" he mumbled, his mouth still full of chocolate chip cookie. He quickly stood, gathered the basket of cookies under one arm, and leaned over, affectionately kissing the top of Danielle's head. "Thanks again, Danny." He looked to Boston and winked. "And thank you for the cookies, Miss Boston Rhodes."

"Thank you, Mr. Vance Nathaniel," she said.

"Is this basket like the large bucket of popcorn at the movie theater? When it's empty, can I bring it back for a free refill?" he asked, indicating the basket with a nod of his handsome head.

"You've gotta be kidding me, Vance!" Danielle giggled. "What…five dozen cookies isn't enough?"

"Well…for now," Vance said, winking at Boston again. They shared a secret, she and Vance, and Boston loved that they did.

"Sure, Vance," Boston said. "Bring it back for a free refill."

"Nice!" Vance said. "Well, you ladies have a good night. I'm off to bed."

"Good night," Danielle and Boston chimed.

Boston watched Vance walk toward the door with her favorite basket tucked under his arm—the bum of his jeans so nicely filled out, the tight, ratty T-shirt he wore accentuating the muscles of his arms and back. She thought for a moment she might miss seeing him so scroungy when he was finished working road construction. No doubt when he started his curator's job, his work attire would vastly alter—and she kind of liked the hardworking construction worker look.

She sighed with disappointment when he'd closed the door behind him.

"Don't worry, Bost. He'll be back," Danielle teased. "If for no other reason than he'll want to fill that basket up again."

Boston looked to Danielle and smiled. She took another cookie from the plate and said, "You know, I feel like I've been drifting down a river…that I'm starting to come out of a heavy fog bank. Or…or that I've been trapped in a nightmare and something finally woke me up."

"I know that feeling," Danielle said. "You are the one who woke me up from my own nightmare."

"And you and Vance are the ones who woke me up from mine," Boston said. She giggled. "I kind of imagine you as this good sort of witch—all dressed in a white, sequin-drenched prom dress…with, like, a little diamond tiara and pink, pink cheeks."

"I like that," Danielle giggled. "But what about Vance? Is he, like, a prince or something?"

"Naw. Princes are always too…too…I don't know," Boston sighed. "He's more like…I don't know…maybe Bruce Willis in some action movie. Or at least Huckleberry Finn…only with an education."

Danielle burst into laughter, choking on her milk and coughing wildly.

"Are you okay?" Boston giggled, pounding her on the back several times.

Danielle nodded, choked once more, and then said, "Bruce Willis or Huckleberry Finn? Oh my heck! What kind of combination is that?"

Boston smiled and bit her cookie. "A perfect one," she mumbled with her mouth full. "Especially if this Huckleberry Willis is a hottie with a naughty body like Vance Nathaniel!"

"Huckleberry Willis?" Danielle asked, still mirthful.

"Yeah," Boston began. "You know…tough, capable, protective, witty, smart…that would be the Willis part."

"And the Huckleberry part?"

"Insightful, wise, a survivor, a little rough around the edges, secretive…and somehow a little haunted…maybe a little neglected." Boston said. "So then you add Vance's handsomeness, musculature, and determination, and you've got Huckleberry Willis…my dream man."

"So now he's your dream man? This Huckleberry Willis?" Danielle teased. "After looking at me like I'd asked you to show up at work in nothing but your leopard-print underwear when I suggested it the other night?"

Boston raised an index finger. "Huckleberry Vance Willis should be his full name, I guess. And yes, I admit it. I've thought about it a ton since Dempsey's party. And even though you assure me Huckleberry Vance isn't a cannibal—even though I'm still scared to death—I remembered how much I like Christmas."

Again Danielle choked on the combined efforts of laughing while drinking milk. "What in the heck does the fact that you like Christmas have anything to do with it?" Danielle squealed. "I think your mind is one step short of nutbutter!"

"No, I'm serious," Boston said. "I mean, I haven't really enjoyed Christmas since I've been living with Steph…not really. She always made it so awful—demanding this, planning that. Only her decorations could go on the Christmas tree and stuff…which, actually, now that I think about it, I'm thankful for because it would've been so mean for my well-loved, pretty little ornaments…to stick them on the same tree with her expensive, giant-sized ones. Anyway…I love Christmas! It's why I loved working at the North Pole so much. To me, it's what life should be—perpetual kindness and thinking of others, doing kind things, smiling. Remember how our cheeks used to hurt from smiling? Everyone's cheeks should hurt from smiling…all the time! Don't you think? It's a beautiful season, when even the crankiest people think of others…even Steph in her own way. People do things for others, and hopefully that causes them to remember and linger on the ultimate sacrifice made for the world…remember what is really important…which, in turn, makes them less selfish…which makes them do more nice things and smile and even though they're tired and stressed…if they remember why they're doing it, the reason we celebrate Christmas with beautifully decorated Christmas trees slathered in twinkling lights…why we smile while we're wrapping gifts and hum 'Silent Night' whenever we see a little nativity scene." Boston paused to draw a breath and sigh. "I love Christmas! It gives me hope, makes me smile, makes my heart light, makes me forgive people for their shortcomings…the way I should…the way Christ did and does. I love Christmas and what it does to me…who it makes me strive to be. And Vance, he does the same thing—makes me happy…more happy than I've ever imagined. Just being around him makes me want to never leave, to be better, to be worthy of winning him. That's what I'm trying to say…even though I'm still afraid he might turn out to be a cannibal instead of…instead of…"

Danielle sat smiling, her eyes alight with admiration and joy.

"Instead of Huckleberry Willis, your own personal Santa," she said.

"Exactly!" Boston exclaimed. "See, Danielle? It's not so hard to understand me, now is it?"

Danielle giggled. "No…not compared with trying to imagine Vance as Huckleberry Willis Claus."

Both girls reeled with giggles, and Boston wondered why she'd ever let Stephanie Crittendon pull her off the path of warm friendship and self-confidence. Oh, deep inside she was still terrified that in allowing herself to admit she was in love with Vance, she might be opening herself up to devastation. Still, the Boston Rhodes she once was, and now was again, knew she couldn't not love him. And that was that, no matter the outcome.

Vance exhaled heavily as he let his forehead rest on the large steering wheel of his pickup for a moment. He was tired—completely worn out. He'd always had a great admiration for the men and women who worked road construction. All his life he'd thought that it took a pretty tough person to work that way, either because of the physical labor required or the monotony some of the tasks might produce. Still, in that moment he was thankful for his great fatigue, for it meant his mind couldn't linger too long on one thing. It couldn't linger on present concerns, such as the misery of staying in the ratty motel he'd moved into—or the fact he was feeling something for Boston Rhodes. Feeling something? He was becoming downright obsessed! Every waking moment she was in his mind. She lingered in his dreams every minute that he slept. It had happened so suddenly. He'd let his guard down, and she had sifted into his soul almost before he'd known it. He'd seen it in her at once, even through the poison that Steph chick was dampening her bright spirit with. Vance had seen in Boston Rhodes all the good things he craved. She was kind, nearly to a fault—yet kindness was never a fault. She was an optimist, an eternal one, or so he suspected. She was clever and funny, empathetic and compassionate, witty, wise, and wonderful, and she scared him to death! He couldn't even think about his physical attraction to her. If he did that, he'd be back in the apartment in a heartbeat, flipping out the light and having his fill of the sweet flavor of her kiss.

Again he thought of how grateful he was to be so tired. He was so thoroughly worn through that his mind felt like mush. In that state, he couldn't think of any one thing too long—other than Boston, of course—but not any other one thing, and that included the past. Thus, Vance enjoyed fatigue—the kind of fatigue that made his mind too tired to think of the past.

Drawing a deep breath, he turned the key in the ignition, and the truck rumbled to life. As always, whenever he started a car engine, the hair on the back of his neck stood on end, and his stomach twisted with anxiety. But he shrugged it off—too tired to think about it—reached over, and took another cookie from Boston's basket, shoving it in his mouth. He thought for a moment that Boston's cookies tasted almost as sweet as her mouth—almost.

Shaking his head, however, he tried not to let his thoughts nest on his sister's best friend—no matter how cute, bubbly, babbly, and fun she was—no matter how often the word *love* ricocheted through his mind. Still, the fact was, she made him feel better. Whenever he was around her, he felt better, as if things might eventually be okay, as if scars could heal. He knew some scars would never heal, of course, but Boston somehow made him think they could. When in Boston's company, Vance could almost envision himself walking up the path of his little house after working at the zoo, little dark-haired toddlers throwing tiny arms around his legs, carrying them into a home fragrant with homemade chocolate chip cookies to be greeted by a pretty, loving wife named...

Before he knew it, he was pulling into the motel parking lot. He decided to leave the basket of cookies in the pickup. He figured there was less chance of a cockroach finding its way to them in his truck than in his room. Being the honey-homemaker Boston obviously was, she'd lined the basket with cellophane before arranging the cookies in it. Vance popped one more cookie into his mouth and tied the cellophane closed at the top with the orange ribbon Boston had provided. He looked at the basket, smiling as a clever idea began to ooze into his tired mind.

Yep! He'd return the basket for a refill all right. He would definitely return the basket for a refill—but he wouldn't return it empty. No siree!

෯

"I just want it understood," Danielle began as Boston entered the apartment Thursday after work.

"You want what understood?" Boston asked. The expression on Danielle's face was gleeful, somehow even a little triumphant.

"That I get to say, 'I told you so,' at the wedding," Danielle said. "Just once. I'll only say it once…but I get to say it."

Boston laughed. Danielle's playfulness only added to her good mood. She'd been offered the assistant news scriptwriter's job that afternoon, Vance had texted her after lunch letting her know his cookie basket was empty, and there hadn't been a cloud in the sky all day.

"Wedding?" Boston asked. "Danielle…what are you talking about?"

Danielle stepped aside, gesturing toward the kitchen table. "My idiot of a brother had your cookie basket returned today."

Boston gasped. There, in the center of the kitchen table, sat her cookie basket. It was definitely her cookie basket; she would've known it anywhere, even without the enormous flower arrangement sprouting from it.

"What?" she exclaimed.

"Oh, Vance is wrapped around your little finger, honey!" Danielle giggled. "There's a card…but I was strong enough not to read it, thank you!"

"Oh my heck!" Boston breathed as she hurried to the table. "It's…it's massive!"

"Oh, yeah! Vance never does anything average—a barrel of Tootsie Pops…a field of flowers."

Boston shook her head, unable to believe the beautiful arrangement was actually sprouting from her simple cookie basket! The basket was stuffed with butterscotch daisies, miniature sunflowers, orange and yellow mums, orange lilies, and Leonidas roses that were rather terra cotta on the inside and creamy yellow on the outside. Stems of dried wheat and red berries embellished the already beautiful arrangement, and a small gift card was held by a plastic florist peg protruding from its center.

"I have just one question," Danielle began. "What did you put in those cookies?"

Boston shook her head, still awed by the beautiful floral arrangement on the table. "Nothing. Nothing different from what I usually do…except I used milk chocolate chips instead of semisweet."

"Well?" Danielle asked with pure impatience.

"Well, what?"

"Are you going to read the card?"

"Oh! Yeah…I guess so," Boston said. Carefully, she removed the small card from its little plastic peg. She smiled as she read her name on the envelope, sprawled in nearly illegible man-writing (as she and Danielle liked to call it).

"Read it to yourself first…in case he says something I might feel compelled to chew a hole in him for," Danielle suggested.

Boston giggled, opened the envelope, and removed the card.

"*Boston*," she read aloud, ignoring Danielle's suggestion for the sake of her own zeal. "*More cookies, please. Be sure the lights are out when I come over to pick them up. Love, Vance.*"

"Love?" Danielle squealed. "Love? Oh my heck! I knew it, I knew it, I knew it!"

"Danielle," Boston began, "he's just being nice. I'm sure…I'm sure he signed it that way out of habit. We all do it." Still, Boston's heart hammered like a train rolling down the tracks as she looked at the word *love* scribbled in Vance's sloppy handwriting.

Danielle seemed to ignore Boston, however, and simply exclaimed, "Oh my heck!" She snatched the card from Boston's

hands and read, "*Be sure the lights are out when I come over to pick them up.*"
Danielle smiled a knowing smile. "To the best of my knowledge,
whenever the lights go out with you and my brother in the same
room...oooo! Muchas smooches! Oh my heck!"

Boston couldn't help but catch hold of Danielle's excitement.
The Steph-poisoned Boston was afraid to believe Vance meant the
basket flower arrangement as anything more than a kind way of
thanking her for the cookies. Yet the true soul of Boston Rhodes
dared to hope differently. After all, there was nothing trivial,
mediocre, or casual in such an effort, expense, and insinuative
inscription.

"Maybe he'll come over tonight!" Danielle said. "Dempsey called
and wants me to run over and see the new ad campaign he's working
on. Maybe while I'm gone...maybe Vance will come over and turn
out the lights for a little while."

"And if not?" Boston asked, hopeful that Vance would drop by.
She knew the job he was working on had run late the past few
nights—but she hoped anyway.

"If not," Danielle said, picking up a large Priority Mail box from
one of the kitchen chairs. "Then you can start going through these
for me!"

Boston gasped, opened the box, and squealed with delight when
she saw its contents.

"The pictures?" she asked Danielle. "The pictures you've been
begging your mom to send so you can start scanning them?"

Danielle nodded. "Look how many there are," she said. She
balanced the box on one arm, reached inside, and pulled out an
ancient, sepia print. "I mean, I know this one. It's my Great-Great-
Grandmother Nathaniel." She tossed the picture back in the box.
"But when I got to digging through them, I found these three...that
I thought our weird, sort of morbid curiosities about the past might
find interesting."

Boston watched, entirely intrigued, as Danielle reached into the
box and withdrew three old, Victorian-era photographs. "Take a

look," Danielle said, handing them to Danielle. "I don't recognize the names on the back…first names anyway."

Boston looked at the three photos. Her eyes widened; a chill prickled the hairs at the back of her neck. One photo was of an elderly man, the other two of young women. Instantly, Boston knew why Danielle had thought them intriguing.

"Postmortems," Boston whispered.

"Exactly," Danielle whispered in return.

"I'm already wigging out," Boston said as she studied the photographs taken of the subjects following their deaths.

"But you're intrigued too, huh?" Danielle said. "I know I am. I figure when I get back from Dempsey's, we can go through the box. But it might be interesting to start with these."

"Are there any more in there?" Boston asked, glancing into the box.

Danielle shrugged. "I don't know. Mom sort of sent a conglomeration. There are old ones…really old ones…but there are even some of my old school and prom pictures mixed in. It'll be fun to organize them. Don't you think?"

"Oh, totally!" Boston agreed, still studying the three postmortem photographs in her hand.

Boston loved photographs, especially old ones, and the thought of going through Danielle's old photographs with her was like anticipating the grandest adventure.

"Okay," Danielle began as Boston placed the three postmortem photos back in the box, "so if Vance doesn't show up—which I think he will, simply to see if you liked the flowers, if nothing else—then you can start going through the photos."

"Oh, I'll love looking through them!" Boston exclaimed.

"Not as much as you'll love making out with my brother," Danielle said. She giggled, grabbed her purse off the kitchen counter, and headed for the door. "I'm off to Dempsey's. See you later!"

"Have fun!" Boston called to her. As Danielle closed the door, however, she remembered that in all her excitement over the flowers, she'd forgotten to tell Danielle she'd gotten the assistant news scriptwriter's job at the station. Oh well. It was no big deal. She could tell her later.

Boston turned, sighed, and smiled as she studied the beautiful flower arrangement. It was September, and the orange, crimson, and gold colors arranged in the basket caused Boston's already grand appreciation of the beginning of the season to heighten. She leaned forward, sniffing each rose, caressing a lovely orange mum with the tips of her fingers. She hoped Vance did come by to see if she liked the flowers—she just hoped he came by at all.

Yet as six o'clock spent its hour and then seven, Boston wondered if a long day working the stretch of road between the city and Mustang had been too wearing for him. She tried not to think of Vance trapped in that crummy motel. She wished the previous owners of his house would move out early.

Sighing with disappointment in the lack of Vance's presence in the apartment, Boston turned off the TV. Yawning, she went to the kitchen, retrieved the box of pictures Danielle's mom had sent, and returned to the sofa to leaf through them.

There were so many photographs—and from so many eras! To Boston, it was like opening a treasure chest and finding a wealth of gold pirate treasure.

Slowly she leafed through the photos, giggling when she came upon an awkward school dance photo of Danielle. Brace-faced and with a giant zit protruding from her chin, Danielle still looked beautiful—even at fourteen, fifteen, or whatever teen year she was enduring at the time the photo was taken.

"*Sadie Hawkins*," Boston read on the back of the photo. She reached into the box and drew out another photo. This time Danielle had shed her braces and the monster zit on her chin. Boston turned the photo over. "*Junior Prom*," she read. She giggled and pulled out the postmortem photos instead.

"Who were you?" she whispered as she studied the photos. "Why did you die?" The thought intrigued her. Oh, she knew most people would think she was morbid for finding the photographs interesting. Yet she laughed—another human hypocrisy. People still took postmortem photographs, only usually they took them at funerals, when the deceased were already in their casket. But wasn't it really the same thing? She'd even heard a lady once at a funeral commenting on how disturbing Victorians were for taking photos of their dead to remember them by. Boston had then watched the same lady walk up to her late uncle's casket and take several photos. She'd always thought it was a connection with the past. People of bygone centuries did take photographs of loved ones before burial. It was a reflex borne of mourning, a desperate attempt to hold on, to always have a part of the loved one there, tangibly in view. People still mourned, still felt the need to hold on, still took photos of loved ones not for morbid reasons—but out of pure love, because losing someone hurt so thoroughly that the human spirit, heart, and mind often wondered if endurance of the loss was even possible. That's why people took photos of loved ones before they were committed to the grave. It was why the Victorians did it, and it was why people still did it. And to Boston—well, she'd always understood it. Especially since her grandmother had passed away some years before. Oh, how she wanted to keep her image—even her last image—forever.

Boston turned the photograph of the elderly man over.

"*Noble Angus Nathaniel,*" she read aloud. "*39th New York Infantry Regiment.*"

She smiled, her mind suddenly alive with possibilities. Boston hopped up and made for her bedroom. She knew Civil War infantry lists were often available on the Internet. If she could discover something on old Noble Angus before Danielle got home from Dempsey's…

CHAPTER TWELVE

Vance listened to Dempsey. He'd been talking to Dempsey on his cell almost all the way over to Danielle and Boston's apartment. It seemed Danielle was at Dempsey's place and that he had called Vance to make sure he approved of his starting to pursue Danielle. Vance had found Dempsey's call kind of touching—completely unnecessary, but touching.

Naturally, Dempsey had turned the tables and asked Vance when he was planning to turn up the heat with Boston. Danielle had told Dempsey about the barrel of Tootsie Pops and now the basket of flowers. Dempsey already knew Boston and Vance had spent eleven minutes of bliss in the pantry at his party, so Vance hadn't denied his attraction to and interest in Boston.

Gradually, their conversation had taken a different venue. Vance was now coaching Dempsey on how to get past his own fear of rejection.

As he parked and climbed out of his pickup, Vance said, "It's easy, dude. Just coax her into the pantry, turn out the light, and go for it! I can't believe you're nervous." He chuckled, "You always look like you've got it all together."

"I'm a wreck, man!" Dempsey said as Vance sauntered toward Boston's apartment. He'd been even more excited and more impatient to get over to Boston's place when he learned that Danielle wasn't home—that Boston was probably home alone. He'd been sweating over his plans all day, trying to build up his courage. Vance had decided to ask Boston out. He figured if she was willing to kiss him in the dark, maybe she would be willing to go out with him. He was scared to death, of course—but he couldn't keep away from her any longer and needed to try. He'd begun to hope she could accept him—even for his past.

"You're a wreck?" Vance laughed, forcing his mind back to Dempsey's predicament. "Dude! She'll be putty in your hands. I know my sister."

"You don't know how long I've been in love with your sister, Vance," Dempsey admitted, lowering his voice. "What if she, like, throws up or something?"

Vance laughed again. "She won't throw up, man. Just drag her into that pantry and lay one on her! It's like a magic room, dude. I promise."

Dempsey inhaled a deep breath. "Okay, man. But if she slaps me…I'm coming after you."

"Deal," Vance said. "Now go drag your woman into the cave and have your way with her."

"All right. Thanks, man," Dempsey said.

"Anytime, my friend."

Vance closed his cell and dropped it in his pocket. He looked down at his dusty, dirty shirt and worn-out jeans. He considered that maybe he shouldn't have come straight from work. He wasn't a very appealing sight, all covered in dust and smelling like road base and tar. He lifted his arm and sniffed his armpit. Raising his eyebrows in surprise that he still smelled more like deodorant than sweat, he raised a fist and knocked on the door.

Fear washed over him for a moment. What was he doing? She'd run away as fast as she could if she ever found out the truth about him—when she found out the truth. In that moment, he knew Boston Rhodes deserved so much more than he had to offer. He almost turned around and hightailed it—but he'd already knocked. Nothing left to do but man up and take a chance.

Boston startled—a terrified, yet quiet, yelp escaping her throat as there came another knock on the door. Trembling, she snatched her cell from the kitchen counter and crept toward the door once more. Tears brimmed in her eyes as she flipped open her cell and pressed 911. She didn't press send but let her thumb hover just over the send button.

She brushed a tear from her cheek as she raised herself on tiptoes and peered through the peephole once more.

"Vance!" she cried in a whisper, relief and hope flooding her soul.

Quickly—desperately—wildly she turned the deadbolt, unlocked the doorknob, and opened the door.

"Vance!" she cried.

"Hi," he said. He'd smiled when she'd first open the door, but his pleased expression quickly turned to a deep scowl as he looked at her. "What's the matter?"

Boston reached out, taking hold of his wrist and pulling him into the apartment with her. Frantically she locked the door once more, twisted the turnkey on the dead bolt, and burst into tears.

"He'll come back! I know he will!" she cried, throwing herself against the sure protection of Vance's powerful body. She closed her cell phone, not even caring that her trembling caused her to drop it. Sliding her arms around Vance, hugging him tightly for reassurance that all would be well now that he was with her, Boston was instantly comforted as he returned her embrace.

"Who? Who will come back?" Vance asked, thoroughly perplexed. "What's wrong?"

At once, Boston broke into one of her characteristic strings of babble.

"I was in the bedroom. I came home, and Danielle had gotten the package of pictures from your mom." She paused, smiling even for her fear and tears. "And the flowers are gorgeous, Vance! I've never seen anything so beautiful! I can't believe you'd—"

"Just tell me what's wrong...what happened," he interrupted. It was obvious he was concerned, and Boston thought perhaps he should be.

"Well, Danielle got the box of photos from your mom today, and she found these three that we were pretty sure are postmortem photographs. So, like an idiot—'cause I know I'm a chicken at night—but like an idiot, I thought I'd just look on the Internet for some information on the man in one of them...because his name is on the back...so he must be your guys' relative, and his infantry number's there too. So I thought I might be able to find something...but instead I decided to do a little research on postmortem photography of that era, and pretty soon I was getting totally freaked out because—let's just say it—Victorian postmortem photography can be disturbing if it's night and you're home alone...and I was totally wigging out anyway because I *am* here all alone and shouldn't have been looking that stuff up at night. So then I was afraid to go to bed or to get in the shower because...well...to be honest, I've just seen *Psycho* too many times, and that part when Janet Leigh gets shanked in the shower just freaks me out completely. So I didn't want to get in the shower because I'd been scrolling through pages and pages of those creepy old photographs, and then I started thinking about Tony Perkins in *Psycho*, all insane and stabbing Janet Leigh. So I thought maybe I'd watch TV or something and get my mind off of it, but then there was a knock on the door. So I looked through the peep hole, and it was some guy, a guy I didn't know, so I didn't answer the door...because...hello...I didn't know him, and I'm here all alone. So I didn't answer, so he starts pounding on the door and yelling about how he's going to come back because he knows I'm here. And he was cussing...not like you cuss but, like, really bad words...and so he left, and I was totally freaked out then. But he came back, like, five minutes later and started pounding on the door again...and I thought I should maybe call 911. But they say to only call 911 if it's matter of life or death...and so I wasn't sure...and then he left...but he came back a third time, and I have no idea who he is or what he wants. He just keeps yelling about how I'm in his parking spot and he's ticked off…though he used different verbiage than that, of course…and I don't know what the heck he's talking about. And I'm sure he'll come back, and I can't quit thinking about Tony Perkins stabbing Janet Leigh in *Psycho* in the shower…and those Victorian postmortem photos were really creepy and I…I…"

"Shh…okay…it's all right," Vance soothed, his powerful arms banding tightly around her. He rested his chin on the top of her head. This gesture lent even more comfort to her than his simple presence did, and she melted against him—feeling safe, protected.

"First of all," Vance began, "you should never pause to dial 911 if you have even the slightest feeling you might be in danger, Boston."

"I know…I know," she sniffled. He was right, she knew he was. She shouldn't have paused in calling for help—but she'd been so rattled!

"You didn't recognize the guy at all?" Vance asked, still holding her, his breath warm in her hair at the top of her head.

"No," Boston answered. "I've never seen him before."

Boston yelped as a mad pounding sounded on the door then.

"It's him!" she gasped. Vance released her so he could peer through the peephole. Instantly, the stranger began shouting.

"I know you're in there!" the man shouted, adding a thread of profanity like Boston had certainly never heard pass from Vance's lips. "Open the door!"

Vance reached into the pocket of his dirty jeans, pulled out his cell, dialed 911, and handed it to Boston.

"Tell them what's going on," he said.

"Hey, man! Settle down!" he shouted then.

There was silence on the other side of the door for a moment, but only for a moment. Boston startled as the stranger on the other side of the door started beating at the door, kicking it. "Who are you, man?" the stranger shouted. "Open the door! That chick's in my parking spot!"

"911, what's your emergency?" a woman's voice asked. Boston's hands were trembling so wildly she feared she might drop Vance's phone as well.

"Someone is at my front door...trying to get into my apartment!" Boston stammered. "He's trying to beat the door down! He's furious, and I don't know him!"

"What's your name, miss, and are you calling from a cell phone?" the woman asked.

"Cool off, man!" Vance shouted.

"Open the door!" the stranger roared. He let go a rope of threats and profanity that would've knocked Steph Crittendon on her backside.

"Boston Rhodes and, yes, ma'am, I'm on a cell," Boston said.

"Please verify your physical address, Boston, and I'll have officers dispatched."

Boston rattled off the apartment's address as the man continued to throw his body against the door.

"He's gonna kick the door in, Boston," Vance told her. "Go in the bedroom and lock yourself in."

Boston nodded and hurried to the bedroom.

"Is there someone with you?" the emergency operator asked.

"Yes, my friend Vance," Boston said. "He told me to lock myself in the bedroom."

"Officers are on the way, Boston," the operator said. "I want you to stay on the line with me until they arrive, all right?"

Boston nodded and brushed tears from her cheeks.

"Are you there, Boston?" the operator asked.

"Yes, ma'am," Boston said.

"Good. Just stay on the line with me. The police are only two blocks away."

Boston could hear the stranger beating on the door; she could hear Vance shouting back at him. All at once the pounding on the door stopped, however, as did the shouting.

Terror gripped Boston, crushing her soul in its cold fist. Had the stranger managed to break down the door? Had he hurt Vance?

"Everything went quiet!" Boston told the emergency operator. "What if he got in? What if he's hurt Vance?"

"Stay where you are, Boston," the operator said. "Officers are on their way. They're just around the corner."

"What if he's hurt Vance?" Boston breathed. Her concern for Vance beat down her fear for a moment, and she unlocked the bedroom door. Peering out into the living room, she couldn't see anything, but she could hear a scuffling noise, the sound of a struggle.

"I think he's in the apartment!" she told the operator.

"Stay where you are, Boston," the operator said. "Assistance is almost to you."

But a new fear was fast overtaking the old one. What if Vance was in danger or hurt? Quietly, Boston stepped from the bedroom and crept to the living room.

She gasped as she saw Vance struggling to restrain the man.

"He's broken in!" she exclaimed into the phone.

"The police officers dispatched are pulling into the parking lot of your complex now, Boston," the operator said. "Stay back as far as you can."

But Boston was stunned, paralyzed with fear—fear for Vance's safety. The stranger was insane—kicking and punching! Vance managed to avoid most of the blows the stranger threw at him, landing several consecutive punches to the stranger's jaw. The stranger reeled back, stumbled, lost his balance, and crumpled to the ground just as two police officers arrived.

"It's him," Vance said, raising his hands and nodding toward the stranger. "My sister lives here," he said to the officer who held his hand over the gun at his gun belt, ready to draw if need be.

The vision of policemen, Vance's hands at his side, and a stranger in her apartment was horrifying! Boston rushed forward, throwing herself against Vance and sobbing with relief.

"Are you Boston, ma'am?" the officer asked.

"Y-yes, sir. Boston Rhodes," Boston stammered. The officer nodded, and Boston felt the strength and protection of Vance's arms around her once more.

"And, Miss Rhodes, you do know this individual?" the officer asked, nodding to indicate Vance.

"Yes, sir," she managed. "But not him," she said, pointing to the stranger. The second officer held a gun on the stranger as he stood.

"Are you all right, Boston?" the operator's voice asked. Boston had all but forgotten she still held Vance's cell to her ear.

"Yes, ma'am," Boston said.

"Please hand the phone to one of the officers, Boston. You'll be fine now," the operator said.

"Yes, ma'am," Boston breathed. "Thank you."

She handed the cell phone to the officer and listened as the policeman identified himself and assured the 911 operator that the situation was under control.

"What are you doing here, sir?" the other officer asked the stranger.

"That dude just beat me up, man!" the stranger shouted, pointing to Vance. Boston felt the muscles in Vance's arms and torso tighten with restrained aggression. Instinctively, she snuggled against him— embraced him more firmly in an attempt to settle him.

"That guy's wasted," Vance growled. "Did you drive here, man?" Vance addressed the stranger.

One of the police officers held a hand up to Vance, an indication he shouldn't speak to the stranger.

"That dude hit me, man!" the stranger shouted again. "I want to press charges!"

"Well, apparently you were trying to break into his girlfriend's apartment," the officer said. "And, sir, it looks to me like you hit him. Were you trying to break into Miss Rhodes's apartment?"

"Yeah…but so what?" the stranger growled. "That don't give him the right to mess me up!"

"I'll ask you again, sir. What are you doing here? Why were you trying to gain access into Miss Rhodes's apartment?" the officer asked again.

"She parked in my spot," the man said, wiping the blood from his nose on his shirt. "She parked in my spot!" The drunken man let go a slur of violent profanity.

"Watch your language with me, sir," the officer threatened.

"She's parked in 1-G, and that's my spot," the man continued.

"I'm parked in 1-E," Boston told the officer questioning the man.

"This guy is totally wasted," Vance mumbled. "Lock him up before he kills somebody!"

"Please, sir," the officer said to Vance. "Please let us handle this."

"He'll kill somebody!" Vance shouted, however. Boston felt every muscle in Vance's body tighten, felt him trembling with sudden rage.

"I'll have to ask you to step back, sir…and control your temper," the officer said.

"Vance," Boston said, placing a hand on his cheek. He looked down at her, and she was astonished to see moisture in his eyes. The expression on his face was that of pure rage, but in his eyes she saw fear—and pain.

"Have you been drinking, sir?" the officer asked the stranger.

"Maybe I had a few," the stranger confessed. "But I ain't over the limit for driving…and that chick's in my spot!"

The first officer handed the cell phone back to Vance.

"Thanks," Vance growled, dropping the phone into his pocket.

"Do you want to explain to me what happened here, sir?" the second officer asked Vance.

Boston was still trembling, residual fear causing her to literally quake. Yet Vance's state of mind worried her. She wasn't surprised by his anger, but there was something else. The situation had hit a nerve, and she wondered why.

"Of course. For starters, that dude is blitzed," Vance repeated, pointing at the man. He released Boston, quickly unbuttoned his shirt, and removed it, handing it to her. "Put that on," he said. "You're cold."

Boston nodded. She wasn't cold, but Vance must've interpreted her quaking as such. Either way, she put on the shirt, knowing that, if nothing else, it would comfort her simply because it would further calm her nerves to have his shirt on. It wasn't the same as having the protection of his arms around her, but it was emotionally somehow similar. The warmth of Vance's body still clung to his shirt, and Boston's entire body rippled with goose bumps for a moment at the realization. His shirt smelled of Speed Stick and smoke—she figured the construction crew had barbequed their dinner again. She realized she did feel oddly comforted, even for her lingering fear and the seriousness of the present situation.

"I arrived here, and Boston told me this guy had been trying to beat down her door," Vance explained. He was enraged—the quaking in his voice revealed that, and the fact his hands were clinched in tight fists. Yet Vance continued to explain. "She was still telling me about it when this drunk shows up and starts pounding on the door again. I had her call 911 and sent her to the bedroom because I was afraid he'd beat the door down and get in, which he did."

"And you were here why?" the officer asked.

"Man! He's the drunk! He's the criminal! What are you coming after me for?" Vance raged suddenly. "The guy could have killed somebody driving home! Who knows what would've happened if he'd busted in here and I wasn't here!"

"Calm down, sir," the officer said. "I realize you're upset. I'm just trying to gather all the details."

"The details are that this guy is driving drunk, threatening women when he's drunk, beating down doors when he's drunk, breaking and entering when he's drunk! That's what's happening here!" Vance shouted.

"Sir, if you don't calm down, you'll find yourself in trouble too."

"What?" Vance raged with fiery indignation. "Why should I be catching any heat? I'm not the one trying to kill people!"

"Vance!" Boston said, taking hold of his arm. "It's okay. They know he's drunk. They're just trying to get the information they need."

Vance looked at her, still raging, tears still gathering in his eyes. He inhaled and exhaled several deep breaths as he looked at her. Then he nodded and turned to the officer.

"I'm sorry, officer," he said. "I've just had too much experience with this kind of thing to keep a level head about it, I guess."

"I understand, sir," the officer said. "Let's continue."

Boston listened as Vance explained what had happened. He repeated to the officer that he'd arrived to find Boston upset because of the stranger's threatening behavior. When the guy showed up again, Vance had been certain the stranger would break the door down and had instructed Boston to call 911, sending her to the bedroom. The stranger had continued to beat against the door, and when the locks burst through the door frame, allowing the stranger entrance, a struggle had ensued between Vance and the stranger. Several times Vance reiterated that the stranger was intoxicated, and the officer nodded his agreement.

Boston then relayed her version of the story to the officers as another set of policemen arrived. They talked with the officer who had now handcuffed the stranger. The strange man swore and shouted at them as they told the story, and the officers continued to reprimand him.

Boston explained she'd been home alone, that the man had come to the door, pounding on it and threatening her, shouting about how she was "in his spot."

"You are in my spot!" the man shouted.

"Don't speak to the lady," one of the officers said. "Don't even look at her."

"Why not?" the jerk asked. He smiled at Boston—studied her lewdly from head to toe. "If I'd known she was this hot…I would have gotten in here sooner."

Boston gasped and stepped out of the way as two of the officers restrained an enraged Vance Nathaniel.

"Quit looking at her, you drunk piece of—" Vance shouted, moving to lay the stranger out again.

"Settle down, sir," one officer said, taking hold of Vance's arm. "Ruiz," the officer said to one of the other policemen, "get that guy out of here. Question him in the car."

"You're still in my spot, baby," the stranger slurred to Boston.

"How much have you had to drink this evening, sir?" the officer named Ruiz asked as he and his partner led the man away.

"I told you...I'm under the limit," the man lied.

Thirty minutes later, when the police had gone and the apartment manager had promised to have the door fixed first thing in the morning, Boston stood tired and still trembling.

What would she have done if Vance hadn't dropped by? she wondered. What would she have done? She felt insecure and fearful, as if she'd never sleep well or find beauty and joy in the world again.

"I guess...I guess Danielle must really be having a good time with Dempsey," Boston said as she stood watching Vance rubbing his temples.

"I guess so," he mumbled. "It's after eleven."

"Wanna go for a walk?" she asked.

"What? Now?" Vance inquired.

"Yeah," she said. "I think I'd like to get out of the apartment for a few minutes. Here." She removed his shirt and held it out to him. "I wouldn't want you to catch cold."

Vance nodded and took the shirt. He quickly put it on.

"I guess we won't bother locking the door, huh?" he said, forcing a grin.

"I guess not," she said.

Leaving the apartment, they meandered down the sidewalk toward the park on the other side of the apartment complex.

They didn't speak at first. Boston glanced at Vance. It was obvious he was more upset than she was about the incident. She thought it odd—she thought it telling. Excess moisture still rose to his eyes now and then, and he walked with his hands shoved in his pockets and his broad shoulders drooping.

Boston's heart began to beat madly inside her chest—the mad beating she always felt when she was being compelled to do something, when she knew that if she didn't do what she was being driven to do, the consequences would be bad. Vance was in pain—in deep emotional pain—and Boston knew it had been triggered by the intoxicated man that had succeeded in breaking into the apartment. She offered a silent prayer of thanks for Vance's timely arrival. She glanced to him again, the pounding of her heart only increasing—it was almost painful! She somehow sensed—knew—that this was a defining moment in her life, maybe in Vance's as well. She didn't know why—she just knew it.

Inhaling a deep breath of courage, she looked up to him and asked, "What are you always running from, Vance?"

"What do you mean?" he asked, though she suspected he knew very well what she meant. "You mean because I run in the evenings?"

"I do think that is a physical response to something emotional you're feeling," she said. It was a brave thing to say—brave or stupid. "I just feel...sometimes I feel like you run to run from something...not just for the exercise."

Vance held his breath. He felt sick—wanted to vomit as the memories began to wash over him. What if he did tell her now? Would she be the one running from something then—running from him?

He glanced down to Boston. He wanted her—in every way a person could want another person. He'd even come to the apartment, convinced he might be able to win her. He'd always known he'd have to tell her sometime—either that or she'd find out on her own. He and Danielle had made a pact long ago—a secret promise to never talk about what had happened—not ever, not to anyone—not until they were each certain the time was right. Danielle had obviously kept her promise. Boston knew nothing of what had happened.

Still, as Boston looked up at him, her eyes conveying a promise of understanding, Vance wondered if the time had come to tell her. He wondered if she cared for him enough to work past it. He wondered if she could love him in spite of it.

They were coming to a bench sitting under a streetlight on one side of the park path.

"Do you wanna sit down for a minute?" he asked.

Boston could see the pain and fear in his eyes. He doubted her. Whatever it was—whatever secret he'd been hiding, whatever haunted him and caused him to run—he was afraid of it, and it caused him great pain.

"Sure," she said, smiling.

They sat down on the bench. Boston rather brazenly, but also instinctively, snuggled up against him. Vance smiled and put an arm around her shoulders.

"So," she ventured, "what is it you're always running from?"

He paused a moment. Unexpectedly, he reached into his back pocket and pulled out his wallet.

He tossed it in her lap and said, "Remember how I told you that you missed something before?" he asked.

"Yeah?" Boston said, opening his wallet.

"I...I had promised myself that if you were thorough enough to find what's really in there...that I'd tell you then," he said. "I'd promised myself I'd tell you the truth...if you found what I was afraid you would. So...give it another try. It'll be easier for me if you can find a clue first."

"Okay," Boston said. He was afraid to tell her—but why? Danielle had said Vance had baggage. Again Boston wondered what kind of baggage would keep him running—keep him swimming in such obvious fear and pain.

Slowly she opened his wallet. Nothing had changed that she could see—other than the fact he now had seventy dollars in the cash section. She looked at his credit cards, his driver's license—found a little compartment in the middle of the wallet, but it was empty. All that was left were the photos. Quickly she flipped through them. They hadn't changed—no additional photos, none missing. There was the one of Samantha, Vance and Danielle's little niece. Boston flipped to the next photo, Danielle and Vance at a football game, the football player and his sister the cheerleader. As before, the next photo was of Danielle at perhaps fourteen or fifteen, a school photo Boston remembered having seen in Danielle's boxes of unorganized photos many times. She flipped to the next photo—the second photo of Danielle—again in her mid-teens. Boston frowned, thinking again that she'd never seen this school photo of Danielle. She turned to the last photo, a wallet-sized portrait of Vance's mother and father. It was in that moment that something struck her as strange. Why would Vance carry two photos of Danielle at approximately the same age? Why not a more current photo?

She felt Vance's muscles tighten as she turned back to the two school portraits of Danielle. She studied them, side by side. It was then she noticed the difference, as if one of the portraits had been printed backward. Danielle had a small mole on her right cheek—and in one photograph the mole was there—on her right cheek. But in the other photograph, the mole was on Danielle's left cheek. A horrifying understanding began to wash over Boston then. She thought of the summer she'd first met Danielle—the glorious summer at the North Pole, the summer that hadn't started out as glorious for Danielle Nathaniel. She thought about the hidden pain Danielle had endured that summer—of Danielle's recent confession of having contemplated suicide.

With trembling hands, Boston removed the second photo of Danielle from the little plastic wallet photo holder. She held her breath and turned the photograph over.

"Annabelle Nathaniel," she read in a whisper. *"My junior year and I still love you more than anybody, Vance. Thanks for being my big brother. Love, Annabelle."*

Boston couldn't breathe as she replaced the photo. Something else struck her then, and she turned back to the photo of Vance and Danielle in their high school uniforms for cheerleading and football. The photo of Samantha covered the back of the photo of Danielle and Vance, of course, so she would have to remove it to see if there was any writing on the back of it—to find out if it was of Vance and Danielle as she had thought or of Vance and Annabelle, Danielle's mirror twin sister.

She removed the photo of Vance as a high school football player to find part of the photo had been folded back. There, as she unfolded the small photograph, stood Vance—hugged tightly between two identical twin girls.

"Identical twins," she breathed. "Mirror twins. What happened to her?" Boston asked, though as her mind quickly fit pieces of the puzzle together, she could almost guess. What she didn't guess at was what Vance would answer.

"I killed her," he stated.

Inwardly, Boston was astonished at his response. Yet for his sake, she would not let him know how troubled she was. For one thing, she was certain there was more to the story of Annabelle than that— and second, she wouldn't give Vance any reason to feel she might think badly of him.

"I'm sure there's more to it than that, Vance," she said. "Tell me...tell me about Annabelle."

She saw a tear trickle down his face. She reached up and tenderly brushed it from his face.

"She and Danielle were seniors in high school," he began. "It was spring. They were making all their plans for graduation. You know, the stupid caps and gowns, the announcements...everything guys hate and girls love, right?"

"Right," Boston said. Guys did hate the pomp and circumstance of events like high school graduation. She had brothers—she knew.

"Anyway, Annabelle didn't want to wait until the next day to pick up her stuff," he explained. "Someone had called about the announcements and stuff...that they had arrived. They were at some kid's house, and the kid had said everyone could drop by and pick them up if they wanted to. Otherwise they'd have to wait until Monday when the kid brought them to the school." He smiled and shook his head as he continued, "I swear I thought she was going to nag my head right off my shoulders! She wanted her stuff… and she wanted it that night. But I was really tired. I'd been working road construction to save for a couple more semesters of college, and I was tired. But Annabelle kept begging me and begging me to drive her over to this kid's house. She didn't like to drive at night. She was seventeen and only had her license for a few months, and driving at night freaked her out for some reason." He paused and exhaled a heavy sigh. "Well, as always, she talked me into it. So we got in the car and started for the kid's house."

Tears were already streaming over Boston's tender cheeks. The empathy she owned was in full flourish, and her heart was already beginning to ache in sharing Vance's pain. She didn't say anything— just let him continue—snuggled closer and wrapped her arms around his strong one.

"I know I didn't nod off or anything," he said. "How could I? Annabelle was talking a wild streak all the way…going on and on about this guy Phil that she liked." He smiled a little, no doubt at the memory of a sweet, effervescent sister. "I didn't nod off…was driving just as alert as I normally do. But even so, I didn't see the guy run the stop sign. He T-boned us on the passenger's side. They figure he was going over fifty miles an hour. And it pushed us off the road…slammed the driver's side into a tree." He paused to brush a tear from his other cheek. "I was trapped—my left arm and shoulder were broken…my collar bone and my left leg too—and the tree had smashed the front of the car so my door wouldn't open. I looked over to see Annabelle…"

Through her own tears, Boston could see the tears streaming down Vance's handsome, tortured face. He paused—put a hand over his mouth to still his trembling lips.

His deep voice broke with emotion as he said, "She was…I won't describe it to you…but things were severed. She was already gone, and we'll leave it at that." He closed his eyes a moment, and Boston knew the image was as fresh there as it had been when his brain had first registered it.

"She was already…already gone…and I've always been glad that if she had to die…it was quick," he said. "Even though…even though I saw her…I couldn't quite wrap my head around it…and I was struggling to break free so I could maybe help her…somehow. Plus the guy who had hit us…the drunk driver who had hit us…" He paused a moment. "It's why I freak out whenever I think someone's been driving drunk…like the guy at your apartment tonight. I just…I just relive it all…get so angry. And the drunk driver that night, he was screaming for help…screaming and screaming for help. And it sounds strange…but I wanted to help him. So I actually tried to get to him. I tried to move but my right leg was pinned." He chuckled a bit, "And if there's one thing you'll learn about me, it's that I don't like being restrained. So somehow I managed to pull my right leg away from whatever had it pinned." He glanced at her, his tears slowing but excess moisture still welling in his beautiful eyes. "Ever notice that nasty scar and chunk of flesh missing from my right leg? Well, whatever had me pinned, when I pulled my leg out, it just took a hunk of skin and muscle with it." He forced a grin and whispered, "It nearly killed Danielle too…to lose Annabelle, you know."

"I know," Boston said—and she did. After so many years of being Danielle's friend, she finally knew what had tortured her heart and soul so thoroughly that summer they'd first met. It was like someone had turned on a light—a light of pure understanding—and Boston's empathy for Danielle and her brother only grew.

"But Danielle made it through…and it wasn't your fault. Still, knowing you as I do, you're always the hero…and you pinned it all on your own shoulders…so that nobody else could possibly ever blame themselves for any of it—not Danielle, not your parents…not anybody."

"I was driving," he reminded her.

"Yeah," she admitted. "Safely and sober."

"I don't think anybody ever gets over something like this," he said. "I'm pretty damaged goods, Boston Rhodes."

"Everybody is damaged in one way or the other, Vance. And nobody ever does get over things like this," Boston admitted. "In a way, they shouldn't. Experience is what makes us who we are. Depending on how we choose to apply it in our lives, it can make us better people…more understanding, patient, and compassionate. But we still have to learn to live with bad, horrible, painful things. This is your baggage…I understand that. Everybody has baggage to some extent. Not like this, of course—yours is a lot heavier than what most people carry…not because it was your fault but because you lost someone you loved so suddenly, so violently, so needlessly…and you felt responsible. But you're not." She smiled at him, adding, "And you're not damaged goods. You're excellent goods."

Vance grinned—a sad grin perhaps—but an expression of hope and relief accompanied it. He reached up and brushed the tears from Boston's cheeks.

"You know you didn't kill your sister, don't you?" she ventured. The horrifying event haunted him—it always would—but he had to know it wasn't his fault.

"Yeah," he admitted. "It took a long time and a little counseling from my family…especially Danielle. Her support meant the most to me…because she'd lost as much as I had…maybe more…yet she didn't blame me at all. She understood not only my pain but my guilt."

"You mean your *feelings* of guilt," Boston corrected.

"Okay…my *feelings* of guilt," he chuckled.

He looked away from her then and asked, "So…what do you think of me now? Would you still let yourself be locked in Dempsey's pantry with me?"

Boston smiled. He was in pain, she could see it—feel it aching inside him. He would always feel pain when he talked about it—thought about it—but she wouldn't let it linger long—not if she could help it.

"Of course," she said. "Knowing this—the fact you would tell me about it—it only makes me love—like you more."

He looked to her, frowning. "You almost used the L-word," he said.

"I...um...I..." Boston stammered, feeling the crimson of a raw blush rising to her cheeks.

"Do I make you think of the L-word, Boston Rhodes?" he asked. He was smiling—teasing her. She was sure he was still in pain, but he was coming back to her now—she could sense it.

"Maybe," she admitted timidly. It was a frightening confession. Boston actually wondered how she'd managed to confess it at all.

Vance's smile broadened. "You know, I was coming over to ask you out tonight. Can you believe that? Before all the drama interfered, I had worked up enough guts to ask you out...but I guess that point kind of got thrown in the slammer."

"Do you mean, like, ask me out on a date? Like a date-date?" Boston asked. In her stomach, butterflies were busting out of their cocoons by the trillions. He'd meant to ask her out? She could hardly contain her excitement, even for the heavy heartache he'd just shared with her.

He smiled at her. "Yes...on a date-date," he chuckled. "But now, being that you almost used the L-word to me, maybe I'll find the courage again to ask you if you'd let me take you out this weekend." He paused and shrugged straightened shoulders. "I mean, the L-word thing...kind of encouraged me. I might not be able to promise a riveting adventure of eighteen holes of golf..." He smiled—the smile of impending mischief Boston loved so much. "But I can promise you a good time...and maybe a pantry or two to check out along the way." He frowned. "Of course, you've never let me kiss you in the light. Maybe you won't like me with the lights on."

"You never tried to kiss me with the lights on," Boston teased. "And you call yourself Vance Romance."

"To be honest, I thought you wouldn't let me kiss you with the lights on...so I just always made sure it was dark." He seemed thoughtful for a moment and then added, "Except that last time, the other night after Dempsey's party in my fancy hotel suite, you're the one who turned out the lights and kissed me first."

"Maybe I did," Boston giggled.

Vance's eyes narrowed, and the pain lingering in them a moment before seemed to vanish, replaced by something else—something that made Boston's heart leap in her chest.

"You know," he began, "I've been thinking a lot about the L-word lately too."

"You have?" Boston asked, breathless as he took her chin in one hand. Could it be true? In a matter of less than three weeks, had Boston found the one man she would love forever? Surely not—surely she was only dreaming.

But Vance nodded.

"But do you mean the L-word as in lamp or linoleum…or even lollipop?" she asked.

"No," he chuckled. "I mean the one…the queen of L-words. As in…I think I love you, Boston, L-word."

As tears of joy trickled down Boston's cheeks, she said, "You don't even know me."

"Yes, I do," he said. "I've known you from the very first time you walked into Danielle's apartment and that psycho ex-roommate of yours told you to stay away from me."

Boston gasped. "You heard her say that?"

"I don't miss much," he told her. He traced her jawline with the back of his hand, and his caress sent goose bumps rippling over her arms and legs. "But do you think I have a chance with you? Now that you know my baggage?"

Boston placed a soft palm to his whiskery jaw. "No one else could have a chance with me now…not since the moment I first saw you," she confessed. "But…I do feel that I should be honest with you. I have a problem…an addiction. It's been going on for some time now."

"Let me guess," he said, smiling. "Could it be chocolate Tootsie Pops?"

"Not exactly," Boston said. "It's you. I think I love you too…Vance Romance."

"Think?" he asked.

"You said think," she reminded him.

"That's because I'm a chicken," he chuckled. "I was afraid you might jump up and run off screaming if I told you that I'm in love with you before we've even gone on one official date-date."

"Really?" Boston sighed. Her heart was full—radiant with joy! She'd taken a chance, taken a risk, hoped that Vance could be hers—and he was.

"Really," he said. "I love you, Boston."

Boston smiled. "I love you, Vance."

"Enough?" he asked.

Boston frowned, puzzled. "Enough for what?"

"Enough to kiss me when the lights are on," he explained.

"Why don't you find out?" Boston asked.

Vance smiled and glanced up to the streetlight above them. "Why don't I?" he chuckled. He stood, taking Boston's hands and pulling her to her feet.

Boston was surprised by a sudden wave of bashfulness as Vance took her in his arms. He would be able to see her this time as he kissed her, and it somehow worried her.

"What if I'm not good at it in the light?" she whispered.

"You're forgetting, baby," he began, "this is me. You twist me up like a bread tie…light or dark."

"A bread tie?" Boston giggled, letting her hands slide up over his shoulders to the back of his neck. "You're comparing me to a bread tie?"

"Shh," he breathed.

Vance's mouth was watering for Boston's—watering so profusely he had to swallow twice. Surely he was imagining it all. Surely she didn't really love him—surely she wasn't standing there under the streetlight wanting him to kiss her. Yet the feel of her small, warm, curvaceous form in his arms and against his body as he tightened his embrace—her hands at the back of his neck as she wove her fingers through his hair—he couldn't possibly have misunderstood. She loved him. Even for the painful, dark secrets he'd harbored, she loved him.

He gazed into the soft jade of her eyes for long moments, reveling in what he saw reflected there—himself. Oh, he'd kiss her all right, like she'd never been kissed before—even like he'd never kissed her before. Somehow he'd managed to win the heart of Boston Rhodes, and he'd make sure that, if nothing else sealed it as forever his, the way he kissed her would.

Boston was breathless—awash in delight as she watched Vance's face slowly descend toward hers. She felt his hands fisting the fabric of her shirt at her back—felt his massive chest rising and falling with the labored breath of restrained passion. And then, finally, there under the bright radiance of the streetlight, Vance Nathaniel kissed her! Instantly lost in a heated, moist, affectionate exchange, Boston quivered, awash in bliss as his hands at the small of her back held her firmly against his body. There, under the bright street lamp light, Boston surrendered to passion—to love. In that moment, there was no fear in her—only bliss, joy, and insatiable desire. She pressed her mouth more firmly to his, orchestrating a ferocious kiss of her own. He did not pause but met her instigation full willing, the measure of their exchange finding a common measure as she was one moment submitting to him, the next moment offering her own demands.

Vance Nathaniel loved her! Boston's mind struggled to believe it. Even as they stood wrapped in each other's arms, mouths melded, she couldn't believe it. He was her hero and in so many ways—and no girl actually won her hero, not in real life.

Yet he was her hero—for enduring what he had endured so bravely and successfully, for being the man he was, for saving her from Steph's poison. He'd even championed her that very night—saved her from who knows what at the hand of the drunken stranger!

The added emotion of intense gratitude only further spurred Boston's desire for Vance, and her hands left his hair and neck and traveled down over his chest to slide under his arms and embrace him. This action seemed to ignite Vance somehow, and Boston gasped as he broke the seal of their lips to place a driven, moist kiss to her neck. He kissed her neck hard, several times in succession. She imagined he was trembling a little—surely she imagined it—a quivering about him—within him.

"You kissed me…in the light," she breathed.

He smiled at her, his eyes warm with admiration and love. "You used the L-word about me," he teased.

"It wasn't the first time, you know," she said.

He frowned. "I think I would remember if you'd ever told me you loved me before just a minute ago," he said.

"I told you last week," Boston said. "Remember?" She raised herself on her toes, put her lips to his ear, and said, "I love you, baby. Smile."

Vance did much more than smile—he laughed.

"Ooo! You smiled! You lose!" Boston giggled.

"You're right, you win," he said. "So what's your prize?"

Boston reached up, running her fingers through his soft hair. "Can it be anything I want?" she asked. "Can it be you?"

Vance took Boston's face in his hands and kissed her softly on the mouth.

"If that's what you really want," he said.

Boston smiled. "Then kiss me, Vance…because I love you."

He did kiss her then—deliciously kissed her until her knees were weak and her heart was sure—sure that it was forever safe in Vance Nathaniel's loving possession.

EPILOGUE

"Anna! Belle!" Boston scolded tenderly. "I told you girls to have Daddy hose you off so you could come in for baths! We need to get everybody ready if we're going to get to the hospital to see Auntie Danielle and Uncle Dempsey's new baby."

"Okay, Mommy," Belle called from the mud hole in the backyard.

"But can we have three more minutes…or two?" Anna asked.

Vance chuckled and used the hose to squirt more water in the mud for the girls. Vance had been working on the landscaping in the backyard. As usual, however, he'd completely lost his focus, not to mention all sense of reason, when the twins had begged him to make one of his signature mud holes. Naturally, he'd caved, and the girls were now covered head to toe in "good, clean, harmless mud" (as Vance liked to call it).

"Okay, two more minutes," Boston giggled. She glanced over her shoulder to Stevie. He seemed fine, still sitting in the highchair, happily rubbing sweet potatoes through his hair. She closed her eyes, imaging the mess cleaning up the kids would leave in the bathroom. Still, she shrugged. It would be a mess, but a mess borne of too much childhood fun—though she wondered if there could really be too much fun in childhood.

She sighed, delighted in watching the girls roll around in the mud hole their dad had created for them.

"One more minute," Vance chuckled as Belle opened her mouth and caught hose water in it.

Boston laughed and wondered that her daughters still managed to be such little prissies most of the time. It seemed they were either dressing up as princesses and twirling about singing at the top of their lungs or rolling around in the mud with their daddy. There was no in between. She felt her smile fade just a little, imagining that Danielle and Annabelle must've been just the same. How she wished the accident had never happened—that Danielle and Vance had never lost their beloved sister. She thought then of the night she and Vance had first kissed in the light, of returning to the apartment afterward, of Vance explaining that the school dance pictures in the box Danielle's mom had sent that day were really photos of Annabelle—not Danielle.

Boston felt tears welling in her eyes as they always did whenever she thought of Annabelle. She swallowed the lump in her throat and laughed as Vance called the girls to him and started hosing them off. They giggled with the pure, carefree joy of delight, and Boston giggled too.

"Now, run in and ask Mommy to start the shower for you," Vance said.

"Thanks, Daddy!" Anna chimed, hugging Vance around the knees.

Boston covered her mouth to stifle her laughter as she heard Vance breathe, "Oof!" as Belle ran headlong at him, throwing her arms around his legs and hitting him squarely with her small shoulder where no man wanted to be hit.

"Yes, Daddy! Thanks!" Belle said before she took Anna's hand, both girls giggling as they ran toward the house.

"Mommy!" Belle exclaimed.

"Daddy says we can go to the new gorilla exhibit at the zoo tomorrow—" Anna began.

"—if it's all right with you and Stevie," Belle finished.

"Okay!" Boston said. "But for now, let's get you girls all cleaned up. You want to see the new baby, don't you?"

"Yes!" both girls agreed.

"But will we ever get a new baby of our own?" Belle asked.

"Yeah, Mommy," Anna added. "Stevie needs a twin too. It's not fair that he doesn't have one."

"Well, we'll just have to see," Boston said. She smiled at her girls, awed by the very miracle of them. "Now you run on into the bathroom, and I'll be right there."

"Okay, Mommy!" Anna giggled, running off.

"Wait for me, Anna!" Belle called, trailing after her sister.

"Boston!" Vance called from the back porch. "Has Stevie finished smashing his dinner into his hair?" he asked.

"Yeah. Why?"

Vance chuckled and put his thumb over the hose so it sprayed more lightly. "Bring him out, and I'll hose him off."

"He's a baby!" Boston exclaimed.

"If he's old enough to walk and old enough to climb up in the cabinet and eat a whole roll of Rolaids, then he's old enough to play in the hose," Vance chuckled.

Boston shrugged. He had a point. Going to the highchair, she lifted Stevie down and said, "Go see Daddy, baby. He wants someone to play with."

Stevie giggled, toddling off as fast as his little eighteen-month-old legs would take him.

"I'll be right there, girls," Boston called. "I'm waiting to bring Stevie in. He'll need a bath too."

"But not with us, right, Mommy?" Belle called.

"Yeah, Mommy…not with us!" Anna added.

Boston watched as Vance gently hosed the smeared sweet potatoes off his son. He laughed as Stevie giggled with delight. Then he turned off the hose and took Stevie's little hand, leading him back into the house.

"I brought your son home," Vance said to Boston. He hunkered down to Stevie. "Go find your sisters, Stevie."

Stevie toddled off toward the bathroom.

"You'll never get that landscaping finished if you don't quit making mud holes," Boston told Vance as he wrapped her in his arms, kissing her soundly on the mouth.

"I know," he said. "But kids don't stay little forever. If I don't get that landscaping finished, it'll still be there. But I won't always have two little girls who want to roll around in the mud."

"That's very true," Boston said. She reached up, running her fingers through Vance's soft, dark hair.

"I love you, you know," Boston said. "Even though you can't resist making a mess just before we're supposed to be somewhere important."

"I love you too, baby," Vance said.

"Ooo, Daddy! Kiss her, Daddy! Kiss her!" Belle giggled as she and Anna ran up behind Boston.

"Yeah, Daddy! Kiss her like a prince!" Anna added.

"Okay," Vance said, kissing Boston slowly, deeply, and with a low moan escaping his throat.

The girls giggled with delight and began jumping around with excitement.

Stevie came tearing around the corner then, bumping into Belle and knocking her over. Before Boston knew it, she and Vance were tumbling to the floor in a heap with the children.

Vance chuckled, rolling onto his back and pulling Boston's head to his once more. He kissed her—the same way he'd kissed her that night under the streetlight. Well, perhaps not exactly the same way, but Boston felt the same love—an even deeper love in his kiss.

"That's it, Daddy! More kissing! More kissing!" the girls chimed in unison. "Kiss him, Mommy! Kiss him!"

Boston giggled, took Vance's face between her hands, and kissed her husband passionately on the mouth. The girls squealed, took hold of their brother's tiny hands, and led him back toward the bathroom.

Boston sighed, "Did you ever think it would be this wonderful?"

Vance chuckled. "Do you mean did I ever think I'd be this sleep-deprived?"

"Well, that too," Boston agreed. "But really…did you?"

Vance kissed her cheek—her neck—her mouth.

He looked into her eyes, and Boston smiled—seeing herself reflected in their deep green.

"Yes," he told her. "I did."

AUTHOR'S NOTE

If you know me, you know how nervous I get anytime a new book or e-book is released. Allowing the public to read your work can be very much like using an X-Acto knife to fillet your chest open, then letting people dig around inside. At least, that's how it sometimes feels to me, and it's especially true with this story.

It took me the first thirty-five years of my life to learn the lesson Boston learns concerning what I term "poisonous friends." Thirty-five years! I did learn the lesson—though it took me another five or so years to learn how to regulate or avoid poisonous relationships. In my insatiable desire to "sift sugar all over the world" and make glad the hearts of others, I've had to learn to see the red flags—the warning signs of poisonous relationships—to balance my associations with people who expected or demanded that I put their wants, needs, and desires ahead of not only my own but those of my family, my physical and mental health, and so on.

Thus, Boston is a true soul mate to me! Even as she realizes the necessity of removing Steph from her life, she still feels bad. She'll always feel bad, haunted by feelings of guilt and failure. Though, thanks to Vance, she began to recognize the earmarks of poisonous friendships, she'll struggle with what she perceives as being "mean" for the rest of her life. Still, I'm just glad she learned the lesson early in life.

A friend said this to me as she was reading *Kiss in the Dark*: "Please! Please tell me this Stephanie character isn't based on your real-life experience!"

Oh, but she is! Not necessarily on one specific person (though I did have an enraged soon-to-be ex-roommate throw a quart jar at my head the day I moved out of an apartment at college) but more on the lessons I've learned about self-preservation, self-advocacy (which I still fail miserably at on nearly a daily basis), and recognizing when you really can't help someone without losing yourself—or can't help them at all, at least at that time in their life.

I also struggle with tolerating human hypocrisy. An admitted hypocrite myself (because I don't think any of us can be born and live our lives without fighting some measure of our own hypocrisy), nothing vexes me more than watching someone embezzle money from the business they work for, as they sit in self-righteous judgment of the guy who's changing a pregnant lady's tire because he's smoking a cigarette. Do you know what I mean? Sometimes it's our imperfections and struggles that end up aiding us with the most personal growth. Furthermore, as far as I'm aware, there was only ever one perfect being to walk the face of the earth—and He is yet the pure example of ultimate humility.

So, as you can see, I've filleted my chest open with this one, at least in my mind. Someone *will* reprimand me concerning Vance's two or three swear words—someone will lecture about how Stephanie was just a poor soul who needed a friend (which is actually true, and Boston knew it—she tried to help her). It's the hard, no-fun part of being an author, of sharing glimpses of your soul with others. A famous vocalist was once quoted as saying (I'm way, way paraphrasing), "Fame is really hard to deal with. Once you're famous, people think they can say anything to you. They seem to think you're made out of Teflon." Still, 99.999 percent of my readers and friends share my feelings, dreams, and struggles—they know I'm not made of Teflon and that I'm as imperfect as the next guy. They are the sugar sprinkles who enrich my life, teach me, humble me, lift me, and make me a better person. (Ahh! I feel a chili-dog-fest coming on.)

Yeck—that's all so serious and thinky! Let's move on, shall we? Now, just for fun, I'll answer a few other questions I've received in regard to this story.

1. Yes! I (like many others) did indeed enjoy rousing games of Kissing Rugby and I Love You, Baby—Smile in my youth. I still think they're two of the most fun party games young people can play. Loved them—right up there with Sardines (also known as Pack 'em In—*Dusty Britches*).

2. Yes, Vance's nickname (Vance Romance) was inspired by a guy I used to date in college. Everyone called him "Lance Romance," and he was way, way cool! 6 foot 4, totally handsome, and played the electric bass guitar in one of the bands I sang in. (Now, *that* was a life lesson—a story, in itself. More later!)

3. And finally…yes, chocolate Tootsie Pops are the only flavor of Tootsie Pops I like.

In the end, I just hope you enjoyed the story. I hope it entertained you and made you laugh—that your day was just a little less stress-filled because of it.

And now, enjoy the first chapter of
Take a Walk with Me
by Marcia Lynn McClure.

CHAPTER ONE

Cozy Robbins exhaled a long sigh. She was tired, and her eyelids felt droopy. Yawning, she leaned back in her chair, running her fingers up through her long hair and stretching her arms over her head. Glancing to the clock on the wall, Cozy wondered how she had managed to finish thirty more Christmas tree ornaments before midnight. Of course, these were only tiny clay mice tucked snuggly beneath hand-stitched quilts in walnut shell cradles. They weren't as tedious to make as the hinged walnut halves with Christmas tree and fireplace scenes depicted inside them. Still, they were far more difficult to craft than the simple gold-paint-dipped walnuts with ribbon loops Cozy also made.

She shook her head, wondering how in the world she had gotten herself into taking so many orders again. Things certainly had escalated in the past five years. It seemed difficult to fathom—the hundreds of ornament orders she still needed to fill—when just five years previous, she'd been astonished at having sold sixty ornaments total.

Cozy closed her eyes and sighed once more in thinking back to the November she had been sixteen—to the first series of finely crafted walnut ornaments she'd made to sell. She'd wanted to purchase something nice for her Grandma Robbins for Christmas that year—a beautiful set of bookends she'd seen in a specialty shop, knights in armor posed in kissing princesses. The moment she'd seen the bookends, she'd known they were just what her grandmother had been looking for to adorn the bookshelf in her entryway. But they were costly, priced at nearly three hundred dollars for the set.

At sixteen, three hundred dollars was hard to come by, especially when it was to be spent on only one gift. Still, the bookends were ideal for her grandmother, and Cozy had begun to ponder ways she could make the three hundred dollars—for in truth, how often did the perfect Christmas gift present itself? Ironically, it had been her Grandma Robbins who had suggested Cozy make and sell her charming walnut Christmas tree ornaments. Though she had no idea why Cozy wanted to acquire three hundred dollars, Dottie Robbins (the very person for whom Cozy was inspired to earn the money) suggested her granddaughter sell the delicately crafted Christmas ornaments.

Cozy's grandmother had always adored Cozy's walnut ornaments. In fact, Cozy had begun making them for her grandmother in the first place. She'd been ten years old and wanting to give her grandma something special. She had seen a plastic walnut ornament in a bin at a second-hand store. The plastic half walnut shell had a little plastic mouse nestled in it, nibbling on a piece of cheese and wearing a Santa hat. Cozy thought it was the most adorable thing she had ever seen and begged her mother for fifty cents to purchase it. The little Christmas tree ornament had fast become Cozy's greatest treasure. To some, it may not have been worth even the fifty cents, but to Cozy it was priceless.

Consequently, Cozy had spent an entire afternoon cracking open walnuts and hollowing out the insides until she found just the perfect shells to make her own ornaments. She used gray molding clay to form little mouse heads. Carefully she'd painted tiny black eyes and noses and nestled them into the shells. With old fabric scraps her mother had given her, she then cut and stitched tiny quilt tops, tucking them snugly around the little clay mice. She had figured out how to fashion a way to hang the ornaments by using lengths of gold thread so that the walnut cradle would hang perfectly from any Christmas tree branch.

Cozy had presented these first walnut ornaments to her grandmother on Christmas Eve that year. Dottie Robbins had been delighted to literal tears, claiming Cozy's walnut cradle ornaments were the most wonderful gift she'd ever received. After that Christmas, Cozy worked on improving her ornaments. Every year she presented her grandma with several new walnut ornaments, and Dottie was always just as excited as she had been the day she received the first ones. Gradually, Cozy began to diversify her craft. She hollowed out walnuts by the hundreds. Some she would glue back together, painting them gold and adding a red ribbon at the top to provide a means of hanging it. Her favorite ornaments, however, were the ones with two walnut halves hinged together. When opened, they revealed either a miniature nativity scene or a miniature Christmas scene—one half having a tiny Christmas tree with gifts at its base nestled within and the other boasting a little fireplace, complete with stockings hanging from the mantel. These required a lot more work with clay and detailed painting, but they were Cozy's favorites. Yes, her walnut ornaments had become quite popular around town.

As Cozy tucked one special ornament into a small white box with her gold embossed logo (two robins sitting on a holly branch, their heads lovingly pressed together and the trade name *Cozy Robbins* beneath them) stamped on the top, she wished she could see the look on the girl's face when her boyfriend handed her the ornament and told her to open it. The young man had contacted Cozy about a making a specialty ornament. She had agreed to do it, of course—to hide the diamond solitaire engagement ring inside a gold, red-velvet-lined walnut.

"How romantic!" she sighed, smiling and setting the box aside. She glanced at the clock again, even though she already knew the time. She had to get to bed. Her shift started early, and she didn't want to be too tired.

Exhaling another sigh of weariness, Cozy rose from her chair. Two more semesters and she'd have her degree. Surely she could stop waiting tables at the café then. She glanced at the table covered with Christmas ornaments made from walnuts. She could hardly believe she'd managed to pay for every one of her winter college semesters with the proceeds from selling such a little thing. Oh, it was a ton of work—no doubt it was. Still, the whole concept that walnuts could pay for a college education was almost unfathomable.

Reaching over to the electrical outlet nearby, Cozy unplugged the Christmas lights she'd strewn over the ceiling of the basement. She blew out the pumpkin-spice-scented candle on the table and turned off the old stereo, and the soothing music she listened to while working at night was silenced. The basement room that had seemed so warm and inviting a moment before was dark and cold and quiet now. Cozy smiled, amazed at what a few Christmas lights, an aromatic fragrance, and some soothing music could do to brighten up a dark space.

Hurrying up the stairs, Cozy brushed her teeth, threw on a pair of pajamas, and fell into bed. Morning and the early birds who frequented the café would arrive all too soon. Still, Cozy smiled, for a vision of her grandmother's delight at seeing the new ornaments Cozy had made for her lingered in her mind like a comforting dream. Grandma Dottie always brightened Cozy's day. Therefore, Cozy decided to look on waitressing at the café the next morning as a means to a happy end. She hadn't seen her grandma in almost a week and could hardly wait to leave work and drive over to see her the next day.

She loved spending time with her Grandma Robbins—she always had. As far back as Cozy could remember, her grandmother had been one of the most wonderful things in the world to her. Cozy knew Dottie Robbins's affection, influence, and love had helped shape her life—still did shape it—and she could not imagine an existence without her.

With one final sigh, Cozy's mind wandered toward sleep with the tender memory of being two or three years old and her grandmother pushing her in the old swing that still hung, faded and worn, from one T-bar under the clothesline in Dottie Robbins's backyard. In her mind, she could still hear her grandma singing "The Teddy Bears'

Picnic" as she gently pushed the swing and then attached a sheet to the clothesline with a clothespin from her apron pocket. Cozy could almost feel the warm breeze on her face as it billowed the clean white sheets hanging on the line—still hear the birds as they twittered around her grandmother's bird feeder—still smell the sweet perfume of freshly mown grass…

❦

"Cozy!"

Cozy turned to see Mindy hurrying after her.

"Have you got any extra ornaments?" Mindy asked, rushing toward Cozy's car. "I know I already put my order in, but I forgot a couple of people."

Though the question rather deflated her enthusiasm, Cozy smiled at her friend. A sale was a sale and meant more money for tuition—whether or not she was getting tired of walnuts. She felt a giggle tickle her throat as Mindy characteristically puffed at the blond bangs on her forehead.

"Sure," Cozy answered with more enthusiasm than she really felt. "How many were you wanting? I'm still making them right now…so if there's something special you want…"

"I want four nestled mice cradle ones and four hinged nativities, if it doesn't stress you out too much," Mindy answered. Again she puffed at her bangs. Cozy felt her heart lighten even for having to make eight more last-minute ornaments. Mindy was too sweet—too kind and supportive of Cozy as a friend and a customer—for Cozy to deny her anything.

"Eight? That's a couple?" Cozy asked.

Mindy shrugged. "I guess it's more like a few, right?"

"I guess," Cozy giggled.

"Do you mind?" Mindy ventured. "I know you like to have the orders before now."

"I don't mind at all," Cozy answered with a just little less than perfect honesty. "Are you sure you want to spend that much though? That's eighty bucks…I mean, forty."

"I'm sure," Mindy confirmed. "Can I bring some cash tomorrow?"

"Yeah...but why don't you just make it twenty."

"Cozy Robbins," Mindy scolded. "You have got to quit underselling your stuff! Your ornaments are so charming, and they're hard to make, I'm sure. Ten dollars apiece is a steal, and you should quit cutting your friends and family that crazy five-dollar discount on each one. I'm paying eighty."

"No," Cozy argued. She hated charging her friends and family anything at all, and she certainly wasn't going to let them pay full price. "I'll take twenty...or I won't make them for you."

"Cozy," Mindy scolded.

Cozy sighed, relenting, "Okay then. Forty. Dang! That's like four movies at the theatre...or a new pair of shoes...or—"

"Stop it!" Mindy giggled. "They're worth it, Cozy. They are the most adorable things in the world! People are willing to pay for adorable...so let them. Okay?"

"Okay." Cozy shook her head, still unable to believe someone would drop even a dime on Christmas ornaments made out of walnuts. Her smile for Mindy broadened—for if there was one thing her ornament sales had taught her, it was who her true friends were. So many people asked for freebies because they knew Cozy personally. Yet she found that her real friends understood she made the ornaments as a supplement to her income. Her genuine friends never tried to take advantage of her or haggle her down. It was a valuable life lesson to her—and an example she followed in her own dealings with friends. Still, she absolutely loathed letting them pay for anything. But she knew it was important to Mindy that she take some kind of remuneration.

"Good. I'll bring cash tomorrow," Mindy said, smiling.

"If you must...but it's still a waste of forty bucks," Cozy giggled.

"Shut up!" Mindy laughed. "I have to get back...so have fun with your grandma. I know she'll love the new ornaments."

"Thanks," Cozy said. Nodding toward the café, she added, "And good luck tonight."

Mindy's eyebrows arched with understanding. "Thanks. I hate the dinner shift."

"Sorry."

Mindy shrugged. "I'm fine. Just thankful to have the job, you know?"

"I do know," Cozy agreed.

"Okay then…have fun."

"You too."

Cozy watched Mindy return to the café, silently reminded herself how glad she was not to have the dinner shift, and felt guilty.

Opening her car door, Cozy turned when she heard a familiar rustle. The leaves of the cottonwoods were quickly changing from green to gold as autumn descended in its full beauty. She paused a moment, for she had promised herself a long time before that she would always, always take the time to watch the leaves transform in the fall—that she would never, never be too busy with ornaments or work or anything else to miss it.

She lingered in watching the breath of the breeze cause the green and yellow leaves to tremble. The air was crisp and refreshing. The moment soothed Cozy even more than punching out from work had, and she felt her smile broaden.

She got into her car, turned the key in the ignition, and pulled out of the café parking lot. She hoped her grandmother had planned meatloaf and mashed potatoes for supper; she loved her grandma's meatloaf and mashed potatoes. In fact, it was the only meatloaf she really liked. There was something special about her grandma's meatloaf—something nostalgic and old-fashioned—and Cozy's mouth began to water as she drove toward the bridge.

"Over the river and through the cottonwoods," she said aloud to herself. With a delighted giggle of anticipation, she began to hum the familiar words to the song that had prompted her thoughts. Secretly, she loved the fact she had to drive over the river and through the cottonwoods to get to her grandmother's house. Cozy thought of the way her mother used to sing the song every time the family traveled to her grandmother's house when she was a child. It was a wonderful little sentiment—a wonderful memory—and it added another measure of joy to her already happy mood.

❦

"Grandma? I'm here," Cozy called as she closed the front door behind her. "Grandma?"

"In here, sweet pea!" Dottie Robbins called from the other room.

Cozy smiled. Her grandmother's voice was like music. How she loved the happy sound of it.

Setting a basket of new walnut ornaments on the entryway table, Cozy hurried toward the kitchen. She could already smell the meatloaf cooking. Supper would be delicious—as was always the case at her grandma's house.

"Hi, Grandma," Cozy said as she entered the kitchen to see her grandmother peering out through one of the windows.

"My angel!" Dottie said, turning from the window and drawing Cozy into a warm embrace. Cozy smiled as the light fragrance of rose perfume tickled her nostrils. "It seems a coon's age since you've been here."

"I know," Cozy agreed. "I'm sorry. I've just been so busy that I—"

"I know, sweet pea," Dottie said. "But you're here now, and we're going to have a wonderful evening!"

"As always," Cozy said as her grandma released her.

"I've got a meatloaf in the oven, and…" Dottie began, clasping her hands together just like an excited child, "and I'm hoping you brought me some new ornaments today."

"I certainly did." She frowned as uncertainty washed over her. "I hope you like them this year. I did a few things differently and—"

"I'll love them, and you know it!" Dottie laughed.

Cozy studied her grandmother for a moment—her smiling, twinkling blue eyes, the sweet little wrinkles on her face. Her grandmother's hair had once been a dark, dark chocolate-brown like Cozy's, but it had faded to a beautiful snowy white. Cozy thought it was very becoming and hoped her hair would do the same—but not until she was in her sixties like her grandmother was.

Dottie Robbins glanced to the window she'd been gazing through when Cozy had entered the room. Cozy frowned, curious—wondering what could be so interesting.

"What are you looking at, Grandma?" Cozy asked, going to the window.

"The handsomest hunk of burning love I've seen in a long, long time…that's what," Dottie sighed.

"What?" Cozy giggled. She looked out the window to see an elderly man raking leaves in the backyard next door. "Who's that?" she asked.

"My new hunk of burning love neighbor, that's who," Dottie answered.

"Grandma!" Cozy exclaimed. She laughed. Her grandma was so funny sometimes.

"Well, just look at him!" Dottie said, nodding toward the window. "Isn't he just the dreamiest man ever?"

Cozy gazed out the window once more, giggling as she studied the man. He was tall, silver-haired, and as tan as leather. He wore an old barn jacket and worn-out work boots, and Cozy shrugged, thinking he was indeed a striking figure. She couldn't see his face very clearly, but it was obvious he was a hard worker.

"He moved in last week," Dottie offered, "and I've been watching out my windows every day since. He's got the deepest blue eyes. They just set my heart to palpitating!"

"Grandma…you have a crush?" Cozy teased.

Dottie smiled. "Of course, angel! Wouldn't you if you were my age?"

Cozy's smile faded just a little. When her Grandpa Robbins had passed away seven years before, the family feared Dottie might follow him too soon. A deep, aching depression and loneliness had overtaken her grandmother. It was one reason Cozy had begun to visit her at least once a week—to remind Dottie Robbins how loved she was and to cheer her up. It had taken a couple of years for Dottie to return to some semblance of the woman she'd been before her husband's death. Therefore, it was surprising to see her puppy-eyed over another man.

Even so, Cozy felt her heart leap a little. It was wonderful to see her grandmother so rosy-cheeked and excited. She thought for a moment that her grandma looked like a schoolgirl in that moment, blushing with the excitement of a new boy in the neighborhood.

"Well? What's his name?" she asked her grandmother.

Dottie's smile broadened. "Buckly Bryant...Buck for short," she answered. "Isn't that a wonderful name? It sounds like he just rode into town on a white horse, doesn't it?"

"Yeah, it does," Cozy agreed. "So you've met him then?"

"Of course! I went over and introduced myself last Thursday while the movers were moving his things in. I swear, Cozy...he put my heart to hammering like a woodpecker!"

Cozy giggled as her grandma placed a hand over her heart as if it were still hammering. "Well, good! You need a little romance and excitement in your life, Grandma."

"Do I?"

Cozy nodded, noting the pink that rose to her grandma's cheeks. "Of course! Everyone needs it...and you deserve it too."

Dottie glanced out the window once more—rather longingly—and exhaled a wistful sigh. "He is a tall drink of water, isn't he?"

"Yes, he is," Cozy agreed.

With one final sigh, Dottie turned her attention from the window and her handsome neighbor in his backyard to Cozy. "Well, as I said...I've got the meatloaf in the oven. We can put the potatoes on in about an hour. Meanwhile..." She paused, gleeful anticipation twinkling in her blue eyes. "Meanwhile, show me what you've made this year. I've been so excited to see the new ornaments! I could hardly wait. I almost snuck down to the basement last time I was at your house...but your father stopped me."

Cozy laughed. "Oh, Dad's very protective about my ornaments," she explained. "He doesn't want the surprise ruined for anyone. Still, it's not like they're really any different than the ones I've made in the past."

"Cosette Robbins!" Dottie scolded. "That is simply not true. Why…every year they're different. And I don't know how you manage it…but they keep getting better and better."

"You're my grandma. You have to say that," Cozy said.

"I am your grandma…but I'm sincere in my compliments."

Cozy nodded. "Okay then, come and see what you think."

Dottie rubbed her hands together like a silent-movie villain as Cozy went to the entryway and retrieved the basket of ornaments she'd brought. Returning to the kitchen, she set the basket in the center of the table.

"Oh, I can hardly stand it. The anticipation is glorious!" Dottie exclaimed, sitting down in a chair and pulling the basket to her.

Cozy sat down next to her and tried to hide her amusement in her grandma's delight. She bit her lip, unable to hide her relief and pleasure as her grandma gasped when she opened the first little white box.

"Oh, Cozy. It's adorable! Simply too adorable for words," Dottie exclaimed as she carefully took the small walnut cradle, complete with a mouse reading a tiny copy of "The Night Before Christmas" and tucked beneath a red flannel quilt. A miniature oil lamp on one edge of the walnut cradle and a tiny green nightcap for the mouse completed the scene.

Again Dottie gasped with awe. "I *love* it, Cozy. Oh, I love it!" She picked up her reading glasses from the old lazy Susan that had lived in the center of her kitchen table for as long as Cozy could remember. "Oh, look at that! How did you ever paint the title on that book? And look at the little lamp. Oh, Cozy…I *love* it! I just *love* it. Just look at the stitching on the quilt! Oh, however do you manage to make the stitches so small? Oh, I love it. I absolutely love it!"

Cozy smiled. She could tell when her grandma was sincere in her compliments, and she was certainly sincere. She felt relieved—and elated.

"Well, if you like that one, then you should freak out over this one," Cozy said, taking another box from the basket and handing it to her grandmother.

Dottie paused and inspected the *Cozy Robbins* logo embossed on the box's lid. "I have to admit, I'm kind of proud of myself for thinking of this—the two little birds…the two cozy robins."

Dottie giggled, and Cozy said, "You should be. It was very clever."

"And memorable," Dottie added. "People remember it. Something this cute sticks in their minds."

"I know…and I'm glad."

Dottie reached out, cupping Cozy's cheek with one hand. "I love you, sweet pea," she said.

"I love you too, Grandma," Cozy said, taking her grandma's hand in her own and squeezing it for a moment. "Now…see if you like the others."

"Oh, I know I will, sweetheart. I know I will."

Cozy sighed. She loved her grandmother so much! What would she ever do without her?

"So? Where did he move from?" Cozy asked, dipping a forkful of mashed potatoes into the melted butter puddle at the center of the far too large helping of mashed potatoes her grandmother had plopped on her plate.

"The east side," Dottie answered. "He said he'd always wanted to live in the valley, along the river. So when the opportunity presented itself, he moved. He lost his wife a few years ago and was having trouble with the blues, as he put it. He's a retired firefighter."

"Wow! A real-life hero, huh?" Cozy asked, smiling.

"Well, he sure looks the part!" Dottie giggled. "I swear, Cozy…I had butterflies in my stomach the whole time he was talking to me! For a minute there, I felt like I was seventeen and he was the proverbial captain of the football team, you know?"

"I can imagine," Cozy said. She smiled as she took a bite of meatloaf.

"What?" Dottie asked.

Cozy shrugged. "Nothing. I was just thinking."

"Thinking what? I know that look. You're up to mischief, Cozy."

Cozy sighed. "I was just thinking that maybe Mr. Buckly Bryant will whisk you away on some romantic adventure. He looks like he's a good kisser."

"Oh, for pity's sake, Cozy!" Dottie laughed. "The things you come up with. What an outlandish thing to say!"

But Cozy saw the merry twinkle in her grandmother's blue eyes. She wished for a moment that her own eyes were blue. Cozy had her father's hazel eyes, but she'd always wished they'd been blue. Still, she contented herself with being glad she had her grandmother's chocolate hair.

"It's not outlandish," Cozy argued. "He's a hunk of burning love. You said so yourself. And you're ravishing. You'd make a perfect couple."

"Now stop that teasing, Cozy Robbins," Dottie playfully scolded. "You're being ridiculous, and you know it."

"No, I'm not, Grandma," Cozy argued. She paused a moment and then suggested, "You should bake him some of your banana nut bread and take it over—you know, as a housewarming, welcome-to-the-neighborhood sort of thing. Once he tastes your banana nut bread, you'll have him eating out of the palm of your hand."

Dottie smiled and laughed a little. "You know, maybe I should." She shrugged. "I mean, it *would* be the neighborly thing to do."

"It would be," Cozy encouraged. "And I still say he looks like a good kisser!"

"Cozy Robbins!" Dottie scolded. "Shame on you."

Still, Cozy could tell by the blush rising to her grandma's cheeks that she was thinking the same thing.

"Grandma…I love your meatloaf and mashed potatoes," Cozy sighed.

"Thank you, darling." Dottie placed a warm palm to Cozy's cheek. Nodding to the small blue bowl of green beans on the table, she added, "And those are the last of the green beans from my garden for this year."

"They're delicious," Cozy assured her.

"I know," Dottie said, shrugging her shoulder with delighted pride.

Cozy laughed. She felt as if she were caught in a moment of perfect wonder. Sitting at her grandmother's table enjoying a supper of meatloaf, mashed potatoes, and green beans—it was peaceful, warm, comfortable, and relaxing. The rhythmic ticking of the clock on the wall was soothing, and Cozy sighed. It was a moment to cherish, as was every moment spent with her grandmother, and Cozy consciously committed it to memory.

"I suppose women my age do still kiss, don't they?" Dottie asked.

"Of course they do, Grandma," Cozy exclaimed. "If Grandpa were still here...wouldn't you still be kissing him?"

Dottie smiled a melancholy smile and whispered, "Yes. Definitely yes."

Cozy's heart ached, knowing she may have caused her grandmother pain in provoking a memory of loss. "I'm sorry, Grandma. I only meant—"

"I know, darling," Dottie soothed, smiling. "And you're right." Her smile broadened. "Mr. Buckly Bryant does look like a good kisser."

Cozy giggled and took another bite of butter-slathered mashed potatoes. The cuckoo clock in the hallway announced six o'clock, and Cozy was glad the time was ticking by slowly. There would always be ornaments to make, bills to pay, and things to do, but there wouldn't always be time with her grandma. At least she had that priority straight.

"So are you dating anyone yet, honey?" Dottie asked.

Cozy sighed. "I went out with Tristan Plummer last Friday."

"And how did that go?"

Cozy shrugged. "Okay, I guess. But he's so...so..."

"Soft?" Dottie suggested.

"Exactly!" Cozy confirmed. "Like I might expect to see him coming out of the nail salon with a new manicure or something. His hands are so...you know..."

"Soft," Dottie reiterated.

Cozy nodded. "Yeah."

Dottie sighed. "I worry for you girls today, sweet pea. Masculinity itself is under attack, it seems. Society is forcing men from their natural, instinctive path. Men weren't made to be cooped up in a cubicle unable to do anything physical. They were made to be hunter-gatherers, to work hard in body and mind. It's hard for men these days…for women too. Femininity isn't what it used to be either."

Cozy sighed, for she agreed—wholeheartedly. Yet what could be done about it? Society was what it was, and it certainly wasn't going to let up.

"Well, Mr. Buckly Bryant looks masculine enough," Cozy offered.

"Yes, he does," Dottie whispered with a wink.

"You definitely need to whip up a batch of your banana nut bread, Grandma," Cozy giggled.

"I think you might be right, sweet pea."

"Of course I'm right," Cozy said, dipping another forkful of mashed potatoes into the butter well on her plate.

Later that night, Cozy sat in her bed, writing in her journal while tucked comfortably beneath a soft flannel quilt. She had had a productive day and a tranquil, wonderful evening with her grandmother. She was tired but truly content.

Still, it seemed contentment never lasted long. Cozy's bedroom door suddenly burst open, and the peaceful moment was shattered as her younger sister Ashley literally hopped into the room.

"Can I borrow your pink sweater for tomorrow, Cozy?" Ashley asked.

Cozy sighed, wishing she could have afforded to live on campus for one more semester at least. The lack of privacy in living at home was so frustrating sometimes. Still, she loved her home—and her family—even if her little brothers and sisters did drive her nuts.

"I guess so, Ash," Cozy answered.

Ashley smiled and hurried to Cozy's closet.

"Why are you in bed so early?" Ashley asked. "It's only ten."

"Why are you up so late? It's already ten," Cozy teased.

Ashley smiled. "I'm totally nervous, that's why! I don't think I'm gonna sleep a wink tonight!"

"Why's that?" Cozy asked—even though she already suspected there was boy at the core of Ashley's discontent.

"Because Kaylee *swears* she heard Braden Lewis telling a friend that Dylan Hill is going to ask me to the winter formal tomorrow night. And if you want to know the truth…I'm totally freaking out!"

"Because you want him to ask you or because you don't want him to ask you?" Cozy asked—even though she already knew the answer.

"You dork! You know I'm totally in love with Dylan Hill," Ashley giggled.

Cozy smiled. "I know you are, and I'm sure he'll ask you…especially if you wear my pink sweater. It's my good luck sweater."

"I know, huh?" Ashley giggled. "Thanks, Cozy," she said.

"You're welcome," Cozy laughed. "Now close the door. I've got the breakfast shift again tomorrow."

"Okay. Love you."

"Love you too, Ash."

Ashley closed the door, and Cozy sighed. Setting her journal and pen on the nightstand, she turned off her reading lamp.

"Wonderful," she whispered, punching her pillow. "My sixteen-year-old sister and my *grandmother* have more exciting lives than I do."

Cozy closed her eyes and tried not to think of the mountain of ornaments she still needed to finish by the end of the week. She giggled then, however—smiled at the memory of the look of delight on her grandma's face when Cozy had suggested that Mr. Buckly Bryant might be a good kisser. It had been a precious expression—purely precious! As she struggled to settle all the thoughts bouncing around in her head, Cozy found herself wondering if her grandma's new neighbor really was a good kisser.

My everlasting admiration, gratitude and love…
To my husband, Kevin…
My inspiration…
My heart's desire…
The man of my every dream!

ABOUT THE AUTHOR

Marcia Lynn McClure's intoxicating succession of novels, novellas, and e-books—including *The Visions of Ransom Lake*, *A Crimson Frost*, *The Rogue Knight*, and *The Pirate Ruse*—has established her as one of the most favored and engaging authors of true romance. Her unprecedented forte in weaving captivating stories of western, medieval, regency, and contemporary amour void of brusque intimacy has earned her the title "The Queen of Kissing."

Marcia, who was born in Albuquerque, New Mexico, has spent her life intrigued with people, history, love, and romance. A wife, mother, grandmother, family historian, poet, and author, Marcia Lynn McClure spins her tales of splendor for the sake of offering respite through the beauty, mirth, and delight of a worthwhile and wonderful story.

BIBLIOGRAPHY

Beneath the Honeysuckle Vine

A Better Reason to Fall in Love

The Bewitching of Amoretta Ipswich

Born for Thorton's Sake

The Chimney Sweep Charm

A Crimson Frost

Daydreams

Desert Fire

Divine Deception

Dusty Britches

The Fragrance of her Name

The Haunting of Autumn Lake

The Heavenly Surrender

The Highwayman of Tanglewood

Kiss in the Dark

Kissing Cousins

The Light of the Lovers' Moon

Love Me

The McCall Trilogy

Midnight Masquerade

An Old-Fashioned Romance

One Classic Latin Lover, Please

The Pirate Ruse

The Prairie Prince

The Rogue Knight

Romantic Vignettes-The Anthology of Premiere Novellas

Saphyre Snow

Shackles of Honor

Sudden Storms

Sweet Cherry Ray

Take a Walk With Me

The Tide of the Mermaid Tears

The Time of Aspen Falls

www.ingramcontent.com/pod-product-compliance
Lightning Source LLC
Chambersburg PA
CBHW060315260626
47160CB00007B/2612